THE
GOLD
OF
ST. CROIX

TOM SEDAR

THE GOLD OF ST. CROIX

iUniverse books may be ordered through booksellers or by contacting:

iUniverse
1663 Liberty Drive
Bloomington, IN 47403
www.iuniverse.com
1-800-Authors (1-800-288-4677)

ISBN: 978-1-6632-0269-7 (sc)
ISBN: 978-1-6632-0270-3 (e)

Library of Congress Control Number: 2020910639

Printed in the United States of America

iUniverse rev. date: 06/25/2020

This book is dedicated to my wife Charlene who's support and belief in me made this book possible.

Also, I have to say thank you to the dozens of people who shared ideas and took the time to review the many drafts of The Gold of St. Croix. You can't write a book without a Village.

Finally, I would like to give a special thanks to my friend DC Current who has taken hundred of hours of his time to make the ramblings of this old man into a coherent book.

Tom Sedar

CHAPTER

The porch in front of the little coffee shop on King Street was getting warm, and as the waitress drifted over and offered one more cup of coffee, I shook my head.

"Are you waiting or just loitering?" she asked, looking bored.

I studied Alli for a few seconds. She was one of those great kids, all smiles, smart, but still working three jobs to survive in paradise. I looked at my watch: quarter after twelve. "I was just waiting for someone, but I don't think they're going to make it," I said.

"Stood up." Alli seemed amused at my fate.

"It happens when you get old." I started to slide my chair back.

"Mr. Cotton?" a voice came from behind me on the street.

I settled back in the chair and turned toward the voice as Alli went inside. The voice belonged to a small, slender woman with long, curly, red hair and no make-up. She wore jeans and a faded T-shirt that said: "POSITIVE IS HOW I LIVE." As she came over, she managed a weak smile. "Sorry I'm late. The damn traffic on the West End was snarled with an accident in Princess."

"Bad one?"

"No, but the police had the right lane closed, and things just backed up."

"Sure," I said as she plopped a huge black purse on the seat next to me and sat down on the other chair.

"Mr. Cotton," the woman said, "I'm Betsy Rourk," reaching across the table and offering me her hand.

I stood up, uncurling my slightly overweight, six-foot frame from the flimsy, fake-wicker lawn chair, and took Betsy Rourk's hand. Her shake was firm but brisk. Like many long-time residents of St. Croix, she had played in the sun too long, and it showed in the hard lines beginning in what had once been a soft face. I didn't figure Betsy Rourk as much older than 35, but in her short years, she'd run a hard race.

"Coffee?" I asked.

She hesitated for a second, staring out at the street, then said in a much quieter voice, "Sure" and moved her gaze to the hands in her lap.

"You OK?" I asked.

Betsy Rourk looked up from the hands, moisture in her eyes, and a slit of white smile emerged from her deeply tanned face. I looked at her for a few seconds, gave my best reassuring smile, and waved Alli over.

To my surprise, Betsy stood up and gave Alli a big hug. "Hi, sweetie," she said as they broke their embrace.

"You should have told me you were meeting Betsy, Mad Dog. I would have told you she'd be late."

"Not," Betsy Rourk said playfully, throwing a right gently to Alli's jaw.

"Is so," Alli replied.

"Just get the coffee, baby and quit telling stories on me."

Alli turned back to the shop, and Betsy sat down. The mist I'd seen in her eyes was gone, replaced by a look of resolve.

"Good kid," I said, watching Alli leave.

The woman facing me paused and said. "Yeah, good kid. But I didn't come here to talk about Alli."

"What was it you came all the way from Frederiksted to talk about?"

"My husband," she said. She paused, and then began again. "I know you're going to think I'm over-reacting, but my husband, Bob, didn't come home last night, and this morning, when he still didn't come home, I panicked and called Mike Taylor down at the dive shop, and he gave me your name. He said you used to be a police detective, and sometimes you helped people on the island."

"Mrs. Rourk," I began as Alli walked over with a coffee for her and a pot for my empty cup.

"Mrs. Rourk," I said, trying to ignore Alli, who

seemed to be lingering at our table, "I'm retired. You need a real detective like Sol Mimi or Kelly Tilson, not an old retired guy like me."

"Mad Dog, that's not true," Alli said. "You found Sandy's car, and Mr. Stilman said you went all the way to San Juan to find his son for him."

I shook my head, trying not to show my annoyance at Alli for butting into the conversation. "Alli, please," I said as I turned to her and raised my hand. The second I did, I felt bad. The wait for the meeting had me edgy, and I knew Alli was just trying to help.

"OK, grumpy," she said, turning and walking away.

When I looked back at Betsy Rourk, her face had erupted into a million-dollar smile, and the very devil was sparkling in her eyes. "Got quite a fan there, Mr. Cotton."

"Call me, Mad Dog."

"OK, Mad Dog. And I'm Betsy.

"OK, Betsy. You don't seem like the type of woman that would panic and call me just because your husband went missing a few hours. What's up?"

"I don't panic. My husband, Bob, is no angel, and him missing a few hours is no surprise." She looked me in the eyes. "Is that a fair answer?"

"Fair," I agreed, sensing there was more to this than just a missing husband.

"The last time I saw Bob, he and Tony Rasser were heading out to Isaac's Bay to dive."

"What time was that?" I asked.

"About five in the evening."

"Night dive at Isaac's?"

"Yeah," she replied, studying her hands. The mist in her eyes was returning.

"Not the best plan," I said.

"Bob and Tony dive three or four times a week. They both know their stuff."

"Yeah," I said. "I used to go out to Cane Bay with Tony when he was doing a lot of underwater photography."

"I thought I recognized you. Bob and I used to teach at Cane Bay Dive Shop."

I thought for a second and then remembered a bubbly brunette who taught at the shop about seven years ago, when I first came to the island. "You dyed your hair."

"No," she smiled, flipping the curly hair on her shoulders. "I quit dying my hair."

"Bob? He's a tall red-headed guy?"

"You got it."

"OK, so Bob and Tony head to Isaac's Bay. Have you tried calling Tony?"

"That's part of the problem. I kept trying to call him all night and finally got hold of Meg Rattles, his new live-in. She said Tony didn't come home either. She thinks they're probably sleeping it off at some beach party."

"Could be."

"No, it couldn't," Betsy said, reaching into the black purse and pulling out a small pack of tinfoil. She sat for a second and held it in her hand, as though deciding, and then cautiously looked around. Finally, she slowly reached across the table and handed it to me.

"Heavy," I said.

Betsy looked down at her hands again and back up into my eyes. "Open it."

Cautiously, I peeled back the foil and looked at what it had concealed, then looked around the street. "Talk to me," I said.

"Two days ago, Bob and Tony went diving at Isaac's Bay and found that."

"Two days ago?" I looked down again into the foil and knew I would have been back making a second dive as soon as I could. "They didn't go back the morning after they found this?"

"Bob didn't, but he spent all day at the Whim Museum doing what he called 'research.' I don't know what Tony did."

"Research on what?"

"I don't know. Bob just came home, gave me that piece of foil, told me not to open it, and left to go diving. I put it in my purse. I figured it was a sappy gift he wanted me to open when he was around."

"But you opened it."

"Yeah, this morning when he didn't come home."

"You know what it is?" I asked.

"I think so."

I started to reach across the table to return the package, but she stopped me and said, "No, you take it. I'm not superstitious or anything, but I think it's evil."

I pushed my hand toward her and said, "Look, Betsy, this is bigger than me, and you need to take this."

"I've been hearing stories about you for years," she answered. "I don't trust anyone else. You keep that damn thing as my retainer. Mad Dog Cotton, you go find my husband."

There was something in her deep, green eyes that ripped into my heart right there at the coffee shop on King Street. I knew, or figured I knew, that Bob and Tony both were dead, but I couldn't say a word.

Staring into my eyes with an intensity that made me want to flinch, Betsy Rourk said, "Damn you, Mad Dog. I don't give a shit what it costs or what you have to do. You find my Bobby, and you bring him home!"

Then, as I sat there in silence, she grabbed the big black purse, stood up, and walked away.

I sat for a long time, spinning the piece of foil in my hand.

Finally, Alli broke my concentration. "Looks like you're stuck with the tab."

"Yeah," I said half-heartedly, and handed her a ten. Alli headed back into the shop.

I stood up, looked around the street like a purse-snatcher getting ready to hit a mark, and walked off the porch, tucking the tinfoil and the crust-covered Spanish gold coin it hid deep into my pocket.

CHAPTER 2

With Bob Rourk's find giving my heart a jolt like it was a new pacemaker, I left the coffee shop. Only two blocks up King Street in a hidden alcove was my first stop, my favorite jeweler and an old friend, Sam Drumand. Sam was a long-time dive buddy and had a fascination with the treasure of the Spanish fleet. His little store offered a large selection of antique Spanish coins.

In the short walk to Sam's shop, I must have processed a million thoughts. What the hell had happened to Bob Rourk and Tony Rasser? Was the coin in my pocket real? How did it get to Isaac's Bay? Was it really found at Isaac's? How had I ended up working on this case?

When I entered Sam's store, his wife was behind the counter.

"Morning, Ann."

"Morning, Mad Dog. Looking for the boss?"

I nodded, and she waved me over to a door. "He's in working."

I walked behind the counter and into Sam's office.

"Got a second for an old friend?" I said as I entered the small cluttered space.

"Sure," he said, pushing a small rolling chair toward me.

Not really in a mood to visit, and anxious to find out what I had, I pulled the foil-covered coin out of my pocket and gave it to Sam.

He looked at me with a curious smile and began to unwrap it. When the coral-crusted coin was free of the foil, I saw it all for the first time. As Sam moved the coin in the light, I could clearly see letters and shapes inscribed low on one side where the crust had been removed. The part of the coin that was exposed, though it was misshapen, looked like it was minted yesterday. The gold flickered and glistened from its corral womb as if screaming to be free. The sight was mesmerizing. For a moment, I could fully understand the insanity such an object could create. I had an irrational urge to take the coin, thank Sam, and leave.

He didn't say a word, just took out a black magnifying loop and put it in his right eye. Although I was watching him closely, I couldn't see the slightest reaction. I made a mental note: "Never play poker with Sam Drumand."

After looking at the coin for nearly two minutes,

Sam took a small metal scraper out of his drawer and looked up at me. "May I?" he asked.

When I didn't protest, he began picking the crust from the coin.

"Someone," he said, "took some of this off and polished away this part here." He pointed to the small part of the coin in which the glimmer of gold could be seen.

"Yep," I said, not wanting to say what Betsy had told me about how it was found.

"I suppose you're gonna not tell me shit about this. That right, Mad Dog?" Sam asked.

"Well, buddy," I said, "I hate to be that way, but that's pretty accurate."

"So, buddy." He mimicked my term of endearment. "Should you get more of these, would you consider letting me sell them out of the shop?"

"Sure," I said giving my old friend a nod. Then he turned back to hunch over the coin, scraping and peering at it, pulling a book from his shelf and reading intently.

Finally, Sam looked up and said, "Old friend, what you have here is an eight-escudo gold coin. My guess, because this is not my expertise, is that it was minted at the Spanish mint in Bogota, Colombia, between 1625 and 1642."

"So," I said after pausing to take in what Sam had told me. "There a lot of these floating around?"

"In a word," he replied, "no."

"The coins were shaped odd back then," I said,

trying to reach into my mind for some treasure fantasy facts stored there.

"Right," Sam said. "The coin you're looking at is a cob coin the Spanish made quickly. Before sometime in the mid-1600s, they made a real pretty coin with fine workmanship. Then they changed the process and made sloppy misshaped ones like this.

"There were cob coins from the wrecks Mel Fisher found in Florida that were minted in the 1700s. This one is much older, and to be honest, I looked once and couldn't even find one on the Internet."

"What's it worth?" I asked.

"A lot."

"Thousands?"

Sam's face finally lost its poker steel, and a large, excited smile rippled across it. "Buddy, this little fucker is probably worth more than your car."

"Give me a break, Sam. My car isn't worth thousands."

"Well, this little coin is worth tens of thousands if it's an original."

After making me double pinky promise to market any coins like it that I got in his shop, Sam called Gene Triller, a professor of history at the University of Puerto Rico and the only one he knew who could give me the full scoop on my coin. "Gene's a real expert on antique Spanish coins," he said as he got off the phone, "and wants to see what you've got as soon as possible. I set up an appointment for you for six tonight if you can get there by then."

I checked my watch and figured that with a little luck, I could make it. Then, with the largest retainer I'd ever received nestled safely in the front pocket of my favorite khaki shorts, I used Sam's phone to call Joyce Baker at the seaplane port three blocks away. Joyce was an old friend of my wife's, but more important, she was also the manager of Seaborne Airlines.

Luck was with me. Sam's professor in San Juan was my best lead. I had to see him soon, and Joyce could get me on a 3:20 flight. But I had to hurry. She'd already be bending the one-hour check-in rule. After we hung up, I took a deep breath for courage and called my wife.

Cheri answered on the first ring, and I told her what I could without mentioning things like the coin that I thought my new client wanted just between her and me. In her silence after I said I'd be on the next plane to Puerto Rico; I could sense her mind analyzing every word I spoke. Cheri had been a deputy U.S. Marshal on the island for twenty years before she retired. I knew she was itching to know all the facts, and like a puppy watching a ball being thrown, wanted in on the game. One of the things I love about her, though it can be a little annoying, is that she's a born sleuth. I knew that as she was hearing my words, she was straining to fill in the blanks.

"Mad Dog, you know we were supposed to go to dinner with Del and Margie tonight," Cheri said with a playful hint of frustrated anger.

"Look, honey, I know, but trust me this is important. This Betsy Rourk woman I met with today really needs

13

help. I talked with Sam Drumand, and he gave me the name of a professor in Puerto Rico who maybe can shed some light on this case. I should be back by tomorrow afternoon."

"You know you forgot your cell phone." Cheri was figuring a way to come to town and get more information out of me. "I can come right in with it and bring my gun and makeup kit."

"Yeah," I said, knowing it was a little lie. I hadn't forgot the damn phone. I left it home because it was like a leash, and I hated being bothered by it. Just this once, though, I wished I'd brought it so I could make some calls on the case while I was in San Juan.

"You want me to bring it down?" Cheri asked. Her voice made it clear she wanted to go with me.

"No," I said, resigned to my phone-less fate. "The plane leaves at 3:20. I'll just wing it."

When I hung up, it was 2:40, and I hurried to the seaplane port. For some reason, I felt ten years younger. I had the hot coin in my pocket and a case I felt getting more interesting with every minute.

I wasn't really sure why I was flying to San Juan instead of hunting for Bob and Tony or going out to Isaac's Bay to look around, but my instincts told me to check out the coin first, so San Juan it was.

I'd parked my old pickup in the lot at Fort Christiansted, so I decided it would be quicker to leave it there and walk. The plane was only five minutes from Sam's shop in a little walkway leading to the Board Walk along the Christiansted Harbor docks. Passing over the old walkway's cobblestones, I wondered if one of the men who owned the coin in my pocket might have walked these same stones hundreds of years ago. The Virgin Islands past was all around me on the street, the buildings that lined both sides silent reminders of their history. I turned right out of the narrow walkway and went down the bustling docks, surrounded by camera-toting tourists and hurrying locals. An east wind carried the familiar perfume flowing over me, a mix of sea breeze, ocean rot, and fish. The air gave the back of my neck a gentle tickle, and the scent of the ocean carried a touch of adventure. My step quickened, and I realized with a smile that I was back in the hunt. It felt good.

When I got to the seaplane office, Joyce said she'd booked me into the last seat to San Juan. I got my ticket and walked over to sit in the tent-covered waiting area between the building and the sea. I had no idea what lay ahead but suspected it would be far different from those few peaceful moments in a lawn chair backed against the security fence, just admiring the boats and dreaming of treasure.

The scene relaxed me, until I noticed the snatches of arguing voices the breeze was blowing my way. I turned toward the ticket counter, where a large black man in a white T-shirt was clearly becoming angrier because he couldn't get on the flight. As I watched, he turned and hurried away. "Definitely not on Island Time," I thought, as he practically ran down the dock toward the shops and restaurants.

After seven years of living on St. Croix, I could never help notice the obnoxious rarity of someone like that. An uptight tourist, I figured, but it wouldn't be long before the island had him sipping rum and lying placidly in the sun.

The pilot came into the tent shade and began calling names to board the plane. As I stood when I heard mine, a hand touched my shoulder. Cheri was standing there on the other side of the three-foot chain-link fence, cell phone in one hand and a small brown bag in the other. "Phone. Keep it on," she said with a stern look. She knew my habit was just the opposite.

Cheri lifted the brown bag, and her look turned to a smile. "Dock kit," she said. "Brush your teeth and shave so you don't look like a bum."

There was no time to talk. Suddenly, I hated leaving her, and I think she saw it in my eyes as she reached both arms over the fence. The hug was a long one. "I can't believe you're going to San Juan without me," she said teasingly, accepting that I'd be going alone.

"Don't worry. I'll be fine," I said.

"I'm not worried about you," she lied. "I just want to go shopping."

"Sir," a voice behind me said. "We need to go." The pilot was the only one left in the waiting area. I looked at him, then gave Cheri a quick kiss and walked down the floating dock to the plane.

Within minutes, I was bouncing across the waves and off to Puerto Rico. God, I love an adventure.

CHAPTER

In San Juan as I was waiting in line for a rental car, my phone rang. It was Sam telling me through the static that Gene Triller had called to change our meeting place. It would now be for dinner at the professor's home in Isabela, a small beach community on the east side of the island.

When I finally got to the service counter, Ana Ramirez confronted me. I knew who it was because I read name tags attached to ample breasts even when eye contact is more appropriate. As I should have expected, my poor Spanish and Ana's poor English instigated the classic dance of hand gestures done to the music of rising voices and diminishing smiles.

After five minutes of this, Honey Smith, a beautiful blonde who looked at Ana's computer screen and said in a South Texas drawl, "Mr. Cotton, may I help?" saved us. It must have been the drawl, but for some reason, it took me much longer to read "Honey Smith" than "Ana Ramirez."

"Mr. Cotton," Honey Smith repeated, "may I help you?"

"That would be great," I said, my voice still at a decibel level that should be reserved for "Stop! Thief" or "Man overboard!"

Honey Smith smiled. "Insurance or no insurance?"

I took a long breath, reminded myself that I was in a business, not a sporting event, and said in my most polite voice, "No insurance, thank you."

Having been saved by Honey Smith, I walked out to my tiny Honda Fit, armed with a map heavily marked in yellow highlighter, a key, my trusty dock kit, my cell phone, my low-limit credit cards, and a sense of direction that could best be described as forward. As I got in the car, it dawned on me that I had no plan, no language skills, and no clean clothes. I also wondered for the first time if Professor Triller spoke English.

The car rental directions proved sound, and I pulled up an hour later at a huge, yellow, three-story duplex. As I climbed out of the car I'd dubbed "little one," I could smell the salt breeze and hear the familiar tempo of waves against shore. "Damn nice place on a professor's salary," I thought as I walked up to the large wooden door and used the brass knocker.

The door opened quickly, and in front of me -- the final light of day shining through a large picture window behind her -- stood a woman whose long brown hair glowed in the dying sunlight.

"Mad Dog," I said, extending my hand as I noticed, against all my years of training, that she didn't have a name tag. "Mad Dog Cotton."

"Mr. Mad Dog Cotton," she said as our eyes met. "Welcome, I'm Professor Triller."

I don't know what my face did at that moment, but she smiled at what was obviously my confusion and said, "Please call me Jean. I take it Sam forgot to tell you I'm not one of the guys."

"That would be a safe bet," I said in what Cheri likes to call my let's-be-stupid voice.

"So," she said, "we're both full of surprises. I'm a woman and you're a Mad Dog. Tell me Mr. Cotton, how does one become a Mad Dog? Does one have to misbehave?"

I liked this woman. Most people kind of ignore the name – maybe they're afraid I'll bite them -- but she just came straight at me.

"I did misbehave a little," I said, "but trust me, the man that gave me the name just wanted to remind me I had a little bit of a temper and needed to control it. I figured back then in my youth if the name helped remind me to behave, it was the name I needed."

Jean Triller smiled at me. "Well, let's hope the name keeps working."

She turned toward the picture window and walked to where a glass of wine was sitting on a small glass table. I followed.

For a long moment, she stood looking out the window. Then, without turning, she said, "Mr. Cotton, may I fix you something?"

"Whatever you're having is fine."

I moved over next to her. Looking out the window dominating the living room's west wall, I was surprised to see that the building was perched high atop a steep cliff which ended in a coastline of rugged stone and surf.

Jean turned from the last pink in the sky and the white froth of the shore, and walked to a small bar, where she poured a second glass of wine.

When she returned, the faraway look was gone, and she brought a warm smile with the cold glass of fruity white wine.

"Good," I said shyly as I sipped it, knowing I liked it but also that I wouldn't know good wine from grape juice.

"You a wine drinker, Mr. Cotton?" Jean asked.

"No, sorry. I'm more a beer and rum guy, but this is great."

"It's called Mer et Soleil."

"Mer et Soleil," I repeated. "Sea and sun," I added, surprising myself.

Jean smiled. "Your French is close enough."

I smiled back. "I had to take a language in high school, and the girls in French were prettier than the girls in German."

"Big honken girls, those German girls."

"Honken?" I said. "I take it you're not one of those Puerto Rico-born girls."

"No."

We both sipped.

"Nebraska," Jean said, taking a last look out at the sea and final light.

"Pardon me," I replied, confused.

"I'm from Nebraska. York, Nebraska."

"You're a long way from home."

She turned to face me, her wine glass still holding the yellow light mingled with the dying orange of the clouds. "No, I'm very much at home."

I thought about how St. Croix had grabbed me when I first came seven years before, and how alien my life back in the states seemed now. "We're almost neighbors," I told her. "I grew up in Wyoming."

"Really," she said, a genuine glow in her eyes. "A cowboy in paradise?"

"Yep," I said.

"Mad Dog, you want dinner or to talk business first?"

For the first time since that big wooden door had opened, I remembered the hard gold in my pocket. "To be honest," I said, "I haven't eaten since breakfast, and dinner would really be nice."

Over a light dinner of poached wahoo and a Caesar salad, the small talk continued. Jean had fled Nebraska with a scholarship to the University of Florida and never turned back. I talked about St. Croix, growing up, and my years on the Denver police force. It was a relaxed time. During that meal, Jean went from stranger to friend.

"Now," I said as the last of the wine emptied from the yellow Mer Soleil bottle, "you want to talk gold?"

I placed the coin Betsy Rourk had given me that morning on the table.

Jean left it laying there and walked over to the wall, where she turned the light up high. She got a pair of glasses and a large, antique magnifying glass out of a small desk, came back to the table, put the glasses on and winked through them. "Hell getting old," she said.

"Tell me," I replied.

"How old?" she asked.

"Me?"

"Yes, how old are you?"

"I'm fifty-two."

She smiled as she began to examine the coin.

"This is in amazing condition."

"You could hardly tell it was a coin before Sam cleaned it up."

"One of the advantages of gold is it's fairly resistant to salt, and the coral may actually have protected it. Where was it found?"

"I can't tell you, sorry," I replied. I liked Jean, and Sam had told me I could trust her, but I owed the Rourks all the confidentiality I could give them.

"I understand," she said, looking over her glasses. "Well, let me tell you what I can. This is a shield-type eight-escudo coin, and it's almost in mint condition. The irregular shape is how it was made."

"How do you know it's almost mint?" I asked, the coin now taking on more relevance."

"With a coin like this, you look for what are called 'chiseler marks.'"

"Chiseler marks?"

"Because the coins weren't round, they were quick and easy to make, but the downfall was once they entered into the marketplace, the vendors and the people carrying the coins could clip or scrape small amounts of silver, or in this case gold, off the coin, and thus, the chiseler was born."

"And this coin?" I asked.

"No chisel marks, so I can assume it came straight from the mint."

"OK, I understand this coin is old and unusual. Anything else?"

"Oh, yeah," she said, standing up and moving into the kitchen, "but I need another drink. How about you?"

"Sorry. I drink anymore and I won't be able to drive back to a motel."

"Don't be silly, Mad Dog," Jean said with a little laugh, opening the refrigerator and pulling out a green bottle. "You're staying here. We have a lot to talk about."

"But …," I said.

"But nothing. It's 10 o'clock and way too late to get a room, and I have a perfectly good guest room right next to the kitchen." She watched me from the counter as she pulled the cork out of the bottle. "Don't panic," Jean said. "It'll be all right. If you want, I'll call your wife and get permission."

Involuntarily, I glanced down at my ring. I must have blushed, but I also pulled out my cell phone and said, "Part of my survival depends on keeping Cheri in the loop. I better call her and tell her I'm in good hands."

Jean smiled. "Ah, an honest man," she said as she handed me a glass of cold white wine. "How refreshing. You'd best call now. It's getting late."

As I explained to Cheri that I was staying at Professor Triller's house, Jean rolled the coin in her hand and waited.

When I hung up, she took a sip of wine and asked, "In the doghouse?"

"Nope," I replied. "Honesty is the only policy."

"Wise man," she said with a smile. Then she gestured to the computer she'd been working at while I was on the phone. "I can only find one other instance where a coin from that era minted like yours has surfaced," Jean said, "and it couldn't be authenticated. There was no way to establish its history, where it came from, and it was just sold for its gold value."

"Where was it sold?" I asked.

"eBay, about seven years ago."

"By who?"

"I can't really tell, but it looks like it was from St. Croix. She pushed her chair back and took a long look at the screen. "I have a geek friend that may be able to get me a name but not until morning."

"That would be great," I said.

"Now, Mad Dog," she said, spinning the coin around

and staring at it, "let me tell you a little more about your cob."

Jean handed me the large magnifying glass and pointed her pen at the coin. "Because it's so clean, I can give you a pretty good history of this coin. First, it was minted in the New World in Bogota." She pointed her pen at the letters NR clearly visible on the face.

"OK. I see the NR," I said. "What does it mean?"

"That's the mint mark that signifies it was minted in Bogota in what's now Colombia. The NR stands for Nuevo Reino, the 'New Kingdom,' which is what the Spanish provinces governed from Bogota were called then."

"Where's the date of the coin?" I asked.

"Ah," Jean sighed, "that's one of the cool things about this coin and most of the coins of that era. There is no date."

"So, we can't date it?"

"Yes. As a matter of fact, we can just about date it to the year it was minted."

"I don't understand," I said.

She moved her pen to another mark on the coin. "See the P here?" I looked in the magnifying glass and saw it clearly.

"Yeah."

"That's the assayer mark. That tells us the assayer of this coin, probably the gentleman in charge of making it, was Miguel Pinto Camargo. He was involved in making all the coins in the Nuevo Reino mint from 1627 until 1632, which is quite amazing."

"Amazing?" I asked, still looking through the glass.

"Yes, Mad Dog, amazing."

"Why?"

"OK. First, your coin is pristine, never in circulation. Second, it couldn't have come from a previously found treasure wreck because the only one that yielded coins from Nuevo Reino sank before this coin was made. That was the *Atocha* that sank off Florida in 1622. Third, a coin from that era that hasn't been damaged or chiseled has shown up only once in the last 20 years, after the big hurricane in '89, and it was found near St. Croix. Finally, I heard a story once from a reliable source that a treasure ship rumored to be carrying 15 tons of gold coins was lost in 1634, and it could very well have been traveling to St. Croix."

"Fifteen tons," I said, my voice rising.

Jean looked up from the soft light of the computer screen, a wild look on her face. "Yeah, Mad Dog, fifteen tons of gold coins.

All I could croak out was the word, "how."

"How much?" she said, the gleam still sparkling in her eyes.

"Yeah. Yeah, money. How much?" I said, trying to catch my breath.

Jean picked up a calculator and tapped in some numbers. She turned it to me and said, "This would be the figure at $500 an ounce, gold right now is listing much higher. The raw coins in the coin market would bring much more."

I looked at the calculator and studied it, then

whistled. "Twenty-four million dollars." I could feel my heart rate jump.

She smiled at me. "Not a big math guy, are you?"

"I can imagine twenty-four million dollars," I said, still looking at the calculator.

"That's not twenty-four million. That's two hundred and forty million. My friend, if the rumors are correct and this coin is part of a salvageable treasure, that treasure is worth well over a quarter of a billion dollars."

"Shit," was the only word I could muster as I felt the room get hotter.

"Of course, this coin could just be a fluke," Jean said, looking back at the calculator.

"Sure," I said nodding at the black numbers in front of us and trying to uncross my eyes so I could see clearly how many 0's were there.

"Mad Dog, this coin is a clue to what could be a huge find!"

Suddenly, I knew she was going to ask me again where it came from. I rushed to get in my own question first: "You said this fifteen tons of gold was a rumor. What rumor?"

The intense glare in Jean's eyes eased, and her body relaxed away from me. I suddenly realized we'd been only inches apart. As she shifted, a slight floral scent I hadn't perceived before remained. I felt a surge of guilt as she moved her arms across her chest for thoughts I hadn't even realized were running through my mind. "This treasure thing is kinda hypnotic, isn't it?" she said.

A softness came to her voice. "There is nothing more

addictive than the chase for treasure. The damn rush makes jumping out of an airplane seem boring."

"Tell me the rumor," I said.

Jean sat back in her chair and looked at me, and then, as if deciding to release a mystery, started to speak: "The story goes like this. In 1628, a Dutch fleet of thirty ships commanded by Admiral Piet Heyn had the Spanish treasure fleet bottled up in the port of Cartagena. The Spanish had about two years' worth of gold and silver on board, and, like our coin, much of it was minted in Nuevo Reino. After months of waiting, the Spanish treasure fleet left Cartagena and sailed north. The Dutch followed and finally trapped the Spanish fleet off the coast of Cuba, near Havana. The Spanish were said to have surrendered their whole fleet and ninety tons of gold and silver without firing a shot. The Dutch fleet then headed back to the Netherlands.

"But there's a little hiccup in the history of Piet Heyn's raid on the Spanish fleet. It seems most scholars agree that Heyn returned with ninety tons of silver cob coins and gold bars and a wealth of jewels but only a small amount of gold coins, but the manifest the Spanish had showed a hundred and five tons of silver cob coins, gold bars, and gold cob coins."

"But it was minus fifteen tons."

"Finally, some quality math on your part," Jean said, her voice becoming more animated. "It seems that during an ugly storm off the coast of Puerto Rico, a ship commanded by a captain named Dirk Chivers disappeared with two of the military escort ships.

"There's a rumor built from reports by men who served with the admiral that during the storm, Chivers' ship broke away from the fleet and was supposedly pursued by two of the attack ships. The story goes on to say that none of the three ships were ever seen again."

"That's not in the history books?"

"No," Jean said, "but at that time, there was good reason for a Dutch cover-up. The Dutch with their new wealth were moving into a position of world power and able to supply a larger navy and army. If Captain Chivers had absconded with such a big chunk of the booty, the Dutch might have wanted to keep that little blurp in the history books under their hats."

"And Chivers disappeared into history?"

"Until now. He had a grandson -- a namesake -- who seems to have followed in his footsteps seventy years later. The guy was a pirate, a small terror in the Indian Ocean for a while. But this Chivers who got the gold was never heard from again."

Jean pushed the coin toward me. "Oh, one more morsel," she said. "In the late 1620s, the Dutch had a colony named Nieuw Zeeland on what you know as St. Croix, and it seems the governor of the settlement was Chivers' older brother, Hendrik."

I thought for a second and did some mental geography. "So, tell me where was this storm that got Captain Chivers and his ship full of gold separated from the admiral's fleet."

"North of the Mona Passage."

I knew the Mona Passage well from years of sailing

the Caribbean, and the answer made perfect sense. "In a storm, the Mona Passage would be a death sentence to any ship like they sailed back then."

"Probably," Jean agreed.

"But," I added, "if you were a truly ballsy guy and wanted to steal fifteen tons of gold coins from a fleet of thirty ships, I can't think of a better place to ditch the fleet."

"And if you survived the passage," Jean said, picking up the logical thread, "and the smaller ships chasing you didn't, all you had to do is sail the southern coast of Puerto Rico and make a short hop to Vieques and over to beautiful St. Croix. There's only one problem: Back at that time, the English controlled the west side of St. Croix and the Dutch the east side.

"Chivers would have known the English were on the west side of the island, and he might have feared that his good friend, the admiral, would check out Nieuw Zeeland for his lost ships. The captain didn't have a lot of places to go."

I felt her logic beginning to corner me.

"Your ship is probably trashed by the Mona Passage storm," Jean said. "You have to go far enough south of Puerto Rico not to be seen by the Spanish who now don't like you. The Dutch fleet might be on your tail and may even be going to Bassin, the Dutch colony on the island's north shore. So, if I'm Captain Chivers and I didn't die in the Mona Passage, I'd skirt wide around the Spanish in Puerto Rico and the English on the west end of St. Croix. I'd sail south and east out of sight of land and then north to the east coast, which is controlled by my beloved brother. But I can't sail into my brother's port at Bassin because the admiral may have figured out what I'm up to.

"I need to find somewhere else on the island where I'll be good and safe."

For what seemed like an eternity, Jean stared at me -- not challenging but knowing – just looking quietly in the dim light of her computer. Finally, I must have shown a crack. She lifted her wine glass and tapped mine sitting on the desk in front of me.

"Yep, makes perfect sense," Jean said, telling herself but telling me, too. "Chivers would have hid out on the southeast end of St. Croix while things cooled down. If I were Captain Chivers, I might think I could send word to my brother and get provisions from him or help repairing my boat."

Jean's fingers changed the image on the screen, and a Google Earth vision of St. Croix appeared. She hit the magnify function, and the island's southeast end materialized, then grew to fill the screen.

The bright red nail of her index finger traced the coastline, touching each bay and inlet a boat might enter. Then her hand stopped, the tip of the long finger frozen on Isaac's Bay. Jean tapped her computer mouse twice, and it grew bigger. "This bay," she said, "this could be a break in the coral, this small passage a way in." Her nail clicked on the screen. "Look at those reefs on all of the others."

I had snorkeled and dove the bay, and I knew the

cut in the coral she'd found. My throat felt squeezed by an invisible hand, my mouth frozen dry. The professor's logic and intuition had unearthed my last big secret.

My professional veneer cracked. "Bob Rourk," I croaked, feeling like a conspirator.

Jean's head turned toward me with a small smile. "Bob Rourk," she repeated.

"He disappeared a day ago. His wife, Betsy, hired me to find him."

"Most women don't hire a private investigator only a day after their old man disappears."

"He found this the day before he disappeared," I said, laying my finger on the coin. "And he was going out for more."

There was a long silence, then, like a school kid giving up his final secret, I said, "He was going to Isaac's Bay."

She smiled, and we both looked back at the map on the screen.

"Southeast corner of the island, lots of shoals," I said, pausing to think of the hundreds of times I'd looked at the bay from the tall surrounding hills. "It could be a ship killer really easy, but no one back then had any reason to go into it."

"Except Captain Dirk Chivers."

"Yep," I agreed in the same way she had. I thought for a second and then asked, "So, Jean, are you gonna murder me in my sleep tonight?"

She reached across the desk and put her hand on mine. "No, Mad Dog Cotton, but as Bogey said in

Casablanca, I think this is the beginning of a beautiful friendship." She shut her computer, leaving us in the dim light shining from the kitchen. Jean stood and pointed through the door. "Your room is on the other side of the kitchen," she said. "If you're up first, you make the coffee."

She stretched to her full height, turned, and walked down the long hallway. Somewhere, I heard a door close.

CHAPTER

4

After midnight, lying alone in the guest room, I was wide-eyed as the day buzzed through my mind. I knew that an extraordinary and beautiful woman was lying in bed under the same roof. Her presence, the wine, and the lure of treasure gold had been an intoxicating combination. My mind slipped toward sleep but then slid back to the heart-pounding sensations of the evening. Was Jean wide-awake like me and thinking inescapably about pirate gold?

"Shit, you're an old fool," I said out loud as I rolled over, hoping the rhythm of the ceiling fan would lull me to sleep."

I was in that semi-coma of being awake-too-long when I heard the crash. At first, I thought it was part of a dream. The second crash and a scream from the kitchen outside my door whipped me awake.

When I heard the second scream, I knew it was Jean. The stream of curses that followed was clearly a man. I jumped from the bed, tangling my legs in the sheets, and falling to the floor like a hobbled chicken. It felt like it took minutes to escape the cotton shackles that trapped my legs, but once I did, I rushed for the door.

As I got there, something hit the wall next to my head, showering glass in every direction. I instinctively pulled my head back into the dark. Taking a deep breath, I peeked around the doorjamb. In the moonlit kitchen, Jean was about 15 feet away, her back against the refrigerator. She held a heavy salt grinder in her right hand, poised to throw at the huge form towering between us. In the dim light, his white T-shirt seemed to shimmer as he moved. As I stood hidden in the dark of the doorway, Jean's arm uncoiled and hurled the heavy saltshaker at her attacker. Like a shortstop picking off a line drive, he deftly caught it and whipped it back at her.

Jean dodged right, and the grinder slammed into the huge picture window. With a pop, the moon-bathed glass cracked into a web of broken light.

Then, suddenly, I recognized the flash of dull metal in the giant's right hand. He raised the large hunting knife toward Jean and growled -- the Cruzan accent unmistakable -- "This is for you, bitch."

The animal had to be six inches taller than me and

at least twenty years younger. I stepped quietly into the kitchen, feeling no fear. The hundreds of hours of combat training I had endured took over. My mind chanted the mantra of survival drilled into me: "Knees. Groin. Eyes."

The thought kept screaming at me as I tensed my body and rushed single-mindedly across the glass-littered floor.

Like the flip of a switch starting a powerful angry engine, a part of me I seldom thought about roared to life. My mind filled with cool calculation as I leaped and smashed full force into the man's solid mass.

My knee struck deep in the heavy muscle just above his knee. At the same time, I reached over the mountain of his shoulder with my right hand and grabbed for his eyes. My left hand gripped his T-shirt, and as his muscles tensed, I hung on his back like a crazed terrier.

Pulling on his shirt, digging in my knee, I tried to move up his boulder-like bulk to tear at his unprotected eyes. To my amazement, the guy's head barely budged despite my violent yanking, and his leg where I'd buried my knee stood solid and unmoving.

As I pulled up his body, feeling the rough beard but unable to reach the softness of eyes and nose, his mass began to ripple and move. In a quick, reflexive surge, he bent forward, lifting my struggling weight and destroying any advantage I'd had.

I felt small, insignificant, doomed -- unable to damage my prey or to let him go. Wrapping my left leg around his thick waist, I dug my fingers deeper into the sharp stubble of his face and yanked with all my might.

Like an enraged bull, he effortlessly threw back his arms and shoulders to slam me against the wall. With a crushing force, we hit a narrow pantry door. The handles ground into my back, then the doors shattered with a crack, and the shelves behind them exploded. Cans, jars, pasta, everything else they contained cascaded on top of us. I was helpless on the floor, my arms trapped by the walls, my body crushed by a suffocating mass of sweat-soaked T-shirt.

Then air rushed into my lungs as the hugely muscled body began to rise. I tightened my grip on his shirt, and a burst of curses exploded out of him like a cloud of black smoke. The pantry sides pressing in my arms held me tight as the monster, struggling and cursing, shook out of my weak grasp and turned on his hands and knees toward me. I fought for breath as his huge black face roared out, "I'll fucking kill you."

Like a slow-motion movie, words from my father flashed into my mind: "Never fucking quit! Never!"

Under my hand was a can. My fingers squeezed tight, and I whipped its weight up into the stubbled jaw, feeling bone and teeth being smashed by steel. The dark face jerked back, but before I could move again, the big right hand reached out and seized my throat.

He tried to move closer, but the same crush of cans and shelves that held me immobile kept his other hand from my neck.

As the huge fingers squeezed my throat, I flailed

weakly with the can. My mind lost focus. I was dying. The powerful grip pinned me in the pantry's wreckage as it crushed my windpipe.

I fought for air, my mind struggling for a way to damage him. I stared at the giant, and again my father's voice spoke: "Never quit! Do something." I swung the can again but only hit weakly against soft flesh and the wall alongside me.

The man's eyes stayed fixed on mine, waiting for the moment my oxygen-starved body went dead. The contorted face was so close I could smell the sour beer on his breath and see my reflection in the deep yellow tint of his eyes.

He was squeezing the life from me. Still, my mind raced, feeling my father there, too, detached from danger and pain. Together, thought-by-thought, we sought ways I could kill this man.

I moved to the left, pushing against the pressure in my neck, and battered the can again into his torso. My dying mind saw not the beast but my father and heard him say with pride in his weathered face, "Nice."

But the force on my neck never lessened.

I was summoning the last bit of strength, my father cheering me on, when I heard the thump. It was the sound of a bat smashing a coconut, and the huge hand on my throat fell loose. I pulled in breath and saw the fevered eyes go glassy. The man rose unsteadily and grabbed the back of his head, then stared at the blood covering his hand. Looking amazed, he pushed the rest of the way to his feet.

"Fuck," he said.

I pulled my left knee to my trapped chest and kicked out at his leg, but he sidestepped it and I missed. I tried to get up from the wrecked pantry but couldn't.

Then I saw Jean. She was standing next to the giant, holding a large marble rolling pin in both hands. I smiled, and he glared at me in confusion, trying to understand why.

She swung the club toward his head again, crushing the marble bludgeon into his temple. The crack was like a whip. His head snapped sideways, then returned to center. As if shocked by the blow, Jean let go of the rolling pin, and it fell to the floor. For a second, the man stood over me, blood soaking from his head into his shirt. He blinked in confusion, then, as if unharmed, turned toward her.

Staggering away from me, he grabbed Jean by the front of her robe and pulled her to her knees. She fell forward next to me. We caught each other's eyes, and I could see her terror.

The man had us both down now, but he didn't attack. Instead, he turned and staggered out of the kitchen toward the dining room. His bulk was a ghostly silhouette as he stopped next to the table, then turned and leaned on it as he looked back at us still huddled in the kitchen. The moonlight framed his body as it streamed in fractured patterns through the picture window.

Like an audience watching a terrifying play it was powerless to change, Jean and I sat helpless. The man stood still with his hands on the table. The blood on his shirt shone black in the yellow glow.

Without emotion, he said, "Fuckin' bad." Then he turned away and lurched forward, into the window's wounded glass – and through it! For a moment, his body flew out in the night, then cascaded down in a shroud of glittering fragments.

The full moon sat as if transfixed, framed by the glass still left in the window. I knew what was below, the rocks and the surf I'd marveled at only a few hours before. Now the body of the man who had come to kill us was there, too, flesh merged as one with the black, unforgiving rock and the cruel, cold surf.

It was over.

Slowly, the violence that had seized me dissolved into rational thought. I turned to Jean on the floor next to me, sitting hunched, drained, eyes emptying into space. Her arms were wrapped around her knees, and she was shaking. I touched an arm lightly. "You're OK," I said.

Jean pulled her knees tighter, rocking and sobbing in huge gasps. I didn't know what else to do. "I must look like an idiot," I thought, cans and bags of pasta pressed against me, and –worst of all – a brown sea of Cocoa Puffs submerging me from a box that smashed when we first slammed down the pantry doors. Never again will I smell Cocoa Puffs without remembering that moment. Never will I eat them again for as long as I live.

The sobbing slowed, and Jean looked up. "It's OK,"

I told her again. Her reddened eyes looked first at me, then out through the shattered glass. I knew what she needed to do.

Forcing my muscles, with a quick twist of my body, I lunged out of the pantry. I stood and took her hand, and she leaned on it a little as she got up. We walked to the window together, pulled by the emptiness outside it.

Below, on the wet boulders 20 feet down, a body lay sprawled in the moonlight. The head's angle on its neck was impossible. Suddenly, recognition flicked through my mind. I'd seen this man before. For a moment, my thoughts were just blank, then I knew: the man at the seaplane, the loud, angry man who couldn't get on my flight and then had hurried away.

"Shit," I said at the thought that this horror could be my fault.

"What?" Jean asked.

"I think this guy followed me from St. Croix."

"What?" she said again, as if in a trance.

"St. Croix," I replied. "I think this guy tried to get on my plane in St. Croix."

"He followed you on the plane?" she asked, trying to understand.

"No," I said. "He couldn't get on the flight. The last time I saw him, he was leaving the airport like his pants were on fire."

Jean turned and moved shakily toward the dining room, stepping around the glass and a fallen chair. "I have to call the police," she said.

"Yeah, good idea."

The thought of the police coming reminded me of what I had on: only the heart-covered boxers Cheri gave me for Valentine's Day. Self-consciously, I looked up at Jean, who was staring at me as she talked on the phone.

I raised my hand in a half-wave and eased out to the bedroom where my clothes were laying on the floor.

I got into them quickly and came back. Jean was sitting on the couch next to the phone, clutching her robe. She smiled a little. "Guess I should throw on something before the cops show up," she said.

"It'll keep their attention on the case," I told her.

But she didn't move, almost couldn't. "What the hell happened?" I asked.

"I came out for water, and he was there in the kitchen."

"How the hell did he get in?"

We both turned to the door. It was ajar but didn't look damaged. "Oh God, I don't think I locked it!"

"Did he go after you?"

"I had my glass. I threw it at him. I don't know what happened then, till I saw you."

"Well, you were doing a pretty good job of fending him off when I came in."

Jean smiled weakly again, then got up and left me alone in the room. I sat down and tried to gather my thoughts. I didn't think the police would have a problem with Jean and me, even with a dead man out the window. It was a pretty clear case of self-defense. Then that thought made me think of the hunting knife, and I went into the kitchen to find it. No problem. It was sticking out of the oak jamb next to the pantry door. If the door hadn't splintered under our weight, it probably would be sticking out of me right now, in the middle of the kitchen floor.

"Jesus!", I thought. My mind shuddered, maybe my body, too. How close I'd come. How lucky I was!

As thoughts of mortality – and the end of my mortality -- poured through my mind, Jean came into the kitchen wearing a pair of Levi's and a long-sleeve white shirt.

"Look at that," I said, pointing to the menacing blade.

"That son of a bitch was playing for keeps."

"Don't touch it. Leave it for the police," I told her. "This'll be a crime scene when they get here." Then I remembered where I was. "Did they say how long they'd be?"

"They said a car was on its way. But who knows?" Jean shared my view of the local cops' efficiency.

"Let's just go wait in the living room and sit down," I said.

We took opposite ends of the couch but said nothing. We both felt awkward. Then I had a thought, one that felt important.

"I don't think we need to mention the coin," I said.

Then I had another thought. "How do we explain what I'm doing here in your home at this late hour, ma'am?"

"We'll tell them I like older men." She smiled, a real one this time instead of the half-tries before.

"You saved my life," I said, serious again.

"Yeah, and my own, too. I swing a mean rolling pin."

The vision of that marble weapon whipping through the air into the black giant's head played again in my mind. It was insane how this woman had saved me.

Jean was still thinking. "You should call your wife," she said.

"What!"

"If I was your wife and you didn't call me right now, I'd be pissed."

I thought about that but not for long. "Yep, I better call my wife."

Cheri answered the phone on the second ring and sounded wide-awake. "Where have you been?" she asked, a mixture of relief and anger in her voice.

"Where have I been?" I said, surprised by her tone.

"Been, you asshole," she snapped. "I've been trying to call you for hours."

"I had my phone off," I said, a feeling of guilt sinking into my stomach.

"Well, while you were enjoying the blissful silence of no phone, all hell has broken loose here."

"Hell!" I said, "What …?"

Cheri angrily cut me off. "Shit, Dog, I've been scared to death worrying about you."

"Why?" I asked, becoming more confused.

"After you talked to Betsy Rourk, you told me you went over to Sam's shop and talked to him. Right?"

"Right," I said, feeling lost.

"Well, some son-of-a-bitch murdered Sam and

Ann right in their shop sometime after it closed last night." She paused, and I tried to choke back a wave of dizziness that began in my gut and was racing to my head.

"I talked to Fred Stanley -- he was one of the detectives that went to the scene -- and he said Sam was cut up bad, like he'd been tortured."

Suddenly, I couldn't breathe. I couldn't think. I couldn't see. I held onto the table, trying to stay on my feet as my mind flashed to the knife still sticking out of the kitchen wall.

Sam! Sam! What did I do to Sam! How did I make this happen? I'd asked him for help. He'd given it like a friend. And now ….

Cheri wasn't finished. "And that's not all, Sherlock. Not ten minutes after you hung up after telling me you were spending the night with the good professor, I got a call from Alli at the coffee shop, and your client Mrs. Rourk had been mugged."

"Mugged?" I repeated, stunned.

"Some gorilla in a man suit grabbed her and tried to drag her into his truck. She managed to get away and run for her life, but she's up at the hospital right now with a broken hand and some pretty damn good bruises."

"Did she get a look at the guy?" I asked, thinking of the gorilla lying in the rocks outside Jean's shattered window.

"How the fuck would I know, you knucklehead? I've

been sitting here on the boat trying to call a guy who turned off his phone."

"Look, I'm sorry about the phone. I wasn't thinking."

"Damn you, Mad Dog. The last people you saw here before you went running off to Puerto Rico are either mugged or dead, and I couldn't get a hold of you. Those asshole cops in Puerto Rico wouldn't even talk to me, and I couldn't remember the fucking professor's name, so – damn it, I've been worried to death!"

Suddenly, all I could hear on the phone were sobs.

"Cheri," I said in my softest voice. "Cheri, I'm OK. I'm fine. I'm sorry."

After a few moments, I could hear her catching her breath. "Dog, don't you ever scare me like that again," she gasped. "Do you understand?"

"Yeah, baby, I understand," I said, feeling my throat tighten more and a tear creep out my right eye.

"Hon," she said, "are you sure you're OK?"

"Yeah," I answered, "but I gotta tell ya something." Cheri never said a word while I described the attack to her and how our assailant ended up feeding the crabs. "It's OK now," I said when I finished.

"No, it's not OK. Someone just tried to kill you, so you keep your eyes open till the cops get there. Do you understand?" The anger was clear in her voice.

"Sure, baby," I replied.

"Good," she said. "I'm gonna call the Federal Marshal in Puerto Rico and tell him you're OK. I called him about an hour ago and asked him as a favor to run you down."

47

"You called Hal?" I asked.

"Yeah," she said. "I got him out of bed and told him to go find you."

"Well," I said, "knowing Hal, he'll be here before the cops."

"Knowing the Puerto Rico cops," Cheri answered, "you'll die of old age before they get there."

Cheri was wrong. I didn't die of old age before the police arrived, but I did get two and a half hours older, and that was -- as I'd predicted -- long after Hal Murdoch, the U.S. Marshal for Puerto Rico, had tracked me down through the rental car's GPS. Hal and Cheri went way back to her early years as a Deputy Marshal in St. Croix. They'd both worked together on the airlift flying inmates from the federal prison in Puerto Rico to testify or for hearings in St. Croix. Hal had gone from being a local Federal Deputy to appointment by the president as the Marshal for Puerto Rico, but he was no politician; he was still pure cop.

By the time the first officer arrived, Hal had called the local coroner to deal with dead knife-wielder, and the three of us were enjoying the sunrise and a hot cup of strong black coffee.

It was noon before the police cleared out and Hal, Jean, and I were left alone.

He'd heard me tell the local cops I never saw the knife guy before and figured he was just looking for a quick snatch – maybe jewelry or a laptop – when I surprised him. But Hal was more than a little bit smarter than the two guys who just wrote down what I said and left.

"Mad Dog, you want to tell me what this is all about?" he asked.

"No, I don't think I can," I said.

"You sure about that?"

"Yep. For now. Maybe over a beer, I'll fill you in sometime."

He wasn't thrilled, but since he was there unofficially, he settled for that. Besides, his thoughts were drifting elsewhere. By then, Hal, a man nearly my age, had gotten around to asking Jean for a date, and wasn't totally discouraged when she told him to call her when she got back to town.

He'd also found out from the dead gorilla's wallet that our attacker was one Mitch Brachure, a St. Croix thug with a rap sheet for murder, robbery, and many other such wonderful crimes. The sad thing was he'd never been convicted of anything. Arrested a half-dozen times for major felonies but never found guilty. Not an unusual circumstance on an island where every jury has more aunts, cousins, and old friends than would go to most of the accused's birthday parties.

"You both need to be careful," Hal said. "Mr. Brachure has a brother that my people in St. Croix tell me is meaner than him."

"Great," I said. "Jean, you can't stay here."

"I wasn't going to."

"Where are you going?" I asked.

"Why, St. Croix, Mad Dog, with you," she said with

a wink. "I'm unemployed right now – on sabbatical to write a book. I need to explore some of the bays on the East End for my research anyway."

"Then St. Croix it is," I said, standing up and heading for the bedroom to retrieve my dock kit. Hal was still talking to her about things they might do when she got back to Puerto Rico.

CHAPTER

5

Our luck was good, and Jean and I were both able to book a flight to St. Croix the night after Mitch Brachure plunged to his death. We'd spent a good chunk of the afternoon doing what we needed most: letting our battered nervous systems recover.

"I'm gone," Jean said after we made the reservations. "See you in a few hours."

"Yep, me too," I told her as I dragged my weary ass to the guest room. The tension still rippled in my nerves and muscles, but little by little, I could feel it fading. Though the few hours of sleep I got were broken and restless, I knew as I woke that it had helped.

When we arrived in St. Croix on the late flight at eleven in the evening, Cheri and my dog, "Dog," were waiting for us. Cheri had her hair pulled back in a ponytail and was wearing her tight jeans and a loose, flowered shirt over a green tank top. With pink sandals and a blue ball cap covered with sparkles, she looked like the perfect classy West Indian lady.

Unlike Cheri, Dog looked like he belonged on the ranch in Wyoming where I'd found him. A short, stocky blue heeler with a thick coat of blue-white fur, he'd come from Colorado with me when I moved. Being lazy at heart, Dog had adjusted well to island life. At twelve years old, he shows his age by trying to sleep twenty to twenty-three hours a day, and then, like many of us older island males, trying to act like an adolescent for the rest of the time. In the seven years he's lived on my boat, he's growled at a stranger once and barked at a tarpon once. After much coaxing, we'd managed to get the marina management to let us have him on the boat, but it is agreed, even after seven years, that he's still on probation.

As Jean and I walked out the terminal door, Cheri ran toward us and threw her arms around me in a hug that said more even than all her emotional words on the phone. There were tears on her face, and I felt tears, for the second time that day, sneak into my eyes. Dog was trying to push between our legs, but no one was paying much attention.

"It's OK. I'm here. It's all OK," I said quietly.

Then we simply held each other, while Dog and Jean made friends. The reality jolt came when my hand touched on the hard presence of the Glock 40 holstered under Cheri's shirt behind her hip. Yeah, this wasn't just a tourist jaunt I was coming back from.

We eased apart, and Cheri seemed to notice Jean for the first time. She stepped back and surveyed my travel companion.

"So, you must be the professor," Cheri said. I knew by the tone it was mostly to me.

Jean moved toward her with a big smile, then a quick hug. Cheri hugged back lightly, then looked at our visitor again.

Feeling a mild panic, I said, "I don't pick 'em, honey. I just get advice from 'em." That stupid statement got me the eye.

I try to make it a habit to give Cheri a little hug when she gives me the eye. It seems to break the evil spell. As I did it this time, though, I realized the eye was probably stronger than usual because I hadn't told Cheri that Jean was coming to St. Croix with me.

I reached behind her and patted her weapon. "Glad to see me?" I asked.

"Don't fuck with me, Cotton," she said under her breath. "I'm still not happy with you."

As I moved away, Dog pushed his wet nose against Jean's bare leg. "Cute," she said, reaching down and rubbing his ears to return the Hi. "Who's this bad boy?"

Dog folded down to his back for a belly scratch, and Jean happily obliged. "That's Dog," Cheri said, joining in the scratch-fest as Dog pumped his tail like a windshield wiper in a hurricane.

"Dog?" Jean asked, looking first at Cheri and then up at me.

"When they both piss me off it makes getting both their attentions easier", Cheri quipped.

Jean laughed, and Cheri quipped, "Mad Dog's not very good at names."

After a few more seconds of Dog worship, the two women started heading for the Jeep, chatting furiously side-by-side about stuff I couldn't imagine.

We all piled into Cheri's old Jeep, and she said she'd drop me at my truck near the seaplane port, then I could follow her over to the Tamerind Bay Motel where she thought Jean could get a room. The Tamerind was a perfect choice, right next our marina, easy to keep an eye on her.

The talk in the front seat quickly focused on shopping in San Juan and haircuts as Dog and I sat in back and just soaked up the air conditioning.

"I can't wait to see the boat."

"He didn't tell you we live on a boat?"

"I used to wear it long …."

"This shirt was only ….."

"Blah blah blah blah blah." By the time we got to the truck, Dog and I had both dozed off.

When we all got to the boat, I was only too happy to hear Cheri and Jean decide I wouldn't be needed at the motel. The plan was to meet again for breakfast at the Deep End around eight o'clock.

The Deep End restaurant is Cheri's and my primary hangout because it's only about 100 yards from our boat, and, like most live-aboard at the Green Cay Marina, we eat out a lot. Since we moved onto the boat, the morning ritual had become either cereal on the back deck or a real breakfast at the Deep End. Usually, it's bacon and eggs at the bar, but this time Cheri, who went over while I was showering, ushered me to an outdoor table for six at the far side of the restaurant. To my surprise, she'd also been busy with social arrangements that morning. When I got to the table, Jean and Betsy Rourk were sitting there. Betsy had a cast-wrapped arm in a sling, and a huge black eye, too. She stood stiffly when I walked up and offered me her good left hand. "Mr. Cotton," she said, "I'm so sorry to have gotten you mixed up in this."

I didn't know what to say. Her battle wounds seemed a lot worse than mine. Cheri looked at me and then at Betsy. "Don't worry about it," she said. "It's what he does."

I sat down and looked around. There were no smiles at the table, no cheerful morning chitchat, just three rock-faced women staring into their coffee. The atmosphere was more like a Defense Department situation room than breakfast. "Betsy, I didn't know you'd be joining us," I said.

"I invited her," Cheri answered. "Bob is missing, this whole mess is tied together, and Jean and I can't help if we don't know the whole story."

"Wait a minute!" I said, raising my hand in protest. Wasn't this *my* case? But Cheri cut me off.

"God damn it, Cotton. We are all in this," she said, anger in her voice.

Quietly, Betsy said, "I've been talking to Jean and Cheri since we got here, and I think they can help find Bob."

This wasn't the way I worked; I was about to tell her. But then Helen came into the corner of my eye, menus in one hand, coffee pot in the other.

"Hey, you guys seem really serious," she said as she made the rounds of our cups.

"Just a little business," I told her. Helen had been a fixture at the Deep End since long before I first walked in. Gray-haired, plus-sized, and motherly, she was one of the main attractions for me. But I wasn't in a gabbing mood even with her. We each took a menu and put it right down.

I looked around the table as Helen left. "Mrs. Rourk," I said, "I didn't know this was going to be an investigation by committee. My sense of these people out there, just from their track record, is they're dangerous. I don't want anyone else getting hurt."

Jean was quick to reply. "You really think even if we don't do anything, they're not going to come after all of us – like that guy came after me?"

I was thinking about this when Betsy cut in. "I know that the man that grabbed me wanted to kill me, just like Cheri told me they killed Sam and his wife."

"The way we see it," Jean said, "we're all in this together."

"Plus one," Cheri said, nodding to someone behind

me. A big hand grabbed my shoulder as I heard a familiar baritone boom. "My old partner tells me you're in a jam," the voice said.

I looked up over my head and saw the beefy, red face of John Canfield staring back.

"Any other surprises?" I asked Cheri as John grabbed a chair and sat down.

"Nope," she said, a big smile crossing her face.

I knew I'd been cornered, but I felt better than I did since this whole thing had started. I had to admit there were times I'd felt over my head before, but now, it seemed as if the cavalry had arrived. John had been Cheri's partner as a Marshal for ten years and was as solid as you could ever want, for backup or anything else. The two of them worked together like a well-oiled machine. And I knew that if bad things were gonna happen, John was a very good man to have on your side.

As he picked up a menu, Cheri shifted into her deputy mode and looked at a list on the table in front of her. "Betsy, Jean," she said, "this is John. John, Betsy and Jean." She looked at the two women. "While everyone is trying to figure out what happened to Bob, John is going to make sure nothing happens to any of us. Is that OK?"

Betsy gave John a smile that made me blush. "Oh, my goodness. Thank you so much," she said.

John just nodded his big bald head.

"You ready to order yet?" It was Helen, back at her efficient best. But none of us had opened a menu. Cheri and I could manage out of habit. "Ham and eggs. We'll split it," she told Helen.

"Do you have eggs *bénédictines*?" Jean asked.

"We sure do."

"That sounds really good," Betsy said, looking at Jean. "You want to split an order?"

Jean nodded. "Sure, that'll be good." Then John piped up, "How many pancakes in an order?"

"Two," Helen told him.

"I'll have three," John said. "Three orders."

"You really gonna eat that?" I asked.

"Yep," John said, "and I ain't splitting with no one."

Cheri laughed a little. Then she turned serious again and looked down at her list. "Now that everyone's here," she said, "I think the first order of business is confidentiality. Do we have an agreement that everything said is in strictest confidence?"

Jean nodded. Betsy just said, "All I want to do is find Bob."

"Great," Cheri said, "second order of business, all -- and I mean all -- cards on the table."

Jean gave me a quick glance. I knew what her question was. "Yeah," I answered, "what we talked about in Puerto Rico needs to be said."

Systematically, as the conversation went on, Cheri pulled information from all of us. After about two cups, I mentioned Mitch Brachure. Cheri blanched and set her coffee down. "I know Brachure," she said.

"Prisoner?" I asked.

"No, Brachure was always in the state system. I

worked at the Grapetree Resort with him and his twin brother, Charlie, back in the late '80s. I was old for the job, just one of the kids waiting tables in the summer my last year of college, and they were busing and washing dishes. They were mean as shit clear back then." Cheri sat silent and thought for a moment. "God, that's weird!" she said. "I watched those two in the paper when they would be charged with something because I used to know them, but they just never got into federal court, so I never had to deal with them."

John knew the brothers, too. "I remember those guys from when I worked the drug task force. They were serious muscle."

"I followed the murder trial," Cheri said, "when they shot the three kids at the theater and the judge dismissed the case."

"That was them?" I asked.

"Yeah," Cheri said. "Small world."

"OK," John said, "so this brother Charlie's a bad guy."

"Oh, yeah," Cheri agreed.

"Should I roust him?" John was always the one for a fun day of harassment.

"No," I said. "If he comes around, we deal with him. Cheri, we'll need pictures. Will you get them? And Betsy, if we give you a picture, can you make an ID?"

"Maybe," she said.

"What about the police," I asked her. "Did they talk to you? What did you tell them?"

"Only a few minutes at the hospital. They didn't seem to care much at all."

Just then, Helen showed up with the food. It looked and smelled delicious, and Jean and Betsy both said their eggs tasted great, but together, they didn't finish half. Not much appetite for me either, and Cheri just picked a little at the bacon. Only John was his normal self. The pancakes vanished like a hurricane had blown them away.

Pushing the bacon and eggs in my direction, Cheri looked down at her list again. Maybe it was the fourth time, maybe the twelfth. I was tired of it. I put the gold coin on the table. "Jean, I want you to tell them everything you told me."

"Shit, man, is that what this is about!" John asked.

"It's evil," Betsy said, shifting away from the shining coin.

Jean picked up the coin and started her story, talking slowly at first but giving a complete course in one slice of West Indies history. When she reached the part about Dirk Chivers and how he could have made it to the east end of St. Croix, Betsy said, "That's where Bob and Tony went."

We all nodded in recognition, and I began to feel like this meeting was finally going somewhere.

When Jean had led us all to Isaac's Bay and finished her story, we sat there for a long few minutes trying to swallow the thought of a treasure that huge.

John finally broke the silence. "So, professor, so who does this big pile of gold belong to?"

"Beats me," she said with a smile, "but possession is ninety percent."

"You can have the money," Betsy said angrily. She was staring at the table, her voice almost choking. "I want Bob back!" Even John quit smiling.

"Cheri," I asked, "when you get that picture of Charlie, can you get a list of his known associates? It would be good to know who to look out for."

"Got it," she replied, marking something off her list. "We need to find out, too, how Mitch got to Puerto Rico. I'll check all the commercial flights, and any other way he could have gotten off the island. And we need to know about any oddball activities out on the East End."

A lot of angles for Cheri and me to chase down. "Jean," I said, "I want you to stay here at the motel for now. And you, too, Betsy. You should be where John can keep an eye on you."

She thought for a second. "Yeah, that would be a good idea."

"One more thing," Jean said, raising a hand. "I forgot to mention that one of these coins showed up on eBay about seven years ago. If I can get on the Internet, I can find out who sold them, and more about Captain Chivers. If he turned up alive somewhere after he was here, maybe his ship didn't go down at Isaac's Bay after all."

I turned to Cheri. "When we're done here, can you bring over one of our laptops? It should work fine at the motel. But if not," I told Jean, "you can work off the boat."

"OK," she said.

"John," I asked, "while we're gone, are you going to have any trouble keeping an eye on these ladies?"

John just gave me thumbs up and his best quarter-of-a-billion-dollar smile.

Finally standing up, I said, "Cheri and I are going out to the East End and meet with a friend."

"Who?" she asked.

"PADI."

Cheri nodded and stood up, too, but John asked, "Patty who?"

"Not Patty, Uncle John, but PADI," Cheri said, "like in P-A-D-I."

"We call him PADI because back in the '80s before Hurricane Hugo, he was a PADI dive instructor," I added.

John understood, but no light bulb went on for Jean or Betsy. "It's the Professional Association of Diving Instructors," Cheri told them."

"So, Mad Dog, why are you talking to this PADI guy?" John asked.

"Because, my friend," I said with a smile, "he is the resident expert on all the bays on the East End. Nothing happens there that he doesn't know."

John stared at me, then a spark of recognition hit him in his blue eyes. "That homeless guy that lives out there? Good luck. He's a whack job."

"He is not homeless, and he is not a whack job!" Cheri snapped angrily.

"Whoa, momma," John said, raising his hands.

"Cheri and PADI go way back, John. She's a little defensive," I explained.

"No problem, partner. Put your claws back in. Sorry. The guy's just a little weird, ya know."

"I'll give you he's a little independent," Cheri said, "but he's not a whack job." Looking up into John's face, she told him firmly, "He's the sweetest little guy on the planet, and if I hear you talk shit about him again, I'll ..." Cheri stopped and smiled her dangerous smile at her old partner.

"Got it, boss," he said.

"Bob knows PADI, too," Betsy said quietly. "He thought he was a nice guy. He used to take him rum and swap it for lobster."

"Well," I said, eager to go, "you kids have fun."

CHAPTER

6

As I drove the narrow, winding roads up toward Point Udall, my mind was running over the dozens of memories of the East End and all the great times Cheri and I had had there with our friend, crazy PADI. We always ran into him on the beach at Jack's Bay or Isaac's Bay. He was always wearing tattered swim trunks and sporting a set of dreadlocks down to his waist. A huge salt-and-pepper beard hung in mats to the middle of his chest. In the seven years since I met him, the only parts of his face I'd ever seen were his bright green eyes and his full set of even white teeth. Cheri had told me he was a clean-shaven southern boy when she met him in the '80s, but after Hurricane Hugo, he'd vowed never to cut his hair again.

When Cheri and I started dating back in 2002, I

had just taken early retirement on a medical from the Denver P.D. I'd moved to St. Croix to recover from a gunshot and memories that a place like the islands can be good at burying. Until I got there, it seemed like nothing could lift the shroud of depression that years as a homicide detective had laid on me.

Before I was introduced to Cheri, I had felt like a stranger in a strange land. My only friend was Pete Sampson, a DEA agent who'd been transferred from Denver to St. Croix. Cheri was with the Marshals Service, and Pete hooked us up for a double date one night. It was lust at first sight.

After dinner, we drove to the marina, where I showed off Itchy Feet and introduced her to Dog. We sat on the back deck of the old boat and talked till the early red hue of the sun began tinting the eastern sky. With the first light, Cheri reached across the small space between us and said, "Sun's coming up. Time for you to take me below."

That afternoon, she put her condo on the market and moved aboard.

The next day, after a night of soft talk and love, Cheri took me to Isaac's Bay, and I met crazy PADI for the first time. It took one look at my pain and the fact that I'd fallen in love with his friend Cheri, and PADI became my island mentor.

PADI is only about five-foot-two and can't weigh ninety pounds sopping wet, but because he spends his days snorkeling the East End reefs PADI is as fit as any man I've ever met.

He was a gift from a benevolent God sent to heal both the hole in my stomach from a .38 Police Special and the bigger one in my soul. His medicine was the underwater world of St. Croix.

Day after day, I would walk in to Isaac's Bay, and PADI and his friends would take me snorkeling. The combination of salt water, daily exercise, and Cheri's love slowly cured the wound in my flesh, but, more important, it did the same for the one deep inside, too. As I drove the broken road, I could hear PADI say, in his usual slight rum slur, "Mad Dog, if your gut and your mind are both in pain, comes to the sea. It'll make you sane."

And Cheri would add, "If you put a pint of rum in PADI, the worst poet philosopher in the Caribbean will emerge," as she passed the bottle back to him.

I reached over and touched Cheri's bare leg. It had been too long since we'd seen PADI, and I was glad we were headed east. Stroking her leg with one hand, dodging potholes with the other, I thought about Cheri's softness – and what it would do to me to lose her, as PADI had lost his love.

That was part of his legend, or really, his legends: the cave he lived in overlooking Jack's Bay, the normal life he gave up after Hurricane Hugo sat on top of St. Croix for two days and ripped his paradise to hell with two-hundred-mile-an-hour winds -- and Sue Horn. Cheri, in one of her blue moments, had told me how Sue was killed by Hugo, and how after that, PADI turned to living alone on the East End, making a meager living selling lobsters and fish to whoever was willing to walk the mile to Jack's Bay or Isaac's – and partying with the dozens of beach bums who were his friends.

Once he'd had another name, but people got to calling him PADI because it was what the dive instructors' jackets said, and after Sue died, he decided, It's my name now. It was just the link to the ocean, I think, the only passion he had left.

To get to the East End beaches, you must park on top of a hill just south of the most eastern point of St. Croix. The dirt lot only holds three or four cars, but it's rare that even one person wanders to the secluded beaches and bays, so there's always somewhere to park.

This day, Cheri and I were the only ones there. We both strapped on belly packs with pistols and ammunition. If this was the hot spot where Bob Rourk and Tony Rasser disappeared, neither of us wanted to face it unarmed. I put our lunch and two bottles of Cruzen Blackstrap Rum, PADI's favorite, in my backpack, and we started the long, slippery, thorn-covered walk to wherever we'd find him. While we moved through the cactus underbrush, Cheri began talking about PADI and how she, he, and Sue Horn had first met.

"I don't think Sue or PADI were more than twenty. It was the summer of '88, and I'd come back home to St. Croix to work during my summer break. I had a job at the Grapetree. My first day, I met Sue, who was waitressing in the dining room, too. After about a week working together, she talked me into going down to the dive shop and volunteering to help run it on my days off for free use of dive gear. PADI was an instructor then, just this very polite, soft-spoken southern boy.

"One day, he offered to take us to Jack's Bay to snorkel the reef. The trip turned into a nightlong party, and by the next day, PADI and Sue were inseparable. I never saw two kids more in love than those two. They were working twelve-hour shifts and still took their sleeping bags and walked the two miles from Grapetree to the beach every night so they could sleep under the stars."

"Romantic," I said, remembering the dozens of nights Cheri and I had done the same thing.

To get to Jack's Bay, where PADI could usually be found, you had to walk the beach across East End Bay, over a tall hill, across Isaac's Bay, and then over a second hill. At the top of the hill overlooking Jack's Bay, we sat down on a large rock. Pointing at the bay, she said in a dreamy voice, "Captain Chivers' boat could have come right into that cut."

"Yeah, if it wasn't Isaac's," I said.

Cheri kept looking down. "I could sure see a ship getting the bottom ripped out of it trying to get in there. But why wouldn't some part of it be left in the sand or on the reef?

"I don't know," I answered, my pirate imagination now turned on. "Four hundred years is a long time. It could have all rotted or been buried in the sand."

"Or never there."

"Or never there," I agreed.

As we spoke, a small figure darted from the underbrush about fifty yards away and moved quickly toward the water. Cheri stood up waving her hands and shouted as loud as she could, "PADI!"

The figure stopped and turned toward us. Even at that distance, you could see the bright smile that was PADI's trademark erupt from the twisted, matted hair.

"Cheri, my love," he screamed, "and Mad Dog. Come, I'll catch a lobster." He bolted across the beach with his lobster snare and catch bag and dove into the bay.

Cheri, wearing her biggest smile, looked at me and said, "Fuckin' nut," then hurried down the hill.

I followed more slowly. By the time I got to the beach, she was sitting watching PADI bob up and down in the surf forty yards offshore. "He'll bring us a lobster for lunch," she said like a little girl.

"Yep," I agreed, plopping down beside her and pulling one of the rum bottles out of my backpack.

Cheri sat her arm on my knee and watched her friend move gracefully over the waves. "He's so free," she said. "Sometimes I wish I was like that."

"Can't be free, baby; you got me."

She elbowed me and said, "Gilded cage."

I poured the rum into two plastic cups and added a little Coke. We sat in silence soaking up the sun, sipping our rum, listening to the waves, and watching PADI for twenty minutes or so until, like a mangy Poseidon, he finally emerged from the surf with a huge lobster in his outstretched hands. "Lunch, my loves, but only if you have rum," he hooted with joy.

I held up the open fifth of Blackstrap, and he gave a hearty "Yaa Hoo" and did a jig of joy. Then he ran from the beach as he yelled over his shoulder, "We need fire."

In a few minutes, he was back with an armload of dry wood he'd picked up in the brush. PADI looked at me. "Well, my friend, where are the matches?" he asked with a smile, glancing down at his wet shorts and mats of beard and hair. "I don't have any."

Cheri pulled a Bic from the pack and threw it at him. "Keep it, you bum."

"I will," PADI said as he knelt to start the fire.

An hour later, the three of us were lying on the sand with the sun baking our swollen bellies. Between us – but mostly PADI – we'd drunk half the bottle, and while he was eating nearly all the potato chips, Cheri and I consumed almost all of the huge lobster.

The plan we'd come with faded as the salt air bathed us in laziness, but after long enough, I remembered and forced myself. We both did. It was time to get down to business. Stretched out in the heat, her eyes closed, Cheri said, "PADI, we need your help."

There was a long silence before he answered. "Cheri, anything, you know that."

"PADI, do you remember Bob Rourk?

"Sure. Bob and his friend -- I don't remember his name -- came to the beach a lot. He had one of those metal detectors and would walk the beach with it. He'd even take it in the water."

71

"Did they ever find anything?" I asked.

"I saw them dig stuff up, but I don't know what."

"Did you ever watch them in the water?" Cheri asked.

"I liked to watch the other guy -- maybe his name was Tony. He was a great spear fisherman. Good instincts for how the fish would move."

"It's a long way to haul all their gear," I said. "Did they have a place they went a lot?"

Again, PADI was quiet a long time. "Most people stay inside the reefs," he said. "Those two spent a lot of time outside. They were both strong swimmers, and I guess the sharks didn't bother them."

"There's a lot more big sharks outside that reef," I told Cheri, remembering days of spear fishing with PADI east of Isaac's when a ten-foot tiger shark kept circling in the gloom just at the edge of what we could see. PADI had just shot a twelve-pound mutton snapper. I think we both saw the shark at the same time. I was plenty concerned, but PADI wasn't. He just put the snapper in his game bag and kept fishing, trailing the bag about fifteen feet behind. When we got out of the water, I asked him, "Did you see that tiger?"

"Yeah," he shrugged. "That's Bruce. He leaves me alone and I leave him alone." That was the day that I realized that PADI was more than just a man who came to the ocean; he'd become part of it. It's hard to describe, but I never looked at PADI quite the same after that. That day gave me a much deeper admiration for the sunbaked little man with dreads hanging like a shirt to his waist. PADI was part of the nature that was this place, like Cheri had said -- he really was free.

"See Bob or Tony last week?" I asked.

"It is Tony?"

"Yep," Cheri confirmed.

"Yeah," PADI said, "saw them in the shallow reefs at Isaac's with that metal detector."

"Have there been a lot of other people around?" I asked. "Maybe people you don't usually see here."

"Yeah, sometimes," PADI said, "but I don't know who they are."

"Have you seen things going on at night? Do you think boats might be coming in and people diving off the boats?"

"No, nothing like that."

Then Cheri asked the question that burned in both our minds: "Have you ever found any gold out here?"

PADI shook his head. "No, no gold mines on this beach."

"PADI," Cheri said, "Mad Dog is trying to find Bob. If you hear or see anything, would you please have someone get a hold of us?"

"Sure," he said. "I'll have one of my visitors give you a call."

"Thanks." Cheri propped herself up on an elbow and looked at me. "Dog, roll over or you'll burn."

I opened my eyes and gazed back at her. "I never burn."

"Roll over, dude," PADI chided with his cackle of a laugh. "The babe wants to look at your ass."

I rolled over, and we drifted back into silent sun worship.

As Cheri and I walked back to the Jeep, we talked about our next move and how to keep the search for Bob Rourk moving forward.

"I think the coin is a major key," I said.

"I agree, but if there's any chance Bob is still alive, the better direction is to chase down Mitch Brachure's brother."

I stopped and looked back at Cheri. Sometimes her logic escaped me, but when she explained, she was usually right. "OK, I don't get it," I said.

"That's because you've taken your eye off the ball."

"How's my eye off the ball?"

"Let me ask you this: Who do you -- I mean we -- work for?"

"Betsy."

"Right, and what does she say she wants?" Cheri paused for effect. "Bob back"

I thought for a second, and as I hesitated, Cheri went on. "You, Mr. Homicide Detective, are already treating this like a murder. This is not a murder investigation; it's a missing person investigation. And until we have a body, we have to assume that time is ticking and every minute we don't get to him and help him is critical -- whether he's trapped in a cave or being held by bad guys."

"You don't think Bob is dead?"

"That's the disconnect. It doesn't matter what I

think. What's important is what actions have the highest chance of saving Bob's life if he's still alive."

I suddenly felt a hit of guilt. I sat down on the path uphill of where Cheri was and looked her in the eye. "We wasted our time coming and seeing PADI, didn't we?"

"No, we didn't. We didn't find anything out, but if we hadn't come and he had some information, we would have regretted it. We should have taken less time with PADI, gotten out as soon as we found out all we could."

"My fault."

"And mine," Cheri said, setting her hand on my knee.

"I was thinking," she said, "the key to this if Bob is still alive is the Brachure brothers. It's our best lead. If Bob is alive, he isn't coming home for a reason. He may be hiding, or someone might be holding him so they can get him to tell them where the coin was found."

"The attack on Betsy might not have been anything more than an attempt to get Bob out in the open or to leverage him to talk."

"Now you're clicking."

"The attack on Jean?"

"Not Jean. She was just there. You were the target. I think we both know Mitch Brachure or one of his friends killed Sam to find out where you had gone in Puerto Rico."

"OK, that's a no-brainer."

"So, Mr. Detective, how did Mitch Brachure get to

Puerto Rico so fast? You and I both know he didn't take a commercial flight, and the seaplanes were done for the day."

"Private plane."

"Good bet."

I thought about my next step. "If I'm going to be looking for Charlie," I said, "I better take someone with me." I knew who that someone would be and took out my phone to try to find him. "No reception," I said.

"So, get off your butt and let's march out of here."

Yeah, Cheri was seeing things better than I was. "I haven't been approaching this right."

"Well, that's not exactly right" she said, following me up the steep dirt track. "You've given us Mitch Brachure as a damn fine lead. We should have asked PADI if he saw Mitch this week."

"Does he know Mitch?"

"Yeah, he and Mitch knew each other from when they both worked at the Grapetree. I don't remember them being buddies or anything, but they knew each other."

"First order of business," I said, "we need to find Mitch's twin, Charlie. He's up to his neck in this, and if anyone knows where Bob is or if he's on the run, it'll be Charlie or one of Mitch's other cronies."

"Bingo, detective," Cheri said, her voice short from the haul up the steep hill.

"We also need to ID how Mitch got to Puerto Rico," I said. "Someone may have seen if someone dropped him off at a plane."

"Good," Cheri huffed, stopping to catch her breath.

"Until we find Bob, the coin's not that important," I said.

"Wrong," Cheri said. "Jean needs to run down the other guy who was selling a similar coin on the Internet. It's a good lead, and we need to talk to him as soon as possible. He may even be behind Bob's disappearance."

"Mitch Brachure might have just been a hired gun."

"When I knew him at the Grapetree, he was not a brain surgeon. He was a thug. He and Charlie barely had the intellect to wash dishes, but they were master head busters."

"They ever mess with you?"

"Nope, I was untouchable."

"Untouchable?"

"PADI and I were close, and back then, that skinny little guy was nobody to mess with. One night at a party, Sol True, one of Mitch's buddies who waited tables, was picking on Sue. This Sol guy was a white guy who acted like a thug. I know Mitch and Charlie both thought Sol was the toughest of the tough. Anyway, we were at this party on the beach and PADI was out snorkeling, and this Sol guy starts making cracks to Sue and being rude. I told him to shut up, but he just ignored me. We were all drinking, and Sol was a mean drunk. When I told him to shut up, he pushed Sue, and she fell, and her arm went in the fire. She didn't get hurt, but it scared the hell out of her.

"When PADI got out of the water, Sue was still crying, and we were sitting at the edge of the party watching Sol while he was playing the bully around the fire, pushing people and just being a jerk. Anyway, PADI came over to Sue all sopping wet carrying some fish he'd speared, and when he saw Sue, he just froze. I just held Sue and nodded at Sol. Sol was about six-foot-three and a tough guy, but PADI walked over as calm as could be and proceeded to kick the shit out of him. PADI and I been tight ever since, and because I was PADI's pal, no one screwed with me.

"Back then, all the dishwashers and busboys thought they were tough because they were from the projects," Cheri said, "and we were just a bunch of soft white punks. That is, everybody was a soft white punk but PADI. After the beating he put on Sol, all the ghetto guys started calling PADI the Bad Boy."

"Never thought of PADI as violent," I said.

"He isn't. He's not violent," Cheri answered with quick smile and a sharp punch to my right shoulder. "He's just tough, like you."

"Thanks, babe," I said in my best Bogart voice as we huffed and puffed on to the top of the hill. When we got there, I threw my backpack in the Jeep and we took off our belly packs. "I gotta get a lighter pistola," Cheri said, lifting hers like it weighed a hundred pounds.

"Let's go to the boat and clean up," she said as she shook sand out of her hair, "and then we can get this little project back on track."

"I've got a plan of attack," I said.

"And …."

"And I'm gonna go find Ray."

Cheri shook her head. "Every time you and Ray even walk down the dock together, you get into trouble."

"My guess is Charlie Brachure won't forget about his brother and will come after me, maybe even you and Jean eventually. Ray is the only guy I know that can get me to him before he gets to us, and I need John to keep an eye on Betsy and Jean so they're safe."

"Don't you want him to protect me, too?" Cheri said, giving me a lopsided smile.

"God help Charlie if he tries to mess with you."

"I'll just kick his ass," she said.

"No."

"I'll just shoot him?"

"Yeah, if he's lucky."

Cheri smiled and punched me. "I need protecting, too."

I shook my head and opened the Jeep door for her.

CHAPTER

7

Driving down the steep East End road, I began thinking about what Ray could find out. Whenever I need information about the local bad guys, he's always been my first stop. Ray Jones must be 55 now – a slender, gray-haired black man with a constant smile and sunglasses on 23 hours a day. He's never mentioned it, but I'm sure in his youth, Ray was a force to be reckoned with. He's one of the rare guys I know who you can always trust when the shit hits the fan -- and I had a feeling the shit was about to hit the fan.

Usually, you can find him at one of two spots: hustling boat repair jobs on the marina docks or drinking beer with his buddies on the corner next to Schooner Bay Market. I set my plan of attack. There were things I had to know: about private planes for one thing, where Charlie might be for another (in jail if I was lucky).

First, I needed to make the calls to get things moving while I drove back – once I got to where my phone would work. Second, shower at the dock and see if Ray was around. Third, if he wasn't there, hunt him down.

"Been awful quiet," Cheri said, sliding her hand over to my leg.

"Look lady, try to be cool. I'm trying to drive."

"You'll think cool," she said, grabbing my leg hard and meeting my sideways glance with a playful grin.

"Cheri, don't. Seriously, I won't let Ray get me in trouble."

"Bullshit," she said, digging her fingers into my thigh.

"No, no," I insisted. "I'll be good."

"Good," she said, finally releasing me and sitting back with a satisfied grin. "You'd better be."

We drove in silence until we passed Duggan's, one of our favorite restaurants, and Cheri asked, "What you want to do for dinner?"

I looked at my watch. It was 2:30.

"I'm still digesting lobster," I protested.

"I'm not cooking."

"I should be done talking with Ray by six. Maybe we can meet with everyone and have kind of a briefing about six thirty at the Greek's." The Pickled Greek was a place Cheri loved for its wild, fun atmosphere, but

I also knew an outside table there would give us the privacy we needed.

"That works," she said. "I'll let everyone know."

"Can I bring Ray?"

"Will he behave?"

I thought for a second and then -- half to Cheri, half to myself -- conceded, "No."

As I drove, it was hard not to be thinking about Mr. Charlie Brachure, a seriously bad man who I knew would not -- and in the eyes of his peers could not -- let the death of his brother go unanswered. He would want revenge, and the police would be no help. Murder for payback is nearly an Olympic sport on St. Croix. Few months go by without a killing where the sole motive is revenge.

In Denver, revenge wasn't a real common motive for murder. Bad people talked about it but rarely acted. In some neighborhoods of St. Croix, revenge was everything. I knew Charlie Brachure was going to come knocking on my door soon. The simple fact was I had to find him before he found me. Not a very civilized fact but a fact, nonetheless.

The hard reality was slowly sinking into me when the phone rang. "Hello," Cheri said, then there was a long silence. After about thirty seconds, she grabbed hold of my leg. Her face was tight with emotion. "OK," she said. "OK." Finally, she closed the phone and looked at me.

"That was John. They found Tony Rasser, Bob Rourk's dive buddy."

"And?"

"He's dead, run off the road on the cliffs on the south road."

"What else do they know? Did someone see it?"

"Some fishermen spotted his Wrangler a few hours ago in the rocks at the bottom of the cliff. They just hauled it out. The paint scrapes are clear what happened."

"No Bob?"

"Just one person, Tony Rasser."

"Shit, he was a good guy."

"Yeah, we have to go to the police or the FBI. This thing is getting out of control."

I looked hard at Cheri. "They can't do anything. We don't have any evidence, just speculation."

We drove on in silence back toward the boat.

The miles moved past us as I kept thinking. Shit, we needed to be *doing* more. I just didn't know what.

But then, like I'd suddenly come to the end of a detour, I did know. "Well," I said, slowing down as I pulled to the side of the road. "Let's go get some good old-fashioned evidence." I swung the Jeep in a wide U-turn and headed back east.

"Where are you going now?" Cheri asked.

"You said the wreck was on the south shore road?"

"Yeah," she said as I made a right at Cheeseburgers junction and headed across the island.

"Call John back and find out where exactly Rasser's Jeep went off."

I sped along the narrow, brush-lined road over the

backbone ridge as Cheri got the information we needed. "Take a left when you get to the south shore," she said, slapping her cell phone shut.

When we got to the spot, it was easy to see where Tony's Wrangler had gone off the road

As Cheri and I looked at the scene, I could sense the pure horror Tony must have felt as his Jeep was pushed suddenly – inescapably -- down the steep slope to the cliff and rocks and sea below. From where we stood, the pattern of road debris and the tire tracks in the sand made a clear picture of what had happened. Tony was driving west when another vehicle had slammed into his back right corner as he topped a hill next to a scrub-covered overlook. Fragments of vehicles still lay on the road and the soft shoulder. Once Tony was forced through the sand, momentum and gravity took over, speeding him faster and faster to his death. Gripped by the awful sense of what had happened, I walked head down along the road, until I saw a three-inch shard of red glass.

"Taillight," Cheri said, peering at its sparkle in the hot sun as I picked up the glass.

"Yeah," I said, setting it back down and looking at a metal headlight rim and shards of clear glass a few inches away. "I bet that headlight's off the truck that hit him."

"You knucklehead," Cheri answered. "How do you know it was a truck?"

"OK, it doesn't matter," I brushed her off. My focus

had shifted to the broken path Tony ripped in the hillside as his truck had hurtled through the undergrowth.

Cheri saw where I was looking. "Shit, Mad Dog. He never had a chance."

"Nope," I agreed.

As we stood at the top of the hill, a stiff Atlantic breeze whipped our faces, and I could see a solitary kite surfer skimming along the lonely shore.

"Lucky anyone found him at all," I said, staring down the steep hill to the black edge of the cliff the Jeep had gone over.

Cheri stood back from me, then walked to the tear the Jeep had made in the scrub brush and cactus. "Come on," she said as she started sidestepping down the steep ground.

I followed. The hill was lightly covered with a combination of greasewood and scraggly cactus. The swath of ripped foliage ended abruptly at a large black boulder below us.

Cheri stopped and tucked her hands in her short's pockets. When I got to the boulder, I could see what had caught her eye. The top of the black rock was smeared with a faint scrape of white paint, and in the sunlight I saw flashes of light that I knew were small chips of metal.

"He hit this rock," Cheri said, pointing to the white blaze. "And then he went airborne." Her hand moved up and out toward the sea.

I looked down the hillside and saw a smashed area of brush fifty feet below, only ten feet from the top of the cliff. "Shit, he hit there and then right off the edge," I said.

Cheri didn't answer, just stared at the ground as she kept sidestepping toward where the truck had landed. I followed, wondering if Tony was still conscious when his truck went flying over the cliff. I hoped he wasn't.

While I cautiously worked my way down the rocky hill, Cheri was already at the spot, crabbing on hands and feet in a search pattern up and down the slope. "What are you looking for?" I asked.

"I don't know," she said, "but maybe there's something that can help us."

I saw her logic and started copying her careful movement, edging across the slope on the other side of the smashed brush. The hill wasn't just steep and rocky but also dangerous because of the loose soil and thousands of small stones.

We had zigzagged slowly for about twenty minutes when I spotted a slit of black leather wedged between a small barrel cactus and a thorn bush. As I half-crabbed, half-crawled over to the spot, I could see it was a cell phone case. I gingerly reached among the spines and pulled it out. I could feel the weight of the phone inside.

"Cheri, I got something," I called out.

She was only about twenty feet away, but it was tough going to where I sat examining the battered phone. "What have you got?"

"I'm guessing this might be Tony's cell phone."

"Where was it?"

"There, up in those thorns," I said, pointing at

the sharp little nest that had kept the phone from plummeting off the cliff.

I was trying to figure how it worked when Cheri got to me and sat down. "Let me see. You'll never figure it out."

I nodded. She was right. I could barely answer my own cell phone and had never mastered such mysteries as voice mail and missed messages.

Cheri pushed some buttons and I heard a female voice say, "You have one new message." She pushed another button, and in a faraway, strained voice, I heard what I knew must have been Bob Rourk.

"Tony. Man, that was crazy. I can't believe that crazy fucker started shooting at us. Look, he winged me in the arm. But I'll be OK. I'm making my way to the satellite tower. Pick me up there. I should be about half an hour. I've got my phone on vibrate, so call me when you get this. Look, I better go. Keep your head down and I'll see you at the tower. Oh yeah, buddy, I been thinking. Whatever you do, don't call the cops, or we may never see a nickel from that treasure." Cheri closed the phone, and we both sat looking down the thorn-covered slope and the rolling sea.

"I'm guessing Tony was dead when Bob made that call," I told her, as I visualized the truck tumbling off the cliff below us.

"Let's get out of here," I said, suddenly feeling uncomfortable on the isolated hillside. Just as I spoke, I heard a vehicle come to a stop above us and a door slam.

I turned toward the hilltop in time to hear the

distinct crack of a pistol shot and see a rock shatter five feet from where Cheri and I were sitting. Instinctively, I grabbed her and pulled her behind a boulder next to us as another shot rang out, sending a small cascade of stones down the hill to our right.

"Shit," Cheri said breathlessly. "I left my belly pack in the Jeep."

I thought of my gun, also sitting in the truck. I pressed down farther into the cover of the rock. I knew the only thing keeping us alive at that moment was bad marksmanship and a rock that didn't feel nearly big enough.

"We're going to have to make a break for it," I said. Looking for options, I saw a bunch of boulders and thorn brush. "I'll go left, and you go right. We got a better chance if we split up."

Cheri grabbed my arm with alarming power. Her eyes showed no fear, only a hard anger. "No, we do this together. We both go right."

I nodded as a third shot rained splintered rock down on us.

"On three, we break for that big one over there," I said, motioning to a large rock about fifteen feet across the slope that could give us better cover.

"OK."

"One, two…." As I shifted my weight to run, I heard a door shut, and I froze. A second later, an engine roared, and the vehicle above us sped away east.

"Keep down," I said, grabbing Cheri's arm and wondering if someone was still waiting to ambush us.

As we stayed heads-down behind the rock, we heard another vehicle come from the west and then pass by.

"I think they hauled ass when they saw that car coming," I said.

"Yeah," Cheri said. "Look!" She pointed at a stretch of road about five hundred feet away where a red car was racing east.

"I think it's some kind of old station wagon," Cheri said.

"Great," I agreed in disgust. "We got ambushed by a family man. Could you see the plates?"

"You gotta be shitting me," Cheri said, making me laugh. "Could *you* see the plates?" she echoed as she shoved me on the shoulder, "You idiot, we could barely see the car" and she began to laugh.

I laughed harder, and for a long minute, the two of us were crouched behind the rock laughing hysterically. But as we calmed down, I looked at Cheri and said, "That wasn't very funny."

She looked at me with tears flowing down her face. "Nope," she said, and then erupted in another round of giggles.

I shook my head in amazement as I stood and looked up the hill. No one shot me, so I reached down and helped Cheri up. She was still giggling a little and put both hands on the big rock to steady herself. A moment more, and the laughing stopped. We looked up the hill.

The spot where the station wagon had stopped and

our attacker fired from was about a hundred feet above us. I realized that the rock we'd been behind gave great cover but dashing to the right would have made us a perfect target.

"We got way lucky," I said, looking around.

Cheri just started scrambling up the loose, rocky hillside.

As I followed behind her, my mind was still playing Bob Rourk's phone message: "I can't believe that crazy fucker started shooting at us." I was convinced the crazy fucker was shooting again, and I knew now I'd chase him till one of us was dead. He'd tried to kill Cheri, and it wasn't business anymore. It was personal.

CHAPTER

8

Once we got to the boat, Cheri and I shared Bob Rourk's voice mail with Jean, who said she'd take it over to Betsy at the motel.

"I'm glad you guys are OK," she said after we told her about our close call on the hillside, "and this voice mail makes me think Bob could still be alive. If he doesn't want the police involved and is trying to lay low, it makes sense he might not call his wife and might be in hiding."

I could see Jean's point, but it got us no closer to finding Bob, so all we could do was keep working the case and keep an eye out for a crazy guy in an old red station wagon.

I needed to find Ray. I left Cheri and Jean chewing over the case and a couple of peanut butter sandwiches while I went out for a quick marina tour to look for him and check on John.

Itchy Feet, the boat Cheri and I live on, is kept at "B" dock, at the first slip on the west side. It's a great location, just a short walk to the parking lot and convenient to everything we need. In our five years there, Cheri and I have eased into the calm and very social life of St. Croix live-aboard. The dock I walked around that day had the friendly, hometown familiarity of what people used to call small town America.

My first stop looking for Ray was twenty feet away up a cement incline. There in the parking lot, I found his 1983 blue Toyota pickup about halfway down the back row on the south side. Judging from where it was, I decided to go back and check out "B" dock first to see if Ray was doing any of his boat cleaning or small repair work there.

Like much of St. Croix, the basic structure of the Green Cay Marina defies logic – except maybe the logic of a dyslexic. "B" and "C" docks are west of "A," but "D" somehow is east of it at a right angle -- and the waterways in the newer parts of the complex make even less sense.

As I walked past Itchy Feet, I could see Cheri and Jean huddled over the dining table.

In the next slip was Racin Rabbit, Ed Miller's sailboat personification of a hillbilly nightmare. Two sinking, mold-encrusted dinghies and a nearly submerged, rotting kayak litter the front. A towering lucky bamboo plant grows on the stern. And the forecastle boasts a wooden monstrosity of a statue depicting the sleek naked body of a woman with the head of a rabbit. Maybe you can't put a full junkyard on the deck of a thirty-five-foot boat, but Ed's given it a damn good try. As is his habit at four in the afternoon, he was sitting under a torn red tarp, chair tilted back dangerously, and size twelve bare feet propped comfortably on the rabbit woman's bountiful ass.

"Seen Ray?" I asked.

Ed closed his eyes, and his face seemed to smash inward in a grimace of thought. Then he unsmashed his wrinkle-crushed face, winked, and said, "Want a beer?"

"Nope."

Ed's grin grew, and he ticked his head toward Itchy Feet. "Who's the hot chick?"

"If it's not Cheri, it must be Jean."

"Jean like in chick named Jean?"

I winked in affirmation.

"She is going to be around for a while?"

"Maybe," I said, knowing that Ed wouldn't tell me anything until he'd fully grilled me about Jean.

"She ought to get some sun," he said, no trace of motive in his voice.

"Like sun bathe?"

"Your bow's a nice place."

"I'll mention that," I said, looking over at my bow and considering Ed's lecherous view. For a man who's approaching eighty years old, and looks like a hundred and ten, there are parts of him that aren't out of adolescence yet.

"Sure you don't want a beer?" he asked again, pointing at the galvanized bucket next to him with three sweating Heinekens on ice.

"No," I said, "just need to find Ray."

"Haven't seen him, but I know he was working inside Bernie's boat yesterday. He may be down there."

Bernie is Bernie Hamilton III, and Bernie's boat happens to be a multimillion-dollar, ninety-five-foot yacht. No one knows what Bernie Hamilton III looks like – he's never been seen here -- but he's notorious for having the most beautiful all-woman crew in St Croix.

Ed followed my gaze toward the towering yacht. "Probably cleaning the bilge. It's a tough job, but someone has to do it."

I didn't respond, just headed for the Eagle Star, Mr. Bernie Hamilton III's floating wonder castle. The captain since I arrived at Green Cay Marina has been Salina Bailer, a six-foot-two blond Amazon who hailed me from the stern deck: "Hey handsome, what brings you to the south end?"

To my relief and dismay, Salina was fully clothed in a narrow, white bikini. I couldn't wait for Cheri's standard question, "Been down looking at tits?" and my answer: "All fully clothed."

"Ed told me Ray was working on the Eagle Star."

"Not today, doll, but he was fixing the salt water ice-maker for the fish chest yesterday."

"Know where he's working today?"

"Saw him on "A" dock about an hour ago."

I told Salina thanks and went to check. "How was

the trip," Ed asked as I passed by, his face squished into one big full-toothed smile.

Should eighty-year-olds be allowed to be that warped?

I just waved.

Ray wasn't on "A" dock, but John was, sitting at the fuel dock, his belly pack strapped on and a small pair of binoculars next to him. "What you doing here?" I asked the big man.

"Sittin'," he said.

"Sittin'?"

"Perfect place," John said. "If the bad guys come by boat, I see them. If they drive in," he pointed up toward the road, "I see them, and I can see the motel through the trees and your boat."

I smiled as I considered the position. "Perfect," I agreed.

"Yup."

"Seen Ray?"

"No, and I don't want to. He's bad karma."

"Karma?" I asked

"Been reading," John said, setting down the binoculars and tapping a white plastic bag at his feet.

"That's nice."

"Yup."

"So, you see Ray, will you tell him I'm looking for him?"

"Sure," John said, his face emotionless, "it's your karma."

"What's sitting here waiting to pop bad guys do for your karma?" I asked him.

"I haven't got that far yet," John said in a deadpan.

"Must be some book."

"Book?" he asked.

"The book on karma."

"Not a book. Reading about karma in the Enquirer. Fascinating stuff."

"Karma?" I asked.

"National Enquirer," John said, pointing at the plastic bag.

"Yep." I turned and started down the dock.

Behind me, John said in a growl, "That Rasser thing was pure murder. I talked to one of the investigators, and there was yellow paint all down the side of his Jeep.

I turned back to him. "I know, buddy," I said. "We were up at the accident less than an hour ago, and some asshole in a red station wagon took potshots at us." I didn't think John needed to know what a close call it was, so I played it down, but just talking about the shots made the pure fear of the moment flash back to me.

"Shit," John said, "they fucking shot at you and Cheri?"

"Yeah," I told him, "but who cares? They had such lousy aim they never came close."

"People like that don't just take potshots. Why didn't you call me?"

"You need to be here, and I didn't want you charging down to the East End."

"Did you see them?"

"Just the car."

"Damn."

"Look, Cheri and I got a phone we think is Rasser's up at the boat. It has a message on it I think you should hear. When you take a break, go listen to it."

"What's it say?"

"Basically, that Bob and Tony got shot at by some guy."

"Jesus, you got that on the phone?"

"Yeah, a message we think was from Bob. Betsy'll tell us for sure if it's his voice, but I'm pretty sure it was."

The concern that had been on John's big red face washed into an emotionless gaze.

"Something happens to you or Cheri, I …." He didn't finish the sentence but looked right at me instead and gave a slight shrug.

"These are bad guys, John. Thanks for being on board."

He twitched his lips, what I'd classify as a smile for John. "Maybe bad people need bad people to fight them. Go find Ray. Maybe his karma will get on the bad guys and not us."

I thought about that and said, "John, I don't think karma works that way."

"You need to read more," he said, his face now back to its mask of indifference.

"Yep," I said and resumed my walk down the dock.

I found Ray Jones on "D" dock, cleaning a small fishing boat. When I walked up, he climbed off to greet me. Ray is about six-foot-two and might weigh a hundred seventy pounds. Once, his short curly hair was black. Now it is the color of light gray. The gray of Ray's short-cropped hair stands in stark contrast against his deep mahogany skin and his ever-present black wraparound sunglasses. Despite his age, Ray moves like a young athlete, with the grace of a professional dancer. He always wears a full smile, showing a perfect set of straight white teeth.

In a conversation over a fifth of rum one night, Ray admitted having been in the military and said the best thing he got out of it was a real nice set of teeth. I told him I didn't know the military did orthodontics, and he just smiled. "Long story," he said, but I never got to hear it.

"What's happening, my man?" Ray said, extending a fist.

I bumped it with my own. "Need ya," I said.

"Done. Talk to me."

"You hear about Mitch Brachure?"

"Dock's alive with the talk." Ray stepped back and looked me up and down. "Word is you iced that bad boy, and him being a strapping young man."

"I didn't exactly ice him."

"Don't matter, friend. Take the juice. They'll respect you more."

"I don't need respect."

"When they come for you, you'll want them scared." He lost his smile. "Scared man makes mistakes. And if they think you iced, Mitch, they be scared, cause he was a seriously bad dude."

"Respect may have worked already then," I said.

"What do you mean?" Ray asked, throwing down a greasy rag he'd wiped his hands with.

"Some guy in a red station wagon took three shots at Cheri and me about an hour ago."

"Just shot and ran?"

"Another car showed up."

"You shoot back?"

"No guns."

Ray shook his head. "It must have been Charlie. You two were lucky, man, like he usually doesn't leave till the deed is done."

"Will you help me find Charlie?"

"Why?"

"I want to talk to him."

"He just tried to kill you."

"I don't know that, and I think someone else is behind all this. They've already killed one man for sure. We found his cell phone near where they did it. And then they shot at Cheri and me when we went there. Cheri opened the guy's messages. There's one from a friend of his who could be dead, too, talking about some crazy fuck shooting at them."

Ray thought a little, then said, "Yeah, Charlie's a crazy fuck all right. That's for sure. And some of his boys are, too."

I nodded. "I need to talk to Charlie. You in?"

"Not if you're just gonna talk to him," Ray said.

"You think he won't talk to me?"

"I think the second he sees you, he will cap your ass."

I patted my belly pouch where my Glock was safely secured, and Ray's smile grew. He patted his back where he carried his own shiny Glock, just like mine, covered by his big, loose T-shirt. Now I smiled.

"John says you're bad karma."

"John wouldn't know karma if it kicked him in the balls. He's reading those girlie magazines again?"

"Enquirer," I said.

"Enquirer?" Ray asked

"National Enquirer."

"John is talking on me about shit in the National Enquirer?"

"Not shit, Ray, karma."

"Well, he's right."

"John is right?" I asked, surprised.

"Yep. For the first time I know of, he's right."

"How?" I asked.

"I am bad karma," Ray said, his voice going flat.

"Good," I said. "I'll help you finish the boat, and then we can go pay Charlie a visit."

"Fuck it," Ray said as he threw his rag into the boat. "Paul and Carol are gone all week. I just need it done before they get back."

"We need cover for Cheri," Ray said as we walked down the dock.

"John," I said, nodding toward the fuel dock.

We walked over to my boat, and I leaned in to tell the girls Ray and I were leaving.

"Ray," Cheri said in a stern voice, "behave."

"Yes, ma'am, Miss Federal Marshal," he answered. "I be good. I be real good."

"Cotton," Cheri said, "call, let me know what's going on. And stay away from the Eagle Star."

"Eagle Star?" I asked, my voice pure and clear.

"Cheri said you were down there looking at tits," Jean chimed in.

"Nope, all clothed," I answered, savoring my chance.

"Yo, who are the ladies?" Ray said, looking into the boat.

"Ray, meet Jean Triller and Betsy Rourk," Cheri answered, pointing to her new friends.

"Pleasure, ladies," Ray replied, tipping an imaginary hat.

"Mr. Cotton," Betsy said, "I listened to the phone you found, and that's Bob's voice."

"Thanks, Betsy," I told her, feeling a touch of surprise at how well she was holding up. She turned away and began looking at the computer screen with Cheri and Jean as I backed out. "I gotta go down to the Eagle Star," Ray said, "get a check for some work. Then we're out of here."

I nodded.

As I stood at the bow of the boat waiting for Ray, Ed waved. He was still sitting in the old wooden chair sipping his Heineken.

"Ready for that beer?" he asked.

"Nope."

"Hear you may be in a little trouble," Ed said.

"I'll be OK," I told him.

"I asked a couple of retired V.I. cops in my bridge club, and they said this Mitch Brachure guy has some bad friends."

"I'll be OK," I repeated.

"You need anything, I'm here," Ed said, his face getting serious.

"I know," I said, feeling a lump in my throat at the old man's sincerity. "Thanks."

Ed just did his face-squish wink, which left an awkward silence till Ray got back.

"Beer?" Ed said to Ray.

"Damn straight," Ray replied, full of joy and goodwill.

In a flash, the old man's hand dropped to the galvanized bucket and came out holding a Heineken by the cap with two fingers. A flick of the wrist shot a chest-high projectile at Ray. As he caught it with a right-handed smack, the pocketknife that had popped into his left effortlessly flipped off the top. He grabbed the cap and then with a flick of his own wrist, sailed it back to Ed, who caught it and set it in the bucket. The whole exchange took maybe five seconds.

I looked at Ray and then at Ed. They both gave me a small smile, and Ray headed down the dock, Heineken in hand.

As I followed him toward my truck, my mind kept seeing the headline: Cirque de Soleil makes Ray Jones and Ed Miller the first beer drinking act in circus history.

When we got to the truck, I threw the three boxes

of pop on the front seat into the bed, and we hopped in. My air conditioner's been broken for a month, so I rolled down my window and Ray did the same.

"I can't believe this piece of shit doesn't have air," he said as he dropped a backpack between his feet.

"Piece of shit?" I asked, looking at Ray's truck off to the right as we pulled away. "No, Ray. Your heap is a piece of shit."

Ray took a deep drink of his Heineken, then said, "Mad Dog, you disrespecting my ride?"

"Yep," I said as I pulled through the marina gate and headed toward town.

"I got money. Let's use it," Ray said, waving a small stack of twenty-dollar bills in my face.

"So, Salina paid you?" I asked.

"Man does the work, man gets paid."

"So, how's Salina doing?"

"As always, my friend, glad to see me," Ray replied, taking another long drink.

"Going to stay sober enough to cover my back?" I asked, getting serious.

"Well, actually I got a plan, and it involves us buying a lot of beer," Ray said.

"Plan?" Ray had never had a plan in his life.

"Sure, a plan. I'll buy your beers for a while and then you buy mine. I got all this fine cash. Let's say you and I go to that little bar in Castle Coakley and get drunk and wait for Charlie and the boys to find us." It was a part of town I don't usually go to, and it was tough to imagine what a bar there would be like.

I turned right on the South Side Road and headed for Christiansted. "So, we just wait, and when we're good and hammered, the bad guys show up and we shoot it out and the whole problem is solved?" I said with a little more sarcasm than I'd intended.

"That works," Ray said, finishing the Heineken and tossing his empty back in the truck bed.

"Can we kind of do this a little less dangerously?" I asked.

Ray looked at me sideways. "So, you got a better plan?"

"We could always go find Charlie and make peace. I've got some questions I need answers to, so shooting him early in the game won't work."

Ray pondered my statement. "I don't like torture," he said.

"I'm not talking torture."

"OK," he said, seeming to be satisfied. "What do you want him to tell you?"

"Who hired him and Mitch to kill all those people and about kill me."

"Then you gonna kill him?" Ray asked, his voice becoming flat.

"No," I said. "Cheri found out he jumped bail last week on a robbery charge. I'll just turn him over to the cops."

"What's gonna get him to talk to you?"

"I got my ways. You just find him for me," I said, though I wasn't sure which way I had in mind might work.

"Done," Ray answered. "Take me to JFK. I got a man I need to talk to."

I was going the right way. The John F. Kennedy housing project sits right on the western edge of Christiansted, just where I was headed.

Ray pulled his Glock out from behind his back and put it between the seats. "This thing's aggravating when a man's trying to relax," he said, then reclined the seat back and stuck a foot up on the dash, arm laying lazy on the window sill, looking just like a man drinking a beer in his favorite chair on a Sunday afternoon.

"You all comfy?" I asked as I changed direction a little to bang into a big pothole in front of the new marine emporium.

"Shit man!" Ray said. "You trying to hit them holes?"

"Yep."

"Why you fuckin' with me?"

"Why we going to JFK?"

"You be happier you don't know."

I looked at Ray, who'd relaxed again. He'd taken his arm off the sill and was holding his nearly empty beer with both hands now. I almost had to swerve off the road to hit the next pothole. The truck lurched as my tires bit into the deep depression.

Ray pulled his sunglasses off and glared at me. I gave him my best "whoops" smile and looked ahead for the next good pothole.

"We gonna go find Horse Man," he said.

"Horse Man?" I asked.

"Horse Man be the last of the JFK old outlaws. He

done seen ten generations of bad boys come and go at the projects, and he be knowing how I can find a man name of Po Po Lane."

"Ten generations! That's forever. Your Horse Man can't be that old."

"It doesn't take long to die around here. Generations come and go quick. Two or three years on the street, and most of these boys are dead."

I thought about what Ray had said. He was right.

"Who's Po Po Lane?" I asked.

"One of the thugs that runs with the posse from the Marley housing project."

"And …?"

Ray pulled the back of his seat up and took his foot off the dash. "We find Po Po, and Charlie will be close. We find Po Po and watch him, and we'll find Charlie. They're tight, those two, and with Mitch dead, Charlie'll be keeping Po Po close to cover his back."

"So, Horse Man and Po Po are tight?"

Ray shook his head like he was teaching a dim student. "No," he said, looking forward as I turned right on Company Street, "but he can get us to Po Po, who can get us to Charlie.

"You solid now," Ray said as he put his seat back again and his size-12 black tennis shoe up on my dash.

"How's Horse Man tied to Po Po?"

"Not."

"Not?"

"Nope."

"Then how does he know where Po Po will be?"

"All the West End boys know Po Po and Horse Man got a serious thing for each other, so when one of the JFK boys, or any of the boys from the West Side, sees Po Po, they tell Horse Man."

"What kind of serious thing?" I asked, looking up Company's narrow confines for a nice pothole to aim at.

"Hate, man. Raw hate. Them two boys both carrying scars from ten years of trying to kill each other. Their thing is a legend, so the grapevine lets Horse Man know where Po Po is, and he'll tell us because he be hoping the white man that put a killing on Mitch is gonna put one on Charlie now."

"You gotta be shitting me," I said, turning the wheel again but this time to miss a big hole. Ray was telling me what I wanted to know now.

"Nope. You happy now?"

"Yep," I said turning right at Times Square and rolling past the downtown police station. "Happy."

"No more potholes?"

"Nope," I said, thinking about the string of logic Ray was using to find Charlie and realizing he actually did have a plan.

The JFK project's low cinder block apartments had been going downhill ever since the feds built them in the Johnson years. As we turned into them, Ray pulled his seat upright, and I could sense his attention sharpen.

To the right, four guys dressed completely in black and all looking alike with huge rows of long black dreadlocks lounged around an old tree. They were all leaning back in fragile looking white plastic chairs their feet propped up on a small bench. A kid in the middle, maybe sixteen, glared at my truck as we cruised by and defiantly took a quick drag of a small joint, then, staring me in the eye, passed the stub to the punk next to him. I gave him a slow nod as he kept his anger fixed on me.

"I love this place," I said as Ray guided me through the maze of dilapidated buildings to the south end of the project.

"Mean streets, man" he said. "Take a left up here and pull into that vacant lot. Park by the line of bush."

The single-level duplexes in front of it looked abandoned. Ray nodded toward a band of deep ruts running through a field of calf-deep shrubs that seemed to stop at a broken-down wooden fence. Beyond it, the bush was deep and thick.

I pulled up to the gate and shut off the engine.

"Got your piece handy?" Ray asked as he picked up his Glock from between the seats.

"We gonna get shot at here?" I asked, eying the set of collapsing horse stalls I could see through the thick brush.

"More likely bit," Ray said as he opened his door and stepped out of the truck.

I got out my side, rolled up the window, and locked the door. "Not a good idea," Ray said. "We might need to get back in real quick." I turned the key the other way and looked around.

Everything was depressing, and real scary, too. There was no way to know what was behind the fence and the thick brush growing up, around, and over it -- or what might come out of the projects.

Years ago, the fence was a barrier between the brush and the yard behind it. Now, it laid broken, flat, and overgrown, but it still screamed: Enter at your own risk. The air was thick with the smell of livestock, like the sheep pens I'd worked in as a kid.

I watched Ray step cautiously over the fence into the open area. His right hand was under his black T-shirt, where I knew it was resting on the Glock. I unzipped my belly pack to make my own gun easier to grab, then started to follow him.

On the other side of the fence, the clearing between the dilapidated stalls and me was a deep mulch of manure. To the right, a lone gray colt tethered to a small post was ignoring us, its head buried deep in a mound of cut green grass. Ray nodded his head to the left. When I looked, my heart stopped. Not ten feet away sat a huge pit bull. A weathered rope held it tied to the makeshift box shanty that was its house. The dog just watched, its small ears straight up, its wide-spaced eyes glaring. I could tell it hated me.

"Shit," I said as I stepped over the fence and crossed into the open yard. The pit bull's gaze followed me.

"Look around, Mad Dog," Ray said softly.

In the chaos of the yard, I saw other pit bulls, just as huge, just as silent, watching from the shadows of their dilapidated shelters. Three of them were lying tethered in the cool shade of the thick brush on the left. To the other side near the colt, two more muscular dogs lay in the darkness of the empty horse shed. I was hoping they were all tied up like the first. But maybe not. Maybe I was in deep, deep shit.

"Ray, this is too many dogs. This is fucking freaky," I said, wrapping my hands around the butt of the Glock. My legs just wanted to turn and run.

"Be calm, man. The Horse Man be close. He come out soon and we talk, and then we out of here."

"OK," I said. The dog I'd seen first was lying down now, resting its huge head on the ground. Its eyes were fixed on me; mine stared back. "So, we just gonna stand here?" I asked.

"Yep," Ray said, his voice low.

Behind us, a loud stick broke. We jumped and whirled around.

My Glock slid smoothly out of the pack and leveled at a small, gray-haired black man standing in front of the truck. In his hands he held the inch-thick stick he'd just broken.

"What bring you to the Horse Man?" the old man asked with a twinkle of glee."

I turned to Ray. He was frozen in a perfect shooter's crouch, pistol aimed with a two-hand grip at the center of the man smiling at us calmly.

"You gonna get yourself killed, you old fool, sneaking up on people like that."

"You getting jumpy in your old age, Ray Man." The old fellow limped slowly toward Ray and stuck his fist forward. Ray extended his own, and the old man punched it hard. "Who's the white man?" he asked.

"Mad Dog," I said, sliding my pistol back in the pack and stepping over the broken gate with my hand out to greet him.

The old man smiled a toothless grin and took my hand, shaking it vigorously. "As in Mad Dog Cotton, the dude what kill that shithole Dicker?"

"Dicker?" I asked, confused.

"Dicker be Mitch's street name, Dog," Ray said.

"Yeah," I answered.

"Cool," the little man said. "I'm George Washington Browne, but my friends call me Horse Man." He paused and looked me over, then said, "You call me Horse Man, and I'll call you Pit Bull."

"It's Mad Dog," I said.

"Whatever, Pit Bull," he replied with a wave of his hand "Why you here?"

"We're looking for Po Po," Ray told him.

"Ol' Pit Bull gonna kill Po Po for me," the old man said, his head shaking in mock joy.

"Let's just say where Po Po go, Charlie will be close behind."

Horse Man considered this and nodded. "Yeah, that's true, especially now that Dicker's gone." He looked me in the eye. "You gonna kill Slider?"

"Who the hell is Slider?"

Ray turned to me. "That's Charlie's street name."

"How do you keep track of all these?" I asked him.

He didn't answer. I looked at the Horse Man. "I'm not killing anyone," I said.

Horse Man turned his gaze to Ray. Ray just shrugged.

"Fuck, I'm gonna make some calls. This is gonna be fun," Horse Man said as he turned and walked back past the truck, pulling a small cell phone out of his dirty jeans.

"Let's get in and relax while he calls," Ray said, walking over to the truck and climbing in.

I sat down inside, too. In the rear-view mirror, I could see Horse Man in the middle of the open field, talking on the phone and gesturing wildly.

"We moving forward now," Ray said. He'd reclined the seat all the way back again and was lying with both feet on the dash and the black Glock between his hands on his belly.

"Mind pointing that thing somewhere else?" I said, eying the pistol aimed straight at my gut.

As we waited for Horse Man to come back, Ray and I drifted into thoughtful silence. Sitting there in the lot, a stone's throw from the silent pit bulls and murderous street kids, my senses were lit up like a jet's radar in a dogfight. Ray, on the other hand, seemed to be napping. When Horse Man banged on my door, I jumped like a whip had hit me.

"Jesus," I snapped as I looked into the aged black man's cheerful, yellowed eyes, "you have to do that?"

"Little jumpy, Mr. Pit Bull," he said.

"It's Mad Dog," I told him.

"Give it up, Dog," Ray said. "Now that the Horse

Man's got your street name, it'll follow you to your grave."

"Or his," I said grouchily, glaring at the small man resting his chin on the top of the glass.

Horse Man gave a small cackle of glee. "All right, Ray Man," he said. "The Pit Bull got an attitude."

"Yeah" Ray answered, still reclined in his seat. "He gets grumpy when the shit's hitting the fan. So talk to me. Where's Po Po?"

"Good news, bad news," Horse Man said, folding his fingers under his chin as he stood crouched and leaning on the truck's window.

I looked down at Horse Man. He was close enough now his stale beer stench was rolling into the truck like a green fog. I turned away and leaned toward Ray, getting a few more inches between the smell's source and me.

"Just the news," Ray said, almost in a growl.

"Po Po gone but stash here," Horse Man said, holding a crumpled scrap of yellow paper.

"You know where his stash is?" Ray asked.

Horse Man lifted his head and reached through the window, passing the slip past me to Ray.

Ray pulled off his sunglasses and read it. Then he looked at Horse Man, whose head was back resting on my open window ledge.

"Sure?"

"Yep."

"Get your head outa the man's window. We out of here," Ray said, sitting up.

Horse Man stepped back and gave me a big smile as I started the truck. "Tell 'em I sent you when you cap 'em," he said.

I pulled away and started dodging the ruts as I inched my way back to JFK. The four punks there had moved to a picnic table, doing the same nothing, staring the same stare.

Ray sat silent behind his wraparound shades. "Where to?" I asked.

"Head for Frederiksted," he said, then pulled the seat back up and punched buttons on his cell phone.

I turned out of the projects and took a left on the North Shore Road, aiming toward the west end of the island. Ray was talking low on the phone, but there was so much wind noise I couldn't hear him even if he wasn't. "What's the deal?" I asked when he hung up. "Where we going?"

"Po Po got him a new woman, and we're gonna go do a little good old-fashioned surveillance. Her house is where my good friend Horse Man says poor ol' Po Po keeps his stash."

"He keeps his drugs at a girlfriend's house?"

"Po Po's not a big drug guy. He keeps his stash of guns at his girlfriend's." Ray was quiet. When he spoke again, his voice was cold. "The kids on this island used to settle their scores with their fists, maybe a knife or a baseball bat. Now, thanks to scum like Po Po, they do a couple months' break-ins and can afford a nice used assault rifle, or maybe a Glock. Po Po was in Iraq and learned all he needed to know about the arms business. When he got out, it was the easy money he was looking for."

I thought of all the killings the island had suffered through since I'd come to St. Croix. I'd always wondered how sixteen-year-olds in the projects got to be so well armed. "Why don't they bust him? If you know the shitbag is selling guns, the cops can't be blind!"

Ray looked at me and shook his head slowly. "My friends at the police station know about Po Po, but they can't get any evidence. His clientele is tight-lipped, and most of the undercover guys here are into drugs. It's kinda hard to turn the people Po Po does business with."

"You gonna give the cops his stash?" I asked.

"Maybe after we're done with what we have to do, but if I told them right now, the odds are one of his buddies in the V.I.P.D. would tell him and we'd lose our best lead to him."

"Makes sense. So, what's the plan?"

"I just called an old friend with an empty building across from Po Po's lady's house. I figure we're gonna stop at the Chicken Shack, get two orders of ribs and a six-pack, and go sit and watch the stash till Po Po shows." Ray reached into his backpack. "And then I'm gonna put this on the bumper of his car, and we're gonna follow him to Charlie and end this thing."

I looked at the small black box Ray was holding. "What?" I asked.

"Radio GPS I built out of a friend's old Garmin chart plotter. Just a fun little project I been waiting for a chance to use. If we're less than a mile from Po Po, we know right where he is."

I looked at the device in amazement. "You gotta be shitting me."

"Nope. This is the transponder from Jack's man-overboard device," Ray said, holding up a little plastic knob that looked like a watch face. "And this is my GPS tracker." He picked up a chart plotter the size of a walkie-talkie, and suddenly, his little toy made perfect sense.

"You took a man-overboard transponder and put it in that black box?"

"Yep."

"And the transponder is tied to the chart plotter?"

"Yep"

I had to shake my head. Ray had taken old parts out of old safety equipment and turned them into a tracking device that might take us where we wanted to go.

"I take it there's a magnet in the little black box with the man-overboard tracker?"

"Yep, that's the only part I had to buy," he said proudly.

"The magnet?"

"Yep. The box is a dry box you gave me. Recognize it?"

I looked at what he was holding, about the size of a cigarette pack, and realized it was a plastic dry box the parks and recreations department had given me when I registered my boat, sort of a welcome-to-the-water kind of gift. I never quite figured why they did it. Maybe the governor's son-in-law makes them.

"So, you had to buy the magnet?" I asked.

"Yep, two bucks at Gallows Bay, and I used some of your glue to hook the magnet to the box."

"How do you start it?"

Ray popped open the black box and showed me the transponder inside. "I just fill the box with water, dunk the transponder in, and the circuit's closed, just like the water closes it if a guy falls overboard. Then my trusty chart plotter starts following the signal."

"What if the water leaks out of the box?" I asked, running my mind through the problems Ray's new toy could have.

"Give me a break, Dog. If the damn box is made to keep water out, it'll keep water in, too."

"True," I conceded. "You ever tried this before?"

"Nope, virgin voyage"

"Cool," I said as I turned into the Chicken Shack for the ribs and beer. I was even going to buy. I figured Ray had earned it.

CHAPTER

9

When we got to Frederiksted, Ray had me park a block south of Custom Street, the main drag, then we walked to a yellow, cinder-block house sitting right on it. After he talked a minute with an old black woman, she gave us two white plastic lawn chairs and opened a door in back that led to a long, dusty stairway.

Up at the top was an empty room overlooking Custom Street. We set the chairs in front of a big picture window with old wooden, louvered shutters, and sat down with our packs and the brown paper bags of food and beer between us. The street was easy to see through the light cotton curtain, but no one was going to see us watching them. We got comfortable. There was no way to know how long we'd be waiting.

Ray pulled out a bottle of Miller Lite and popped

the top with a twist of his hand. A flick of the wrist sent it sailing across the room. "Having fun?" I asked as the cap bounced off the wall back toward us.

"Yep."

"Where's the girlfriend's house?" I asked, looking down into the street.

"Yellow door," Ray said as he pulled a white Styrofoam container out of the second bag and opened it. "Ain't life good?" he said, eying the huge mound of beans, rice, and ribs.

"Yep," I answered, propping my feet on the dusty windowsill and watching the yellow door.

"Bout married ol' Mary's daughter once," Ray said matter-of-factly as he dug into his lunch.

"Who's Mary?"

"The lady that let us in."

"What happened?" I asked, opening my box of ribs and potato salad.

"Failed the test."

"Failed what test?" I mumbled as I bit into the first rib.

"Paternity test," Ray said, "Lilly said I was her son's old man, and I was going to marry her till I flunked the paternity test."

"So she married the father?"

"Nope."

"Then what happened?"

Ray gave me a sideways glance and pointed his meatless rib at me. "You're getting kinda nosy, don't you think?"

"Fine," I told him, turning my attention back to the yellow door and my own rib.

Ray swigged his beer, then said, "Aren't you gonna ask?"

"Ask what?"

"What happened, why I didn't marry Lilly."

"You just told me I was nosy." I pulled a beer out of the bag and tried to flick the cap across the room like Ray had. It spun wildly off my fingers, skipped off my knee into the curtain, and fell to the ground with a dull ting.

"Want me to teach you?"

"How to flick a beer top?"

"Yep."

"Nope. I'll never get enough practice to get good at it."

"Drink more beer."

"I don't want to learn how to flick a beer cap."

"It's a cool skill," Ray said.

"Too late."

"It's never too late for guys like us to develop a skill."

"Like flicking beer tops?"

Ray reached down in front of me and picked up my beer cap. With a quick flick of his wrist, it zipped across the room into the wall.

As it bounced off, I heard a car in the street. A beat-up, four-door, red station wagon was stopping in front of the yellow door.

"Damn," I said, forgetting about the beer cap, giving the old VW my full attention.

"Yeah, I know. It's a cool skill."

"No," I said, "not the beer top. I think Po Po has arrived."

Ray looked at the car, too. "Damn nice ride ol' Po Po got. Must have him a sugar momma."

"That's him?" I asked, sitting up and looking at the large, bald black man climbing out of the car.

"In the flesh."

I was sure the red station wagon was the same one we'd seen on the South Side Road. Po Po opened the back door and reached in.

"I think that's the guy that took the potshots at me and Cheri," I said, setting my beer down.

"I should have figured."

Thinking back to that close call on the hillside, I realized how lucky we'd been.

"He did a tour in Iraq?"

"Yeah," Ray said, his full attention fixed on the man in black and the large duffel he was lifting out.

"How long you think he'll be?" I asked

"No telling," Ray said as he stood up and hurried out the door to the stairs.

I watched Po Po go inside and kept looking at the yellow door. About half a minute later, Ray came walking casually down the middle of the street with his Miller Lite in hand. When he got to the car, he faked a big sneeze and quickly slapped the black box on the inside of the back bumper.

A minute later, he was back in the room, all smiles. "Now let's see if my little invention works," he said, pulling the chart plotter out of his backpack. He pushed a button and a digital voice chirped: "Man overboard."

"Damn, I'm good," Ray said, showing me the display. The little, red circle in the middle, I knew, was Po Po's red station wagon.

I clapped Ray on the back, noticing the empty in his hand as I did. "I'll buy you a beer for that," I said as I reached into the sack to get him one.

"Thanks, man," Ray said, smiling. "I had to pour most of my old one into the box to activate it."

I had a good laugh at the thought that Po Po Lane -- and soon his pal Charlie -- would be in our sights because a man-overboard transponder was drowning in Miller Lite beer.

After packing up the rest of our lunches, Ray and I moved my truck to the next block north and settled in to finish eating while we kept an eye on the red VW.

We didn't have to wait long again. "Lucky we caught Po Po in a hurry," I said as he came out the yellow door and got behind the wheel.

"Here we go," Ray said, setting the chart plotter on the center console.

"Yep," I said pulling away from the curb as Po Po headed south.

"Go ahead and stay back, Mad Dog," Ray said. "This is gonna be easy."

I slowed the truck and felt a slight panic as the station wagon disappeared left around a corner two blocks ahead of us.

"We're cool, man, just keep going," Ray reassured me as he looked at the screen.

I continued on Custom but hit a red light where Po Po had turned. "Damn it!" I cursed.

"We're cool, man," Ray said again as I waited nervously for the light to turn. "Just relax."

"I know. I just like to keep the guy halfway close."

Ray kept looking at the display, then in a dull voice he said, "Whoops."

"Whoops? What whoops?"

"I lost him," Ray said. I glanced at the screen. The little red circle was gone.

"Shit!" No time for red lights now. I pulled past it into the intersection and wove carefully around the honking drivers who thought I shouldn't be there.

"You have to do that right in front of the police station?" Ray said as I drove by the Rainbow Building, home of the Virgin Islands Police Department.

"Just watch the screen, Ray," I told him, speeding up to try to get the truck back in the transponder's range.

"Wonder if the beer screwed with the circuit," Ray said, staring at the blank screen.

Ahead of me, I could see, my speeding was about to end. A long line of cars was crawling behind a twenty-mile-an-hour cement truck. "You see the red car?" I asked.

"Nope," he said as he began shaking the little chart plotter.

"Don't do that!" I said. "If the lights and display are on, it's fine." At that instant, the little box chirped again:

"Man overboard. Man overboard." Ray grinned at me. "I got the touch."

"Do you have Po Po?"

"Yep, maybe about a mile ahead of us and moving away."

I knew if I couldn't get around the cars and cement truck in front of me, we'd lose him again. "Hang on," I said as I wheeled the truck onto the unpaved shoulder and raced through the dirt, spewing dust on the creeping parade as I passed it.

"That's my man," Ray said as I pulled back onto the road and sped up.

"Still got him?" I asked, searching ahead for the red car.

"Yeah, man. This is cool."

As Ray spoke, the police car's siren began screaming behind me.

The officer, showing that sixth sense they can't graduate cop school without, sensed my impatience and shifted into super slow motion to fill out my pile of tickets. When we finally pulled back on the road twenty minutes later, Po Po Lane was long gone.

"Cheri's gonna be pissed when she sees those tickets," Ray said.

"Yep," I said, trying to hide my frustration and regroup.

"What's the plan now?" Ray asked, looking down at the silent chart plotter.

"The island's not that wide. If we keep going east, maybe we can pick up the signal again."

"That works," Ray said, setting the chart plotter down. "Let's go to Schooner Bay on the way, and I'll talk to some of my guys at the market. Maybe they know something."

"And if we pick up Po Po on the way, all the better."

"Right," Ray said. "New plan."

As we turned off the South Side Road down the steep, rut-infested way to the Schooner Bay Market, Ray pointed to the side of the building. "Park over here," he said. "I don't want these guys to know I'm with you."

"Why?" I asked.

"Me and you looking for Charlie will get around, and I want him to feel comfortable for the moment."

"OK."

"Just wait here. I'll be back in ten minutes."

Ray got out and walked down the length of the market and disappeared around the corner. I sat there thinking a few minutes about what he could be up to and then called Cheri.

"I'm in town," I said. "Ray is playing spy."

"What's he doing?"

"I don't know. He had me park at Schooner's and just wandered down the street to check something out."

"That's Ray for ya."

"I guess."

"Jean and I found out some stuff on the guy that tried to sell the coin back in 2002 on eBay."

"What did you find?"

"Well, baby, it ain't good. A lot of bodies, maybe more than a guy can count."

"OK, tell me."

"Jean got some geek on the case from the computer department at the university, and he was able to bring up some records. Give me a second. I'm up on the dock. Let me get to the boat. I've got some notes."

"Fine," I said, feeling an unexplained tension growing in my stomach. Nervously, I checked the mirrors and the parking lot. Nothing seemed wrong, but I still had a strange feeling. I wondered what was taking Ray so long and where he'd gone. "No more secrets," I told myself. "From now on, I'm gonna make him tell me what he's up to." I fidgeted in the car for another minute, then the call came from Cheri.

"OK," she said. "On November 25, 2002, a guy by the name of Brendan Maza from Savannah, Georgia, put one of the coins assayed by Miguel Pinto Camargo, the assayer at the Nuevo Reino mint, up on eBay. Nobody bought it, and he took it off later that month. And no coins like that have showed up anywhere since."

Cheri paused, and I could hear her talking to someone. Then she started again. "Jean tracked down this Brendan Maza guy and talked to his sister in Atlanta. It seems Mr. Maza is in the Army in Afghanistan and can't be reached. His sister did say she'd seen the coin. When Mr. Maza couldn't get a good price for it, he had a hole made in it, and he's got it around his neck as we speak."

"Did she know where it came from?" I asked.

After a short pause, Cheri spoke in a soft voice. "Yeah."

"And?"

"He was in St. Croix with the Army doing hurricane relief after Backward Lenny. His sister said he had the coin when he came back to the states." It all made sense. If anything was going to toss a coin from Chivers' ship to where Maza could find it, it would have been Lenny, one of the biggest hurricanes to ever slam into St. Croix – and even more famous locally because it went the wrong way, west to east, across the Caribbean.

"So, St. Croix again," I said to Cheri.

"Yeah."

"I got to go find Ray."

"Wait," Cheri said, "there's more."

"OK," I told her, "but make it fast. Ray's been gone too long. I need to get moving." The knot in my stomach was screaming that I had to do something.

"Dog, the other coin – there've been two on the market like the one Bob Rourk found -- was put on eBay by Steve Taylor."

"Who's Steve Taylor?" I asked.

"I'm sorry. I forgot you weren't on-Island in 2000. Steve owned a dive shop out on the West Side."

"OK," I said again, becoming more impatient. Ray was gone *way* too long now.

"This is not good. Steve put that coin on eBay on January 3, 2000. And he was shot to death in a parking lot downtown two days later. I think those damn coins got Tony and Steve both killed."

"Yeah," I said, finishing Cheri's thought, "and

probably Bob Rourk. And -- thanks to me -- Sam Drumand and Ann, too."

"John and I have been comparing notes," she said, "and there's something else you need to know."

"Jesus, honey, please! Tell me so I can get out of here. I got to go find the Ray Man."

"In a nutshell, we came up with four more people who disappeared near the East End bays, and two of them were divers."

"Shit, talk to me."

"Kristi Fagan was a gal from California that had only been on-Island for about a month when she disappeared from her home down by Grapetree Beach. John and I didn't have anything to do with the case, but it was odd and scary at the time because there was no evidence of foul play. Just one day she was there, and the next, she wasn't."

"She was a diver?"

"No, I'm getting to that. About seven or eight years ago, before you got on-Island, John remembered two divers whose car was found abandoned at the pullover for the East End bays. They were never seen again. Like Kristi Fagan, they just vanished. And an old friend of mine just when I got back to Island after school disappeared, too, camping overnight at Jack's Bay. Like the others, she just vanished."

"You're making my hair stand up," I said.

"Yeah, I know the feeling. John and I mentioned it to Betsy, and she got really upset. After she settled down, she said she was going down to the newspaper and check articles for other disappearances. I don't think it'll make a difference, but she needed something to take her mind off Bob."

"I don't like it. I don't like her alone."

"John tried to talk her out of it. He told her he had to keep an eye on her. But she insisted. He had to decide who he was going to watch, and it was Jean. He was mad as hell, but there was nothing he could do about it."

"Betsy holding up OK?"

There was a long silence, and I heard a sniffle. Cheri's voice came back weaker. "Betsy's hard-headed, but she's such a sweetheart. This breaks my heart. Mad Dog. If he's still alive, you gotta find him."

"I know, I know," I said. "And I gotta find Ray, too. Now!"

Then from the corner of my eye, I saw movement in the rear-view mirror. He was at the south side of the building waving me over.

"Look, Cheri, I gotta go," I said. "John's still got lots of good contacts. See if he can get the reports on Steve Taylor's shooting from his drinking buddies over at V.I.P.D. And see if Jean can get a lead on what happened to that coin he was trying to sell."

"Got it," she said as she hung up.

I backed the truck up and turned down the wide, heavily rutted dirt road along the east side of Schooner Bay Market. Ray had moved behind the building, and as I pulled near the end, he jogged up and jumped in.

"You see the car at the gas station back there?" he asked.

I looked behind me. A block and a half away, I could see a flash of red behind a gas pump.

"I'm pretty sure Po Po was in that red car at the far pumps." Ray showed me the chart plotter he'd left on his seat. The man-overboard circle was blinking again.

"That's some luck," I said.

"Yeah, but then, they might be following us." Ray kept staring at the little receiver.

"Maybe," I said, "but it's a small island, and maybe he's just gettin' gas. Only one way to find out. Drive someplace, and we'll see if he goes, too."

The dirt road we were on is two blocks long. To the left was a large, vacant lot, and to the right after the market was a warehouse. I drove to the end of the road and turned left. Ray was watching behind us and keeping an eye on his chart plotter.

"Shit," he said and began shaking it again.

"Don't shake the damn thing, Ray." I pulled to a stop halfway down the rutted street to check the receiver myself.

"It's dead," he said, showing me the blank screen.

"Batteries?" I asked.

"It said low, but I thought it wasn't that low."

"Where's the charger?"

Ray reached behind my seat, grabbed his backpack, and pulled out the plotter's charger. "We got to plug it in," he said. "Lotta good this does us." He shoved it back in the pack and tossed the pack behind the seat.

I put the truck in gear and started down the dirt road. "This really would be a great time to know what that car is doing, Ray."

"No shit," he said, looking behind him.

"See anything?" I asked

"Nope."

"I think we should go somewhere safe and charge the chart plotter."

"I got a plan," Ray said, grabbing his pack again and setting it on his lap.

"What?"

"Turn right," he said as we pulled onto the pavement, "and let me out at the No Bones Cafe half a block down on the right. I want to talk to Lola. She's one of Po Po's main girlfriends. She can call him and find out what Po Po's up to."

"And you think he's gonna say what? Oh baby, I'm just out following Mad Dog Cotton and Ray Jones so I can blow their brains out."

"He might say that," Ray said as we approached the No Bones Cafe.

"And she's gonna do this for you because?"

Ray just smiled. "Po Po has lots of girlfriends, but his girlfriends have lots of boyfriends."

He was still smiling when I reluctantly stopped the truck and he hopped out. "I'll let you know what's going on," he said. "Keep your cell phone handy and just drive down toward St. Croix Marine like you're picking up parts for the boat, then circle around and pick me up."

Ray set the dead chart plotter on the seat. "Maybe it'll start again," he said.

"Like it's just taking a nap."

"Yeah," he said as he shut the door.

Ray moved quickly into the little cafe and I pulled away, setting my phone next to the chart plotter on the passenger seat. I looked behind me. No red car, so I drove to the next street and took a right. I was in the Gallows Bay part of town, and if there are any street names down there, I don't know them. Like most of St. Croix, you won't find street signs either. The little lane I was on was lined with mom-and-pop businesses: a T-shirt store, a welding shop, and a small trinket store. In front of me, the street came to a "T" and ended in the parking lot of the Gallows Bay Plumbing store. I drove to the end of the road and looked back again. Still no red car. I turned left toward the center of the Gallows Bay shopping area.

As I approached the next intersection, I was beginning to get mad about the fantasy that Po Po was following us. But as I drove through and glanced to the left, my adrenaline jumped. A red car was turning onto the street two block away.

"Shit," I muttered and looked down at the chart plotter, then thumped the screen with my thumb. The screen lit up and said in a deadpan voice, "Man overboard." The red ring appeared right where the red car had been two seconds before. I sped up and took the next right, which put me on the road to St. Croix Marine.

My heart was racing as I tried to think out all the scenarios. Nothing seemed better than staying on the winding road to the marina. I looked behind me and couldn't see the red car, but the chart plotter showed it was close.

The next time I looked back, the red station wagon was two blocks behind me. My heart lurched, and my mind began to churn in a blur of options. As I approached the entrance to the marina, my instincts said turn. I didn't think any more and just headed into the marina's fenced compound.

I went through the gate too fast, and my truck lost traction as it hit the gravel parking lot and spun out a little. Dust flew, but I just kept going. On my left was the restaurant, where I'm sure some of my friends were watching me drive like an asshole. On the right was a long line of dry-docked boats set up on metal pedestals. I went left and passed by the open-air restaurant and parked in front of the marine store. When I looked back, the red station wagon was coming through the marina gate.

The cold calm that always comes over me before a fight began to descend. I hurried to get out of the truck, but when I tried to open my seat belt, the Glock in my belly pack was wedged against the latch, and for a second I couldn't move it.

As I fought the latch, I felt the cool resolve that was often my edge begin turning into a trapped panic. I took a deep breath and leaned left hard so the latch had less pressure on it, struggling to push the seat belt release through the pack's soft leather. My internal clock was telling me Po Po Lane and maybe even Charlie were getting close.

Finally, short on breath, sweat running down my brow, I managed to push the button. The belt released, and in a single motion, I opened my door and rolled out of the truck onto the ground.

For a second, I froze beside the truck, crouched on one knee, trying to catch my breath and gather my thoughts. The small stones in the hard-packed lot were pushing into my knee.

Staring down into the brown dirt, I regained a little composure. Then I heard something at the marine store behind me and looked up. Staring back was Patty Katz, the marina's accountant, standing in the open doorway with her hands on her hips and staring at me with a "what the hell's happening" frown on her pudgy face. I gave her my "I'm just an idiot" look in return and turned back quick to see what the station wagon was doing.

As I peeked quickly over the bed of the truck, I fully expected a bullet to come ripping at me. The adrenaline running through me was so thick I could almost taste it. I inched above the bed for a second look, thinking, "Damn, Dog, don't look, just run for the boats. Try to hide. Get the hell out of here!" But when I looked for the red station wagon, it was halfway to my truck from the gate already. I ducked back down and began opening my belly pack to reach the Glock easier.

I left the gun in the pouch but turned it so I could draw it out quicker. Then I moved over to where I could look through the side windows of the cab, figuring the reflections might keep the guys in the red car from seeing me.

For a second, I wondered if Charlie Brachure was one of them. Then I decided it didn't matter. They were killers. All of them had most likely killed before, and they were out to kill me now.

As I crouched behind the truck, hand tight on the Glock, the world started moving in slow motion. I'd gone into this state many times as a cop in Denver. My mind was past the panic point, and a cold, calm, calculating mode had taken over. I felt my heart rate drop and my breath slow down.

I looked through the truck windows and saw the station wagon drive over to a spot in the first parking row next to the restaurant, about fifty or sixty yards away.

"Why didn't they come closer?" I thought.

I knew they'd be getting out any second, probably with guns in hand. They wouldn't care who saw them. The crazy bastards could just march across the busy parking lot with guns blazing if they spotted me.

Then, still in my slow-motion mode, I watched as the station wagon's doors began to open. When I saw the back door move, I realized it was at least three against one. My mind raced through the options to escape, but a cold rage was controlling me now, and it insisted: "Stay! Fight!"

Then the other back door opened. Four of them! "Oh God," I thought and ducked down again. I looked back toward the marina store. Patty Katz was still standing silent and unmoving in the doorway, just watching me. Her face wore a frown of concern.

I gave her my half-smile again and wondered what she'd think if I pivoted quick, ran the ten feet to the dock, and dove into the warm blue waters of the harbor. It felt like a good idea, but I couldn't quite understand why.

My thoughts triaged through the options like a mathematical formula. Though I knew I had to fight, I also knew I could never live with the death of an innocent bystander, like a diner at the restaurant or like Patty. I put up my hand and motioned for her to go back into the store, but she just stood there with her face the same mix of confusion and concern.

I thought about running to the empty southwest corner of the marina, getting the four thugs to chase me there. Then we could fight it out darting among the dry-docked boats.

I looked up at Patty again, and something in my eyes must have chased her back inside because she backed up and closed the glass door. Now that she might be safe, I could try to draw the shooting away from the restaurant. I ducked down and moved toward the back of the truck, a few steps closer to the boats.

For an insane instant, I wanted the phone to ring. I wanted it to be Cheri, and a completely irrational part of my mind wanted to answer the phone and tell her goodbye, tell Cheri I loved her. Then I forced the thought out of my mind and locked my full attention on the red wagon.

I knew they'd be coming toward my truck. I needed to let them see me. I'd need to give them a good look. They'd see me easy as I ran around the open water of the loading dock toward the cover of the dry-docked boats. But it wouldn't be much time for them to shoot. They were far enough away they might miss. My chances felt good.

Taking two deep breaths, I put my hand on the Glock but left it hidden in the belly pack as I rose up, giving the four hoods a clear look -- and a clear shot at my head and chest. My heart could almost feel the bullets ripping into it.

My eyes locked on the station wagon. The occupants came into view, the first one getting out the back passenger door closest to me. It was a short black woman with a bush of gray hair and a bright floral shirt.

My mind froze in confusion. I could see what I was seeing but couldn't comprehend it. When my thoughts focused again, all four occupants of the red station wagon were closing their doors and heading toward the entrance of the open-air restaurant. Suddenly, everything was clear. It was Sally Ball and her lunch group. Spirited little old ladies who went to lunch every Tuesday in Sally's red VW station wagon. Widows, retired teachers – not thugs, not my enemies. And they were carrying large floral purses, not guns.

I sank to my knees, almost crumpling on the hard

earth, panting in the parking lot dust. My head hung down. I could feel a deep pain in my chest.

Patty Katz must have been watching me through the glass door of the store. She opened it and walked out again. When she got to the truck, she reached her left hand down and touched my shoulder.

"Mr. Cotton, you OK?"

I looked up at Patty and nodded slowly, then squeaked out a quiet "Yeah." I wanted to say, "Yeah, just a heart attack," but any humor in me was gone.

"You want me to call Cheri?" she asked.

I shook my head no. The world wouldn't stay still as I got to my feet, but gradually the movement slowed, and I could feel strength coming back and my mind clearing. I steadied myself on the truck and looked at Patty. Deep concern showed in her scowl as she put her hand on my shoulder again. "You look like shit," she said. "You sure you don't want me to call someone?"

"No," I said. "Thanks. I just got a little dizzy, too much sun."

Patty looked up at the sky, then back at me. "It is hot. You need to make sure you drink plenty of water."

"Yeah," I said. Across the parking lot, I could see Sally and her three feisty friends seated around a table, probably ordering white wine and salads.

Patty followed my gaze to the restaurant. Then she took her hand off my shoulder and said, "Drink more water" as she turned back to the store.

My phone rang. "Yeah," I muttered into it.

"How long you gonna leave me sittin' here, Dog? We

gotta move. Po Po ain't out for you. He's just out fishing, and he just borrows the red car from his grandma once in a while. You know, Sally Ball. Man, we have been following a grandma. You be wrecking my reputation."

"No shit," I said, climbing back into the truck. "Sorry, Ray. Go out front. I'll be there in five minutes."

"You OK?" Ray asked. "You sound funny."

"I'm fine," I said, "just fine."

I pulled my truck behind Sally's station wagon, climbed out, and retrieved Ray's makeshift tracking device.

As I drove out of the marina, I looked at Sally and her three friends one last time. They were chattering away and sipping wine. "God, this island is scary," I thought.

As I drove back to the Gallows Bay drug store, my heart rate slowly began returning to normal, and the pain in my chest started to fade. In the years I was a cop and since then on the island doing my on-again, off-again investigations, I've been in a lot of tight spots, but my reaction to the red station wagon scared me. As I pulled over to pick up Ray, I was reliving the moment when I couldn't unhook my seat belt. The memory sent a tremor into my shoulders and raised a knot in my back. My own panic could have killed me. My decision to pull into a crowded business could have killed others.

Ray popped open the passenger door and leaped in. As usual, he was hustling on to whatever was next: "Shit, man. We're late. Let's roll."

I looked at my watch and saw it was already five o'clock. "I gotta meet Cheri and the rest of my merry helpers at 6:30 at the Greek's," I said, surprised it was so late.

"We gonna hunt or we gonna chat?" Ray asked. I could tell his eyes were hard with agitation as he pulled off his wraparound shades.

"Chat," I said.

"Fuck, man. Let me off at my truck. While you're doing your chat-chat, I'll go find our man."

"No, not without me."

"Shit, you just be in the way anyway."

I looked sharply at my friend. "Not without me," I repeated. As my mind went back to what had happened at the marina, I knew I needed time to get my head straight before trying to find Charlie again. I reached up and grabbed Ray's arm, knowing that he didn't understand. "Just don't do this without me."

"I'll go shake trees. No killin', just shakin'." he said.

"No killin', just shakin'," I echoed. "We start again in the morning."

"This one's a night man, a vampire. You won't find him when the sun shines."

"Ray," I said, my voice rising, "we wait."

"I'll find you at the marina in the morning."

"Deep End, eight o'clock," I said as I pulled up to Ray's truck.

He didn't say anything. He just got out, gave me a brief nod, and got in the truck. I wondered if Charlie Brachure would still be alive in the morning. All I could do was hope. If Ray got lucky and found Charlie tonight, the Brachure family might have two twins to bury.

When I got to my boat, John was sitting on the back deck smoking a cigarette and watching the beginning of the sunset. "Ladies are inside," he said. "You and Shaft kill anybody?"

"Nope."

"Night's still young," he said, eying the sky.

"Yeah," I replied and pulled up the deck chair next to him.

"Bad deal with Tony Rasser run off the road," he said.

"How'd you get a report?" I asked.

There was a long pause like John hadn't heard me. "Just luck, I guess," he finally said, turning to look at me. "I got permission from your neighbor to stay on his boat tonight."

"Neighbor?" I asked, not sure who he was talking about.

"Yeah, the old pervert in slip three."

"His name is Ed."

"Ed the pervert. That has a ring to it."

"So, you met Ed?" I asked.

"Yeah, him and the crew of women from the end of the dock. He had them all down for beer. He made the big blonde sit on the rabbit woman's ass or he told her she wouldn't get a beer."

"Paints a pretty picture," I said.

"Yes, sir," John agreed, looking back at the sinking sun.

"You drink a beer?"

"Nope," John said, "I'm on duty. But I noticed the Ray Man was consuming."

"I don't think he considers this business."

"No?" John said, turning to me. "If he don't consider this business, what the hell you think he considers it?"

"Just life as usual."

"Shit, the guy is a menace."

"Yeah, John," I said, "but he's our menace."

I left John to the sunset and his smoke, went around the boat, and pulled open the port hatchway.

"I'm home," I said in a singsong voice.

"Welcome," Jean said as I went inside. Cheri was just closing her laptop on the table. "Boy, some characters!" she said.

"Find a few friends of Charlie's?" I asked.

"A bunch. A big bad bunch."

"Lots of charges but not many convictions," Betsy added, fidgeting at the end of the L-shaped bench.

"Where'd you find out who they were?" I asked Cheri.

"Little bird," she answered with a now-you-know-enough nod of her head.

"Those guys ought to all be long gone," I told her.

"They are the cream," John said from the door as he lowered his bulk through the hatchway and sat down on the wooden step that also acts as my tool chest.

"Know any of them?" I asked him.

"Nope," he said, "but I bet your buddy Ray knows

them all. Maybe he's drinking a cool one with them right now."

"I don't know why," Cheri said, looking toward John, "but for some reason, Ray is cool when it comes to Mad Dog. He's on our side."

I nodded as my hand reached toward the small scar on my right wrist. Ray's scar. I had never mentioned it to anyone, not even Cheri. When she asked me about the scar while we were dating, I said I'd cut it working in the engine room. In truth, I'd cut it blocking a knife aimed at a gray-haired black man I barely knew. That man was Ray Jones, and in a split second of reflex, I earned a friend for life. After the young thug tried to stab Ray, he turned and began swinging the knife at my face. Ray caught his wrist in midair and jerked it with a quick, violent snap. Then, like a father scolding a son, he said, "It's broken, boy. Go to the ER and get a cast or it won't heal right."

That night, he treated the young man kindly and with respect – except for breaking his wrist. After the thug was gone, the black man reached over behind the bar and handed me a white rag. "Here," he said, "you're cut." I hadn't even noticed the small gash on my wrist. Ray and I sat down and drank that night away and have done so many times since. It hurt me when John said what he did about Ray, but he was right. Ray was a bad man. He was also my best friend.

I smiled at John. "He's cool," I said.

"OK," John replied. "So, what's the game plan?"

"I think you and I should take turns keeping an eye

on things," I said. "Go on over to Ed's, and I'll wake you at two to spell me. That way, I can get a good five hours' sleep, and you'll be fresh, too."

"I'm out of here. I hope those girls from the end of the dock don't show back up. That old man'll feed them beer all night just to keep them around."

"I hope I'm that frisky when I'm eighty," I told him.

"I'm planning on it," Cheri said with a smile.

As John got up, Jean said, "I thought we were going to dinner."

"Greek's," Cheri reminded me.

"I'll stay and keep an eye on the boat if you'll bring me one of those gyros," John said.

"Done," Jean told him.

"Let's go," Cheri said, "It's going be a long night, and we should all be fresh for the morning."

CHAPTER 10

Like so many other things in St Croix, the Pickled Greek is an odd mix of contradictions. It's home to hard drinking, loud music, and late-night Greek dancing, and sits right across the street from an elementary school.

Half the Greek's seating is an outside area of white plastic lawn chairs and tables on a dirt and gravel floor that probably once was the parking lot. A single speaker that resembles a bullhorn pours loud and rowdy Greek music out into the open air. There's no awning, no umbrellas. If it rains, you get wet. The lighting consists of what drifts over from a city streetlight and the neon "OPEN" sign.

For real furniture and fans, you need to go inside the green cinderblock building. The chairs and tables

149

probably were bought at a garage sale or a second-hand store's closeout. The walls are filled with old signs on weathered raw wood with statements like "Gone Bush" painted bright red. In the local slang, I think it means, "I'm out in the woods."

On the wall next to the bar, a sign says, "COME SOON" in black letters, and in blue letters below, it adds, "FOR TRUE." During the year, the Greek needed to get all his permits and liquor license, the only hint of what was coming was that hand-painted, four-by-eight sign reading simply, "COME SOON." After about nine months, though, he decided "FOR TRUE" was needed as well to keep potential patrons interested. When the Greek finally got his restaurant open, he replaced the sign outside with another saying, "HAVE COME." And the "COME SOON, FOR TRUE" message was hauled indoors to its place of honor by the bar. Then, three months later, the "HAVE COME" joined them to adorn the inside as well.

Tonight we gave up the luxury of the inside seating and dined beneath the stars. We had business to discuss, and outside was where we could get the privacy we needed.

As always, the Pickled Greek was packed, but Cheri led us to a table farthest from the 6:30 insanity.

While we waited for drinks -- water and diet Cokes all around -- Jean entertained us with stories of pirates and treasure. Usually I like to stay on focus in an investigation, but this time, it was nice to relax and just talk about unimportant history. The last three days had been as crazy as any I'd ever seen, and I could feel my body and mind starting to crash. But though Jean's talk seemed to captivate Cheri and Betsy, my mind began to wander. There was a part to the puzzle that I'd seen but couldn't put into place. I felt a changed understanding was right around the corner, but I couldn't quite get there.

When the waitress came with our drinks, Cheri had to nudge me to order. The food is authentic Greek -- no hamburgers, grilled fish, or steaks. Though the menu offers dozens of mouth-watering treats, that night, like a bunch of sheep, we all ordered gyros. After the waitress left, Betsy, who'd been quiet since we sat down, spoke up.

"This gold treasure idea doesn't make any sense," she said. "If Jean is right and these people were killing people nine years ago to protect the sunken gold, shouldn't it all be gone by now? Wouldn't they have just taken as much gold as they could find and move on by now?"

Nobody answered, but her words shook something in the back of my mind where those puzzle pieces I couldn't fit together were tumbling around.

All at once, I knew what was bothering me. "We know the disappearance of Bob and maybe the killing of Tony Rasser, too, happened only one day after they found the coin," I said. Everyone nodded as I paused to think again. "What if there really is no treasure, but someone who heard about the coin thought they saw a chance at a fortune and just got crazy?"

I felt the thoughts that had been simmering out of reach suddenly start to boil. "What if this is all just gold fever!"

It was making more sense as the words took shape in my mind. "What if everything going on now has nothing to do with those other killings? Yeah, people are dead. But that's the only connection. Maybe the fact that they have anything to do with each other is just something we dreamed up in our heads. Maybe it's all just coincidence, and we need to think more about what's happening right now."

Cheri turned to Betsy and asked, "Who would have known about that gold coin other than you?"

"I don't know of anyone," she said. "Bob was pretty clear that he thought it was a big secret."

"What about this Tony Rasser?" Jean asked.

"Tony's whole life circles around his friends. He doesn't have a family," Betsy replied, putting her hands in her hair. She turned to me. "Tony was always looking for a way to look important, to be special. I don't think he really could have kept this a secret. He would have had to brag about finding a coin like this."

"Who were his friends?" I asked.

Betsy looked as though the hands buried in her full red hair were trying to pull thoughts out of her mind. "Just people at the bars, Chicken Charlie's or the Golden Rail," she said.

That left only hundreds of possibilities. The two places were so popular they almost had more regulars than they could handle.

"No one in particular?" I asked.

"Not that I know. I knew Tony from the house. Bob and I would have him over for dinner once in a while, and Bob would join him at one place or another for a beer on the way home from work, but that was it. Except for Meg but they are more friends than boyfriend, girlfriend."

"We need to talk to Meg and the folks at both those places as soon as possible, Cheri said. "We've got to find out if Tony talked about this with anyone. Did someone there show more interest than the rest of the crowd?"

"I'm too beat to do any good tonight," I said, "and you need to catch the bartenders when the places aren't packed, so they can talk."

"We should stop at both places in the morning and find out who was working when Tony went there after they found the coin," Cheri said.

"Can you or John do that?" I asked her. "Ray and I need to hunt down Charlie Brachure in the morning.

"We'll go to the Golden Rail for breakfast and talk to them," Cheri said, "and by the time we start back out to the marina, someone may be at Chicken Charlie's."

"I'm gonna be moving early, so just call me with what you find out," I said.

"That works," Jean replied, giggling as a small Coke burp erupted. "That'll give us girls a chance to brainstorm with John while we drive into town."

As she spoke, a light caught my eye moving in the darkness of the school lot across the street.

"I'll be right back," I said, getting up and heading toward it.

Cheri began to ask what was going on, but I put up my hand to stop her.

As I crossed the street, the headlight winked off. A car roared past behind me, and I walked faster.

I couldn't see inside the truck through the darkened windshield, but I didn't have to. "What's up?" I asked Ray as he sat with his arm leaning out the open driver's window.

"Just keepin' an eye," he said.

"Find out anything?" I asked him. My eyes were adjusting to the dim light, and I could make out Ray sitting behind the wheel.

He had on a black T-shirt and a black do-rag that hid his gray hair. I could see a sheen of sweat on his brow. His eyes seemed to float suspended, his pupils where large, black and surrounded by narrow iris' that were a cat like iridescent green, the whites of Ray's eyes were yellowed and blood shot by years of hard living. In the moon light his eyes seemed to float in sea of black.

Ray blinked and his eyes disappeared, then they came back. His white smile cut a crack in the darkness and Ray said slowly. "Our man has been drunk since he heard about his brother. He's taking it real hard. Word is when and if he sobers up, you're a dead man."

"I'll loan him some money if he wants to keep drinking," I offered.

"Not the worst plan." The eyes were joined again by a crack of white teeth.

"Where is he?" I asked.

"Around, man," Ray said. "He's moving, talking to a lot of people, working himself up, I think."

"Working himself up?" I asked.

"Some folk don't just kill, brother. Some folk need to get themselves in the mood."

"So, he's coming soon?"

"Let's hope so," Ray said. "He's so shit-faced right now he couldn't hit his ass with both hands."

"That would get this over," I said, thinking briefly of facing off Charlie Brachure with a bottle of rum in one of his hands and a gun in the other.

"Yep." The eyes and the smile disappeared, and I could imagine Ray's thoughtful face. "Boss, he may be a bad man, but he's not dumb. He won't be coming tonight. No, when he comes, he'll come stone cold sober."

There was something in Ray's voice, or maybe it was a wisp of cool wind, that made a chill run down my back. My stomach began to knot again as I stood there in the dark, leaning on Ray's door. I looked behind me and could see the three women at the plastic table. Jean had her head back and was laughing. They all seemed so comfortable, sipping their drinks and chatting. They seemed happy, and I felt surrounded by evil.

"Can you find him?" I asked the darkness.

"Maybe," it answered.

I have led a less-than-perfect life. In times of need, I have killed so I wasn't killed myself, but I have never ordered an execution. I knew the darkness was waiting for that request. I knew at that moment without any doubt that if I spoke one word, Charlie Brachure was dead.

I looked back at the women, all of them laughing now in the light. I took a deep breath and let it out. I reached into the truck, found my friend's shoulder and held it. "Go home, buddy," I said. "We'll hunt tomorrow."

His eyes seemed to search into my soul for a long second, then the grin reappeared. "Your call," was all Ray said as the small truck pulled away and left me standing in the dark parking lot, alone with the Greek music and laughter across the street.

I didn't move, feeling somehow that a life-changing moment had just passed. Had I just done the right thing? Had I looked the devil in the eye and said no? Had I just signed the death warrant for myself and everyone laughing at the table across the street? I put my hands over my face and washed the thoughts away, then turned back toward the lights, the music, and the food I could see the waitress starting to serve.

"You OK?" Cheri asked as I sat down in front of my foil-covered dinner.

"Little headache is all," I lied.

"Well, eat. You'll feel better," she said

CHAPTER 11

Maybe it was exhaustion and a full belly, but that night I slept as if I was in a coma. At 1:15, my phone alarm went off and I woke instantly. I was totally alert as I grabbed it off the dresser and killed the noise. Cheri was still snoring lightly next to me as I got down off our platform onto the wooden floor. I grabbed a pair of Levi's I'd set out and a black T-shirt and stepped naked up the stairs to the boat's living area. Silently, I closed the door behind me and got dressed.

I'd set my alarm early so I could look around the marina before I relieved John. I slipped on a pair of black tennis shoes and stepped out onto the side deck. Two boats down, I could see John's shadowy figure sitting on Ed's stern. I waved silently and the shadow waved back.

I walked around the boat, stopping to adjust my eyes to the starlit night, then climbed off and walked down the marina's main cement walkway to the public shower and bathroom under the main building. The path is well lit, but I suddenly realized what a great hiding place the five-foot bougainvillea hedge on the parking lot side could make. I'd never thought much of the hedge before, but tonight, its dark recesses gripped my attention. As always when fear is in me, all my senses seemed on full alert. My eyes scanned the deep shadows for any hint of life. My ears strained for any movement or breath. My nose pulled in the rich night air searching for clues. My heart pounded, and the hedge seemed alive with danger.

When I got to the men's shower room, I grabbed the doorknob and froze. What if they were in there waiting for me? "Bullshit," I told my coward side, but I pulled open the big metal door open with much too much force. It clanged like a gong ripping into the cinderblock. I stared into the darkness, feeling like an idiot but still too scared to move. Finally, as I'd done a thousand times before, I flipped the switch turning on the bank of fluorescent lights. I stared into the brightness and the urinal stared back. I listened, then walked through the lighted shower room. Slowly, the fear slipped away – but not the caution. I checked every shower – no shotgun-wielding hoods. I looked under all the toilet doors. No big pairs of boots with killers' feet inside. At the last toilet, I went in to use it.

Then, as soon as I got fully seated and prepared for

my 1:20 moment of relaxation, I realized I'd come all the way to the shower room unarmed. My Glock was still on the dresser next to the bed. Paranoia does not increase intelligence. As I thought about my mental state and lack of precautions, another critical mistake flashed in my mind. Quickly, I looked at the toilet paper dispenser. A flag of white waved under the gray box. Thank God!

Even after I was finished there, though, I stayed in the relative safety of the lit room for another five minutes. I thought about the fact that I had no gun. I thought about going back on the boat and possibly waking Cheri when I went to get it. I thought about how silly it was to be afraid of the hedge along the walkway. I thought about John waiting for me on Ed's boat. I hoped he had coffee and donuts. I finally resolved that if I got shot by one of Charlie's assholes on the way to the boat – or even by a sleep-startled Cheri if she thought I was a mad attacker -- it was my own damn fault. I was careful this time not to bang the shower room door on the wall as I walked out into the cool dark of the night.

I got back to the boat and retrieved my pistol without incident, and John was waiting when I got to Ed's slip. I really wanted a cup of coffee before heading out around the marina. He just sat in the shadows and looked at me as I climbed onto the old wooden sailboat. I wondered if he knew how spooked I was. I wondered what he'd think if he knew. I didn't like myself so scared. It embarrassed me. As I sat down next to him on one of Ed's small, white plastic chairs, I felt like a kid in school who just realized his pants were unzipped.

We sat in silence for a second. Then the big guy said, "This marina gives me the creeps. Too many noises, too many things moving, too many dark spots."

"Yeah," I said, feeling slightly vindicated.

"Everything's quiet. You want me to stay here with you? I'm not tired."

"No, but maybe you can wait while I make a quick trip around the marina and check in with the guard at the gate."

"Sure, man, take your time."

"Got any coffee?" I asked, looking hopefully at the big thermos sitting next to him.

"Yeah, the old man filled me up before he went below." John handed me the thermos and a Styrofoam cup. I filled the cup and took a sip, feeling the warmth and aroma run through me.

"Good," I said.

"Don't drink too much. Not good to have to pee when you're on surveillance," John cautioned.

"Gotcha," I told him as I stepped over a coil of rope and off the boat, cup of hot coffee in my hand.

I turned left and walked to the end of "B" dock first. I think I chose that direction because it was the least scary of the marina's dark spots. John had been on watch at "B" all night, and anyone who got past him would have had to come by boat. Not likely. I may have also walked to the end of "B" dock to see if Salina and the girls were doing a little late night naked drunken moon bathing. No luck there. The Eagle Star was quiet. Just as well. I needed to keep my mind on business.

As I passed John on the way back, he gave me a slight wave, and I raised the cup in a small salute. I continued to the cement walkway at the end of "B" and then along it to "C" dock. The hedge of bougainvilleas was now on my left, and my paranoia had relaxed enough that I could enjoy the night. The coffee felt warm in my hand, and the cool breeze good on my face.

When you live in a place long enough, you become attuned to the orchestra of its sounds, maybe like someone who lives in the jungle gets used to its screams and rumbles and roars. The loose ropes and guy-wires were beating a soft drum against their masts to the tempo of the wind. Boats moved and sloshed and bumped to the rhythm of the waves. Dock ropes and rigging creaked and moaned. The ancient song of frogs and insects played on and on as the feeding splashes of tarpon punctuated the night. Like a musician hearing a familiar song, you know when it's off-key. I sensed only harmony in the marina, and my fear began to slip aside.

"C" Dock marks the end of the main walkway, and from the corner where they met, I could see the whole other side of the marina. I looked at it all before turning right to walk down "C." All was quiet. One light was on at the motel at the far end. I thought of Jean and Betsy sleeping in safety there, and I hoped they were comfortable. Cheri had arranged to check them in under false names, and I felt confident that Charlie Brachure and the hoods who'd likely be with him couldn't find them for all the gold in the Caribbean. I decided to walk over to the motel and look around quickly before I relieved John. It would take an extra fifteen minutes to walk around the marina to the motel, but I'd be more comfortable if I checked that out, too.

Nothing seemed unusual on "C" dock, so I came back toward "B" and "A." The hedge was on my right again now and for some reason seemed more ominous. I wondered if my right side was more chicken-shit than the left. When I got to Itchy Feet, I stopped and listened. The boat seemed to breathe easily like Cheri deep in sleep beside me. All seemed well. At the head of "B" dock, I raised my cup again to John, and he nodded. I walked on past the marina office and the shower room to "A" dock. It was quiet, too. The walkway changed from cement to wood as it turned into "D" dock. The long row of small motorboats was rising and falling rhythmically as little waves tickled the calm water.

As I turned away from "D" dock, I hit a body – a moving body. Panicked, I pushed it away and backed up nearly to the edge of the walkway, groping behind for the Glock in my waistband. My heartbeat hurt, and my hand wasn't going where I wanted. A second passed and the form took shape. Ted Ringer, in blue swim trunks, holding a yellow towel over his shoulder, stood as frozen as I was. In the dim light from the bulb over the bathroom door, I could see him holding a white box, probably soap. His hair was wet and uncombed, and his eyes were wide with anger and surprise.

"Jesus Christ, Mad Dog, get a grip," he growled.

"Shit, Ted, you scared the hell out of me," I managed to say as I felt my heels nearly at the point of no return on the edge of the dock. "Sorry, man. I'm really sorry. I just didn't see you."

"Yeah," Ted said, shifting the soapbox back and forth between his hands. "I about said hi when I came out of the bathroom, don't know why I didn't. Sorry if I startled you."

"OK, buddy," I said, feeling foolish for about the twentieth time in a day.

Ted gave me a long look and said, "I heard about that deal in Puerto Rico. You should be jumpy. You need anything, you just ask."

I've known Ted Ringer since I moved to the marina seven years ago but never really well. I was surprised by his sincerity, especially since I'd nearly knocked him on his ass only a minute earlier. "Thanks, Ted," I said. "I guess I'm a little edgy."

"No shit," he said, a smile creeping across his face. "That why the moose is camped on Ed's boat?"

No secrets in a marina.

"Yep."

"Good for you. Some punk comes to the marina and tries to hurt one of ours, and God help him." There wasn't any bluster in what Ted said. It was simply fact.

A marina is not just a small town; it's a small town full of crazy sons-of-bitches who'd rather live on four-hundred-square-foot boats than in four-thousand-square-foot homes. It is not a community of pansies. Even the girls are tough. I took a new look at Ted Ringer.

I knew he'd sailed his boat around the world, and I had no doubt he could kick some ass.

"Yep," I said, smiling big as I imagined the reaction of the marina's live-aboard to marauding thugs. "God help him."

Ted adjusted his towel, comfortable his point had been made, then clapped me on the shoulder and walked on down "A" dock to his boat. Some people might say Cheri and I have chosen a strange life, but I do love it.

I waited until Ted disappeared into his boat and then started again to the motel. On the way, I passed the security shack that checks everyone, license plate by license plate, as they enter or leave the marina after six o'clock. For ten years, Miguel Ramos has been the night guard. For twelve hours a night, four nights a week, he's sat in that lonely shack ready to protect us. I'd waved at Miguel day in and day out for three years after I came to live at the marina before I ever knew his name or talked to him. That changed four years ago when a carload of young bandits drove up to Miguel, pistol-whipped him, and proceeded to rob the restaurant. They'd left him bleeding and unconscious at his guard shack.

The next day, Cheri had insisted we visit Miguel at the hospital. When I asked why, she said nothing and just gave me the eye. We went to the hospital with a sack of Twizzlers because Carlos, my good friend and mechanic, told us Miguel had a serious red Twizzler addiction.

When we went into the small, sterile room, he was

alone. A large bandage covered the left side of his face. As we entered, his soft brown eyes flickered open below the bruises, and he tried to rise. Cheri took a step toward him and placed her hand on his chest.

"Don't," she said, pushing him gently back down.

"Mr. and Mrs. Cotton, why are you here?" Miguel asked, a hint of confusion in his voice.

I held my ground about three feet from the bed. I'm not good at hospital visits. But Cheri sat right next to Miguel and took his hand. "You scared us, my friend," she said in her softest voice.

Miguel looked down, and a small hint of moisture formed at the corner of his eyes. "I am sorry, Mrs. Cotton," he said in a quiet, heavily accented voice. "I am so sorry."

"No," Cheri said with a firmness in her voice. I could see her hand squeeze Miguel's. "We all know you were brave and did all you could."

Miguel turned away, and I could hear quiet crying. Cheri just sat there, her hand over Miguel's, and waited. After a few moments, he sat back up and wiped his eyes. "I am sorry. A man should not cry," he said with embarrassment.

When I'm in a highly emotional situation, like most men, I don't do well. My resolution is often inappropriate humor. Laughing is more dignified than crying. So, I stepped up and said, "Don't worry. She makes me cry all the time," and gave him my best "Glad you're OK" smile.

Leave it to history to say that Miguel ceased to be a guard that day and became part of our family.

As I walked up the dark road to his little shack, I could see him inside it watching me. With a big smile, Miguel stepped out to embrace me, the huge gun hanging awkwardly on his small, lean body.

"Mr. Mad Dog, you just come to visit an old man," he said.

"Nope, I'm just going for a walk."

"No, no, not you. I know you're going to check on the ladies at the hotel."

No secrets in a marina.

"Don't you worry, my friend," he said. "I check on them, too, and on you and Mrs. Cheri and Mr. John. He is a big one, Mr. John."

"You know all, Miguel," I said.

"No," he said, shaking his head. "Not all, but I try."

"All quiet?" I asked.

"Oh yes, and with the bad men out there, I will watch much harder."

"Thanks buddy," I said.

Then he gestured toward his little vehicle next to the shack. "You don't walk to the hotel," he said. "You take my golf cart."

"I shouldn't, Miguel. What if you need it?"

"Need it?" he said, looking around. "I watch the gate. You take the cart. And don't hit anything," he kidded as he handed me the small key.

I thanked him and climbed in, turned on the lights, and headed for the motel about a quarter-mile away.

As I drove, Ed and Ted and Miguel all ran through my mind. I thought of Denver. It was a city where I didn't even know my neighbors, and the only people I could count on were other cops. Here, friends willing to help me surrounded me. It felt good. I thought of John and Ray. "God help the bad guys," I said to the darkness.

The marina's motel is a quiet, yellow, cinderblock building. I parked Miguel's golf cart in front and circled it on foot. Everything was normal. I looked at Betsy and Jean's second-floor room. Quiet. No light. All was well.

I drove the cart back and tossed the key to Miguel, then walked back down to the main marina area. John was still sitting on Ed's boat, his feet propped up on the back railing.

"All OK?" he said as I climbed aboard.

"Yeah, all is quiet, and Miguel is watching Betsy and Jean."

"You told him," John growled in disbelief.

"Nope," I said, "he knew."

"This place is a fucking sieve," John said angrily.

"You're kinda pissy," I answered.

"Sorry, haven't done this type of stuff in a while, and I'm sore."

"Get some sleep," I said. "Cheri made up the forward berth for you."

"I'm gonna sleep like a rock," John said, the night's adrenaline clearly fading.

"Yeah, and don't forget, I'll be your protector."

He looked at me for a long pause, then said, "So

much for sleep" as he gingerly moved across Ed's mess of a deck and climbed off the boat.

After John disappeared into Itchy Feet, I laid my Glock next to me on the deck and poured a cup of coffee. I felt wide-awake and alive. I wondered if Salina and the girls would flash me on the way to their showers in the morning. Probably not, but what a great fantasy. If mind reading ever gets perfected, the male gender will be wiped out by pissed off women in a week.

Ray Jones was at my side at six o'clock on the bow of Ed's boat. I couldn't believe it was him materializing suddenly out of the dawn. The sun had just barely peeked over the horizon, but there he stood holding a small, grease-stained, brown paper bag.

"No deep end with the girls today," Ray said before I could speak. "I got something important we need to do."

"I can't go," I told him, amazed that he'd come two hours early. "I need to keep an eye out till John or Cheri is up."

"It's daytime already. It's light! If any shit was going down, it would have done it by now. Come on. I got a ride I want you to take."

He held out his greasy bag. "Do I need to bribe you?" Ray asked. I took it from him and looked inside. In it were four meat *pâtés*. A miracle of Cruzan cuisine, the fried bread dough stuffed with meat and vegetables may be the most rounded breakfast on the planet. No oatmeal and donuts for Ray Jones.

"It's a deal," I said with a smile as I reached inside

and grabbed one of the treats. Ray sat down next to me as he took out another.

Amid the calm and quiet, we ate our *pâtés* and drank coffee from John's thermos, watching and listening to the marina begin to wake up.

At six-thirty, Salina and two of her deck hands I hadn't met came by on the way to the showers. None of them flashed us, but Ray did get a light-hearted laugh when he stood up and gave the ladies a gracious bow.

"You make me crazy," I said.

"The ladies, they like my style," he answered with a big grin.

"Style?"

"Style, man. I got style."

"Drink your coffee, Mr. Style. You're tellin' me we gotta go somewhere."

"Yeah, but we ought to wait till the girls come back," Ray said, looking down the dock toward the showers.

"Nope," I told him. "You're the one all hot to hit the road. Now I want to see wherever we're going."

"Don't worry," Ed said, coming out of his cabin with a steaming cup of coffee. "I'll entertain 'em while you're gone."

"Shit, old man," Ray said, giving Ed a harsh look. "You'll wreck them with all that free beer you give them. They going to be expecting that kind of kindness from all their man friends pretty soon."

"If you can't take the heat…," Ed answered as he shrugged his skinny shoulders.

"Shit, man, we gotta go," Ray said, standing and

turning to me quickly, "or this ol' fool gonna start talkin' and we be here all day."

"Right," I said as I got up. We took our coffee and the trash from our *pâtés* and stepped off the boat.

"Don't worry," Ed said from the stern. "I'll take care of things while you two are off wandering."

For better or worse, I knew he was the man of the moment there at the dock, so I followed Ray to the parking lot.

When we got there, he pointed to a huge, raised-up black Jeep. "Your chariot awaits," he said with a smile.

It was a monster, the body a full foot higher than normal, the tires as outsized as the rest of it, rust and dents splattering the paint. There were no doors, a four-inch pipe roll bar for a roof, and a huge winch on the front.

"What if it rains?" I asked.

"We get wet," Ray answered, admiring his new toy.

"Where'd it come from?"

"Don't ask."

As we drove by the guard shack, the gate was up, and Miguel was just closing the door for the day. He gave us a wave and a smile, and Ray, in an unusually good mood, waved back like he was the grand marshal of some imaginary parade.

The road out of our marina is a minefield of potholes, dips, and speed bumps. Ray hit every one of them, and with each jostle and jump, his grin grew. I wondered if my kidneys would survive the day.

"We gotta worry about the cops stopping us in this death trap?" I yelled over the wind.

"Nope," Ray yelled back as he popped the clutch and left a patch of hot rubber. "Can't catch us."

We went east from the marina and then turned toward the South Side Road, Ray silent all the while. It was clear he was enjoying driving his monster. As we skidded around a corner, he popped a Tina Turner CD into the stereo. I tugged my ball cap down as far as I could and pulled my seat belt tighter. It was a kind I hadn't seen in twenty or thirty years except on a plane.

"Where'd you find the fancy seat belts?" I asked.

Ray just looked at me and laughed. "You're lucky it's not a piece of rope." He was right. Anything that could keep me alive in that heap of a Jeep was a gift to be thankful for. I held on for dear life.

I hadn't wanted to wake Cheri when I left, but I knew I had to tell her why I wasn't at the boat. I got lucky, though. She sounded up when I called.

"Look," I told her, "Ray and I left early. We had to head out to talk to someone."

She paused, not quite understanding what we were doing. But I didn't really understand either. "Keep in touch," Cheri said. "Don't let him get too crazy."

I knew what she meant. She'd known Ray almost as long as I had.

"Don't worry. We're just going to talk to someone," I told her, hoping I was telling the truth. "Nothing to worry about," I repeated. "We'll be careful."

"OK, thanks," Cheri said.

"All right, see you later."

I hung up and looked at Ray. He just looked at the curves that kept coming at us. I could only stand it a couple of minutes more before my curiosity took over. "Where we going? What's the plan?" I yelled.

Ray quit bouncing with Tina, pulled off his sunglasses, and looked at me – maybe for too long for how fast he was driving. He slipped the glasses back on, looked ahead at the road, then yelled back, "Our man may be hiding in the rainforest."

"Where?"

"Butler Bay. I think his grandma lives up in the hills."

"Never been there," I said, trying to place just where Butler Bay was.

"There's an old woman up there took care of me a long time ago, when I was a kid and my mom would go off-island," Ray said. His voice sounded distant, even over the wind that was whipping through the Jeep.

"How old is this lady?" I asked.

"Mabel's probably about ninety-five or so, I'd say. She was in her forties when she took care of me."

"What was she like?"

"She scared the hell out of my young ass."

"Why?" I asked, surprised Ray would admit to ever fearing anything.

"Shit, man, you'll see," he said, laughing loudly as he shook his head. "When I was ten, I was convinced she was a voodoo witch, and I'm still not sure if I wasn't right."

"You ever see her since she took care of you?" I asked as we turned right at the Hess refinery, heading for the main highway to the west side of the island.

"I see her every year at the ag fair. She brings bundles of herbs and potions to sell, and every so often, I make it up to her home in the hills to visit."

"Potions?" I yelled.

"Yeah, like to cure a cough and stuff like that." Ray gunned the Jeep up a hill toward the highway turnoff.

"Work?" I asked.

Ray took the turn too fast and charged onto the highway, the ugly black bomb lurching as he shifted it up to eighty in a handful of seconds. Maybe he answered my question, but I never heard over the roar of the engine.

I kept quiet for the next few miles because Ray was scaring the shit out of me. The Jeep was hitting seventy and eighty between all the highway's stop lights. Luckily, we got everyone, or God only know how fast he would have gone. I had visions of me, Ray, and that damn Jeep rolling like a brick down the hill off the side of the road. Amazingly, we covered the whole Melvin Evans Highway and still stayed in one piece even though we did it in world record time.

There is no doubt when you enter the rainforest. The sky disappears under an umbrella of huge trees, and the road disintegrates into patches of asphalt between car-sized potholes – and that stretches the fact just a little. Once the pavement's ended, the main road holds the average driver to a safe speed of about thirty miles an hour. Ray was pushing fifty with the huge Jeep and leaving me clinging silently to the dash.

"You could slow down," I said when my nerves began succumbing to the fatigue of long-term stress.

"Yep," Ray answered as a huge smile played across his face. He kept shifting gears like he was racing at Le Mans.

"Come on, give me a break, Ray. I'll be good. Just ease off," I begged.

I could see my face in his black glasses as he took a long look at me. Finally, the Jeep slowed down. "You're getting old," he said.

"No," I told him with relief. "I just want a chance to get old."

Ray smiled, but his speed stayed at reasonable fast instead of crazy fast. After a few more hills and curves, I asked him, "You know where we're going?"

"Yeah," he replied. "First thing, we meet with Auntie Mabel. With a little luck, she can tell us where Charlie Brachure's grandmother lives."

"We're not running the risk of running into Po Po and Charlie and all the boys up in the forest, are we?" I asked.

"Nope, if we find Charlie here, he'll be alone. This is his grandma's home we're looking for, and bringing guys like Po Po to his grandmother's home would be wrong even for Charlie."

"Great," I said as Ray turned up a dirt road that made a cattle trail look like a freeway. The big Jeep crept over roots the size of my body and rocks that had to be three feet high. Ray looked at me with pure glee in his face. "Fun, ain't it?"

It took all my control not to just unbuckle my belt and jump out. "No," I told him. "I think we should walk."

Ray shook his head in mock sadness, shifted gears, and began attacking another huge root. The engine growled and stones the size of fists flew out behind the huge tires. Like a surging bull, the Jeep lurched over the root. But ahead was a whole row of roots just like it, at angles I felt sure would roll us over.

Ray just looked more determined as he attacked them one at a time. I gripped my seat with both hands and prayed for a crash helmet. Then suddenly, at the end of the row of roots, a green meadow opened unlike any I had ever seen in St. Croix. I just stared at the thatch of foot-deep grass about half the size of a football field. Huge mahogany trees and heavy brush surrounded the meadow on three sides. The brush was in flower, a rich wall of red, blue, and yellow. To the north, the sky was pure blue, flowing slowly and gentle down to the ocean horizon.

CHAPTER

"Wow," was all I could say as Ray eased the Jeep into neutral, stopped, and put the brake on.

"Pretty enough for you, Mad Dog?" he asked as he popped open a Bud light from the cooler.

"Beer?" I asked

"Breakfast," Ray answered, looking out over the land and sea. "Want one?"

I thought of Charlie Brachure. I thought of the near-death experience I'd just finished riding with Ray to this secluded meadow. I thought of the gun in the belt holster behind me that I might have to use later. I thought of what Cheri would say if she knew I was having beer for breakfast while I was on a dangerous manhunt. I thought again of the drive up here with Ray, and said, "Yeah, beer sound good."

He gave me a nod of approval and passed one over. The cool metal felt good, and the beer felt even better. Ray took out a big slab of jerky and tore me off a piece to balance out my second breakfast of the day.

"So where is this witch?" I asked as we finished eating. Ray pointed his empty beer can at a cut in the brush. "In there," he said as he grabbed a backpack out of the Jeep and started walking. I followed.

"This going to be a long way?" I asked, stepping carefully through the small rocks hidden by the meadow's heavy grass.

"Nope," Ray answered.

"Then why the backpack?"

"Presents for Auntie Mabel."

"The witch?" I asked as I caught up to him.

Ray stopped and turned with a serious frown. "No more with the witch stuff, OK? She may hear you, and it would piss her off, and I don't need that grief."

I nodded my head as we plunged into the cut. The brush there was just as rich with thorns as it was with color -- every bush, twig, and branch. The path was so narrow that slow was the only way to keep our clothes and skin together. As we entered the brush, the light died and the path became a damp, dark, silent hole. The leaves underfoot killed all sound of our passing except the occasional whispered brush against a bush. Then after about twenty yards, we emerged into another sunlit meadow, surrounded like the first by colorful brush and huge mahogany trees on three sides. Framed against the blue sky and ocean to the north was a large white home.

The house was a perfect example of Dutch Caribbean architecture. The front was a huge porch with an arch, pilasters, and a terra cotta roof. The walls extended above the roof on every side. Windows dominated both stories, all with red wooden shutters and ornate black metal grating. On the first floor, each one had a red window box overflowing with flowers of every color.

The path we'd just come on seemed like the only access to the house. All around it was a lawn that someone had cut out of raw meadow long ago, bordered by a three-foot rock wall. On the far side, behind the house, a cliff dropped to the sea. The white house itself, beautiful and well kept, looked surreal in the isolated meadow.

Twenty yards away, what looked like a pile of rags sat in an old rocking chair on the porch. As we got closer, the pile parted and a small black woman in a bright cotton dress emerged from an ancient quilt. Auntie Mabel was no taller than five foot, and if she weighed eighty pounds, I would have been surprised. Her deep black skin was heavily wrinkled with the shine and richness of polished rosewood. Her entire body was framed from head to hips by a heavy mass of gray hair laid out in classic thin braids.

The woman's stance shifted a little, and she leaned in to see us better. When she moved forward, the huge mass of braids seemed to flow toward us, then fall back over her body in an undulating wave.

"I see a bad man," she said in a surprisingly strong voice as the back flow of hair exposed her slender body.

"Why you call me a bad man?" Ray asked as if this was a game they had played before.

"A man drinks in the morning and sleeps in the day and at your age runs with wicked women all night and has to ask this old woman why he is bad is not just bad he's blind to his own evil."

"I may be a bad man and I suppose you're an angel?" Ray countered loudly.

As he spoke the word "angel," an odd movement the old woman made – maybe a breeze -- turned her hair into the fluffing of large wings.

"A dark angel," she countered, her face erupting into a brilliant smile.

Ray walked ahead of me up the stairs and enveloped the small body in a huge hug. Her arms snaked around him and patted his backpack.

"This is full of presents from a bad man," she said, still holding Ray and patting the pack.

"Of course," he said.

Auntie Mabel's small hands scurried expertly down his back to the bulge in his waistband.

"Ah," she said, "and the bad man comes to my home with a gun, I see."

"Of course," Ray said, still embracing her. "Only a fool would come to this strange place unarmed."

Ray and Auntie Mabel stepped away from each other. In a businesslike voice, she said, "You're not here just to visit?"

"No," Ray said, standing back and finally acknowledging me. "My friend and I are looking for Charlie Brachure."

For the first time, the small black woman moved her eyes in my direction. "You are the one," she said in a flat voice. Her smile was gone, and her face was emotionless.

"The one?" I asked, feeling suddenly uneasy.

"I saw Mitch Brachure in my dream, and you were the one who sent him into the abyss," Auntie Mabel said. Her voice had become a dreamy slur. Her eyes were closed.

When she opened them, she smiled as if her words had not been said. Her small right hand beckoned to us. "Come, you need tea. I can tell," Auntie Mabel said as she turned quickly into the house.

I looked up at Ray on the porch, and he smiled at what I'm sure was the pure confusion on my face.

"Come on in, Mad Dog" he said. "The fun is just beginning."

As I got to where he was standing, Ray punched my shoulder playfully. "She is something, ain't she?" he said.

I didn't answer. I just went in. The room was drenched in sunlight and the scent of fresh flowers. Though the house had looked like two stories on the outside, I could tell now it was just one, with twenty-foot ceilings and a second row of windows high above the first.

The room I was in was about twenty feet square. A

small antique table in the middle was the only furniture. On it, a huge, cut-glass vase was filled with clear water and a four-foot bouquet of fresh flowers. Lilies, roses, huge yellow blooms I'd never seen -- a mix any wedding would be proud of. The scent drifted off the table and filled the room.

We walked across the dark, polished floors, the sound of our shoes coming back off the stark, white walls. All the windows were open, and a cool breeze tickled the hair on my arm. Or at least I thought it was the wind, but it could have been goose bumps, too.

A doorway in the center of each wall led out of the room, and we could hear pans clanging through the opening in front of us, the only door that was open. Ray took three roses from the vase as he passed it and handed me one.

Auntie Mabel's voice called out, "In here, Raymond, and I'll cook you up some breakfast. That beer you two have been drinking will just cloud your mind."

Ray looked at me and winked. "Busted" he said.

I followed him into the kitchen, one part of me shuddering at the thought of my third meal in three hours, another part salivating at the aromas filling the air. Auntie Mabel stood in front of a huge commercial stove and oven, dancing between simmering pots. Ray held out his two roses toward her.

"You stealing my flowers again!" Auntie Mabel snapped.

"No, no. It was his idea," Ray answered quickly, nodding toward where I stood with my lone red rose.

The old woman laughed. "See how the bad man is," she said. "He blames everything on someone else."

Auntie Mabel turned toward the backpack Ray had leaned against the kitchen wall. "Do you have what I think you have in there?" she asked. "Show me how bad you are."

"Oh, there's only good things in there," Ray answered. "It's all as good as you are." He picked up the pack, opened it, and reached inside. Out came his hand with a liter of Cruzan Blackstrap Rum. A smile filled the old woman's face. "I can see you are sometimes not so bad," she said as he handed it to her.

Ray reached in again and brought out two more big bottles. "Tabasco! Is that Tabasco?" Auntie Mabel exclaimed. "You know I hate Tabasco!"

"Yeah, but I love it," Ray said calmly, putting them down next to the stove.

The little woman just turned away and hefted a bubbling pot off the range. "I'm boiling a basil potion for James down at the Domino Club," she said. "He has a cold."

Carefully, she carried the pot across the kitchen and dumped the steaming mix into a colander in the middle of a large stainless sink. Steam and the powerful smells of basil and mint filled the kitchen. My sinuses burst wide, and I could feel air moving in parts of them I didn't even know I had.

"Wow," Auntie Mabel exclaimed as the steam cleared, "that's a good one."

"That's the potion you use on me," Ray said. "You need to teach me that one."

"You are not ready," she answered.

"You better get teaching pretty soon, old woman, or you'll die, and no one will learn."

"Don't worry, bad man," she said. "The way you behave, I will live to bury you."

Ray laughed and nodded his head.

"You see, Mr. Cotton," Auntie Mabel said. I was startled she knew my name. "Raymond is an aspiring student, but he is so busy being a bad man, he does not have time to learn."

"Not true," he protested as she moved back over to the stove and uncovered a huge smoked ham hidden under a white cloth. With the speed and grace of a swordsman, she drew a huge kitchen knife from a slot in her cutting board and sliced off a massive chunk. In a single set of movements, she wiped the knife, set it back in the slot, replaced the cloth, and tossed the lump of ham into a large black skillet. Smoke and the sweet smell of sizzling ham erupted from the pan, which was red hot and waiting like she'd been set to make us breakfast all along.

"Did you know we were coming?" I asked the small woman, amazed at how ready things seemed.

"I always knew you were coming," Auntie Mabel replied without looking up.

As her answer sank in, she and Ray went on chatting while she cooked. I sat next to him at the counter, thinking about what she'd said, marveling at my surroundings, and lost in daydreams of the years before Itchy Feet, when Cheri and I had reveled in our condo's gourmet kitchen. The next thing I knew, Auntie Mabel was setting a steaming plate of ham and eggs in front of me with a huge cup of pungent tea. Then she gently placed down one of the big red bottles Ray had come with. "Here, have some of this. I just got it," she said.

Ray grabbed the Tabasco and laughed as he opened it.

"Eat," Auntie Mabel said. "If you're going after Charlie Brachure, I wouldn't want you to die on an empty stomach."

Her words ended the magic of the moment. Ray got down to business as he dug into the mound of food in front of him. "Is Charlie hiding out at his grandma's?"

"I don't know, Raymond," Auntie Mabel said thoughtfully. "Both those boys run back to here when they're in trouble, but I don't know."

"It's been years since I went to that part of the forest," Ray said. "Can you tell me where her place is?"

The old woman sat on her tall chair silent and unmoving. She moved her hands slowly over the steaming cup of tea they were holding, as if to warm them. "If you wait, he will come out of the forest to kill Mr. Cotton and his family," she said at last. "It would be easier to get him then."

"He may not even be up here," Ray said.

As I listened to the conversation, I realized there

was a lot more to this old woman than I'd imagined. She nodded as Ray talked.

"Waiting lets him make the time and place," he went on.

Auntie Mabel studied me.

"Yes, waiting has its problems, but going to his lair is always dangerous." She said her eyes focused on the steaming cup.

The turn of conversation made me lose interest in my food, and I just concentrated on the little old lady and my best friend, surrounded there by the room's rich smells and serene atmosphere, calmly discussing the best way to kill or catch Charlie Brachure.

"Mad Dog doesn't want him killed," Ray said, bringing me into the conversation.

Auntie Mabel raised her eyes from the cup of tea and seemed to study me some more. "Mitch Brachure was an evil man," she said. "He killed many people on my island. Your act saved many lives. I have known Charlie since he was a small child. He will kill you and the woman and your family if he can." There was little emotion as she spoke. She was stating a simple fact.

"I didn't really kill him. He fell," I said, remembering the helplessness of being wedged in the pantry as the big man reeled through the window.

"You and the woman did enough, and now, you, the woman, and your families are at risk. Evil men don't know the gray, only the black and white."

Auntie Mabel reached across the table and put her small brown hand over mine. It pressed tight, and I could feel a heat radiate out. "Let us finish our food in peace," she said.

Ray nodded and forked a big scoop of egg into his mouth. The yolk dripped, and without comment Auntie Mabel reached over and wiped it. Ray kept eating.

When the meal was done, he insisted on clearing and washing the dishes. Auntie Mabel and I talked.

"Since Charlie was small, he has been a hunter," she said. "Killing is natural to him."

"I can't just kill a man," I told her too forcefully, wanting to shift the conversation.

"Then what will you do?" she asked.

"At this time, Charlie is wanted for a series of crimes, including jumping bail in the Territorial Court. If Ray and I can get him to the authorities, I don't think he'll be out of jail for a long time."

Auntie Mabel looked at me for several moments, then said, "I can see in your eyes that you see the flaw in your plan."

I did see the flaw. The flaw was the nature of what often passes for justice on the islands. Deals, mistakes, technicalities, payoffs. If Charlie walked away a free man, he'd be far from the first scum to do it on St. Croix. In my heart, I knew that a million things could go wrong.

"Yes," I agreed, "but it's what I have to do."

Auntie Mabel nodded and patted my hand. "You are a good man," she said, a sadness showing in her voice and eyes.

"No," I said, knowing the truth. "There are just some things I can't live with."

"We will see" she said. "Can you go outside? Raymond and I need to talk."

"Sure," I said and started out the door. At the kitchen entryway, I turned. Auntie Mabel was watching me and smiled. I felt a strange kinship with the little woman who had so much love yet could contemplate seemingly without emotion the death of someone she'd known all his life.

I went outside and was drawn to the little rock wall. When I got to the north side, the view was breathtaking. Endless sky and the ocean lapping lazy and quiet. Seventy or eighty feet below me, it seemed to caress the huge black boulders along the shore.

I sat on the wall. Far across the sea, I could see the outline of St. Thomas and St. John rising out of the mist. The peace and quiet flowed into me. My thoughts turned to Cheri, to climbing onto Itchy Feet with her and slowly cruising away from the Charlie Brachures of the world. I could see her at the helm, all smiles, sun in her face. We could cruise to St. John and the BVIs, then down the other islands to Venezuela and beyond. We had talked of this often, and maybe now was the time.

A voice in the back of my head said, "Run, Cotton, no reason not to." But I knew the reason: Jean and Betsy Rourk and Bob. I owed them. "Owed them what?" the little voice asked. A week ago, they were just acquaintances. Then the image came back of Mitch

Brachure, flying in a shroud of glass into that lost Puerto Rican night.

I sensed a presence beside me. Auntie Mabel was two feet to the right, also looking out at the sea. "You were thinking of Mitch Brachure falling," she said calmly.

I didn't speak. I just kept my eyes on the horizon.

"This is a special place," she said.

I still locked my eyes on the sea. Auntie Mabel turned to face me. "I can see men and women and children leaping off these cliffs," she said. "Like Mitch Brachure. When I sit here, I can see that, and it is awful, but I still love this place."

I was silent, my mind empty and listening.

"The Maroon were the runaway slaves," she said, her voice dreamlike. "When the slave hunters came, the free men, women, and children threw themselves off these cliffs to escape."

I closed my eyes, the thought of dozens or scores of twirling Mitch Brachures filling my mind.

"I know they jumped from this very cliff. That is why I bought this property."

"How…?" I said, my mind still seeing the falling bodies.

"How do I know they jumped here?" she said. "The ghosts, Mr. Cotton. The ghosts are here."

The sun was hot on my face, and the wind was little relief, but a chill ran over me. I looked down at the boulders below and saw the bodies that were there. They were all Mitch Brachure, his head at that impossible angle of the last moment I'd seen him.

Auntie Mabel was looking at the sea again. "When the Maroon jumped from this cliff," she said softly, "they were running away, and could not bring themselves to believe they could survive and be free."

She paused, then said grimly, "They were wrong. They were very brave, but they were wrong. They should have fought.

"If they failed, they could escape again. When they jumped, they didn't give themselves the chance to be free."

"And…." I said.

"You can't run from evil. It will always catch you and the people you care about. Your time is now, Mr. Cotton. You must fight now, or you will be jumping off a cliff like those beautiful free people." She laid her frail hand on mine for the second time that day, and again, it felt hot on my skin. "This is not something you can run from," she whispered. "I know."

I looked out over the ocean, and a feeling of helplessness washed over me. I felt my eyes sting and reached up to them. They were wet. I wiped at a tear and looked with embarrassment at Auntie Mabel. She was gone.

As we left Auntie Mabel's, Ray and I were each lost in our own thoughts. Somehow, the old woman had moved us both. At the Jeep, Ray took out the map she had drawn to the home of Charlie Brachure's grandmother. I looked at it and then at Ray. We both began to laugh. The map was something straight out of a Robert Louis Stevenson novel.

I read it and asked, "Tree where no monkey climbs? We take the road to the right at the tree that no monkey climbs?"

Ray nodded his head. He was clearly pleased with my awe. "It'll be easy to spot when we get there," he said as he started the Jeep. I strapped myself in, and we started down the brush-chocked road we'd come up only two hours earlier. I looked at my watch and was amazed to see it was only ten in the morning.

Five minutes later, Ray pulled to a stop and pointed at a huge tree covered with inch-long thorns. "Tree that no monkey climbs," he said, admiring the massive mix of tree and bush.

I looked at the tree and then the road to the right of it. "You can't be serious," I said, feeling my stomach grow tight. "That's not a road. It's a bad excuse for a drainage ditch."

Ray didn't respond, just gunned the engine and charged toward the break in the brush. He held the Jeep at a steady thirty miles an hour as we passed more and more trees that no monkey climbs. The dirt track's twenty-degree angle would have put us in the thorns if we rolled, but Ray seemed not to care. Before I could gather my senses, we were topping the hill and plunging into a rock-filled dry stream bed. I reeled from the whiplash as Ray gunned the engine again, and we lurched out of the stream bed and back up a thirty-degree grade covered with small boulders. The Jeep rolled and wallowed in a motion that had to resemble being on the back of a lame elephant. Finally, bouncing from one rock to another, it emerged into an open area about as big as a basketball court.

A canopy of huge trees blocked most of the morning sun from the deep grass. As the road went on through the meadow, a small army of old, rotted cars that were half hidden in the deep bush lined both sides forming rust encrusted hedges. At the end of the rusted gantlet stood a small, white, wooden shack. The cars looked like part of the landscape, huge bushes growing beside them and sometimes even in them. "Old man Brachure liked cars," Ray said as he gestured toward them.

"How'd he get all them up here?" I asked, remembering the torturous drive we'd had.

"Don't know, but he had a pretty good collection." Some of the cars were stacked on each other, and others were set on their sides to make more room. I just shook my head at the iron jungle.

Ray had stopped the Jeep when we got to the clearing. Scattered puddles were left over from a morning rain. The house ahead of us behind a small parking area seemed cheery and bright. It had new paint, and both sides of its short picket fence were covered with bright yellow flowers. The small white gate was open. A rocking chair on the porch sat next to the door.

Ray put the Jeep in gear and looked at me. In his eyes, I saw the old hunter coming to life. He reached behind his back, and a large revolver was suddenly in his lap. I thought the Smith & Wesson he was holding bordered on insanity. It held only five rounds, had a four-inch barrel, and probably weighed three or four pounds. The Glocks that Cheri and I used weighed a pound and a half, and with the extended clip I had, carried 17 rounds. Ray's advantage was that if Charlie Brachure was hiding in a nearby '57 Chevy, he could easily punch a hole in the Chevy and in Charlie as well. The beast of a gun would blow holes in one-eighth-inch steel while my little forty-caliber rounds might just bounce off. I knew Ray also had a Glock like mine and wondered if it was on him but hidden.

"Ready," he said.

I leaned forward and took my Glock out of the back holster where it had been rubbing me raw all through Ray's bouncing off road trek. I pulled the slide back enough to see a shell in the chamber and said, "Yeah, let's go."

Ray started driving slowly past the weed-encrusted cars. I felt like a duck at a shooting gallery, but there wasn't a better way to approach the little house.

When we were halfway down the road, the door suddenly burst open, and a very large black woman helmeted with a white Afro filled its space. A simple white and blue flowered dress hung to her knees. She held a broom in her right hand and gazed at us hard.

Ray kept going forward slow and steady. The woman in the doorway stayed standing like stone. As we got closer, her true size became apparent. Charlie

Brachure's grandmother was close to six and a half feet tall and must have weighed three hundred fifty pounds.

"Mrs. Edna Brachure," Ray said, nodding in her direction.

When we stopped at the gate about fifteen feet away, she turned sideways and moved onto the porch. "Good morning," Ray said with the politeness that's drummed into every island school kid.

Neither of us moved to get out of the Jeep. "Morning," the woman said in an amazingly light soprano voice.

"Auntie Mabel told me how to get here," Ray said.

The woman's great black face sliced open in a thin smile, revealing a line of small white teeth. "You're Ray Jones," she said.

"Yes ma'am," Ray said, climbing out of the Jeep.

"And this one?" she asked, eying me with suspicion and moving the brush end of her broom in my direction.

Ray looked at me, then back at Mrs. Edna Brachure, who was now resting her huge right arm on the top of the broom. "This is Mr. Cotton," Ray announced in a formal voice.

The woman's small smile disappeared, and she eyed me for a long moment. I could see her hand twist and tighten on the broom. "Mr. Mad Dog Cotton?" she said.

"Yes ma'am," I answered, staying in my seat.

A sadness came over the big woman, and her head nodded slowly. "The Mr. Cotton that Mitchy tried to kill."

"Yes ma'am," I repeated, wanting desperately to hide from her view.

After a long pause, she made full eye contact with me and said, "It's a hard thing."

I wasn't sure what she meant, but I repeated, "Yes ma'am."

"He was a wicked man," she started, still looking hard into my eyes. "I did what I could, but his crazy mother and my no-good son didn't give them boys even a chance to be decent. You look like a good man, Mr. Cotton. I'm sorry for any grief my family may have brought to you."

"Thank you," I said, stunned by the woman's forgiveness, and feeling both sorrow and admiration for her.

She shuffled forward to the steps and sat down. The wooden stairs creaked with her weight. "Come sit," she said, pointing to two white lawn chairs just inside the gate."

We sat down and waited. "Why are you here?" Mrs. Edna Brachure asked.

In the back of my mind, I thought guiltily, "Maybe to kill your other grandson."

Then, like a mind reader, she answered her own question: "Charlie." It was a flat statement. Her eyes were fixed on Ray.

"Yes" I said, and Ray nodded.

"He's Roger's last child, the last of his line."

"Your son?" I asked.

"Roger Eliza Brachure, my fifth son and the only one that ever gave me pain and grief, but he gave enough to make up for the other eight good ones."

"Eight?" I said.

Mrs. Edna Brachure straightened, and a proud look came over her. "Six boys and three girls altogether," she said. "Roger was the bad egg. The others all are well and happy, and never hurt people like Roger and his boys."

"Is Roger...?"

The woman raised her hand, understanding my question. "No, killed in a bar room in 1989."

I nodded.

"Roger only had Mitch and Charlie," Ray said.

"He only claimed those two," the big woman added, shaking her head.

"We need to find Charlie," Ray told her, his voice flat, his eyes fixed on Mrs. Edna Brachure.

"Not here," she said. "They have their house they got from their father at the back there, but neither of them been home for about five days."

"Sure," Ray said, his voice still flat.

"They come home, they drive right down that lane," she said, pointing the brush of her broom the way we'd just come. "They park right there." She motioned again toward a rutted parking area in front of two rusted green trucks.

"Mind if we look?" Ray asked. She was probably right, we both knew, probably telling the truth, but we also knew that too much trust could get us killed.

Mrs. Brachure considered the question, then turned her gaze to me and said with a hint of sadness, "Look. It's open."

"Thank you," I told her as we all got up. Again,

the wooden step gave a loud complaint. Standing on the stair there, the woman in the white and blue dress towered over us, and I could not help but see Mrs. Edna Brachure and Auntie Mabel together in my mind. The two women could not have looked and talked more differently, but both had an earthy dignity and compassion that was rare and beautiful. I wanted to say more to Mrs. Brachure, but she turned and walked back into her house. As she closed the door, her body left a faint hint of jasmine on the air.

I stood staring at the door, smelling the perfume, until Ray nudged me. "Let's go take a quick look and get out of here. This is a dead end."

We walked over to the two rusted trucks that Charlie's grandmother had pointed toward, and found a well-worn path leading into the bush. We'd put our guns out of sight when we climbed down from the Jeep. Now I pulled my Glock out of its holster in the small of my back and saw that Ray was holding the big Smith & Wesson again.

I was raised in the mountains, and there's something very scary and claustrophobic to me about bush so thick you can't see three feet off the trail. The early rain had evaporated off, but the ground was still soft and soaked up our footsteps. Ray took the lead and I hung about ten feet back, so only one of us would be in sight if an ambush was waiting. The plan had seemed good when we entered the bush, but now, with the deep shadows and Ray often just a movement or glimpse of black ahead of me, I began feeling edgy.

The rainforest seemed ancient and primordial. Above, the view was all vines hanging from huge mahogany trees. At eye level, it was a chaos of shrubs, brush, and moss-covered deadfall. With the wind shifting through the trees and the chatter of birds and frogs, there was no way to hear anyone who might be hiding, or even hear Ray a few feet ahead.

As a blessing, the path was only about fifty feet long. We were in and out in a minute, but the eeriness felt lots longer. The small, cinderblock house in the light of the little clearing seemed like an anticlimax. It was the size and shape of a single wide mobile home, about forty feet long. A small set of steps went up a narrow door in front of us. Plastic mini-blinds looked turned down and closed on the two small windows. The institutional green paint on the house seemed new. The only other thing in the clearing was a big gas weed-whacker leaning against the right wall. The grass and brush had recently been cut back. Nothing was out of place. Nothing in the clearing moved.

Ray studied the house, then stepped back into the cover of the forest. "What now?" he said, surprising me.

"What now?" I asked.

"We ready to go toss this place?"

"Edna told us we could," I replied, wondering for the first time what a judge would think of her saying, "Look. It's open."

"OK," Ray said, looking like a black Dirty Harry as he walked boldly into the clearing with the big revolver at arm's length next to his thigh. I watched him swagger, and before I could follow, Ray was walking in like he owned the place. No gunshots. No angry yells. Lucky me.

When I got to the door, he was in the middle of the front room, his gun still hanging down in his hand. "No one's here," Ray said.

My police training screamed that we should clear every room, look under every bed, check every closet. Instead, I said, "Sure?"

Ray tucked the gun behind his back. "Yep, sure," he said.

Like a complete amateur, I followed Ray's lead and holstered my Glock.

Ray shook his head. "I can't believe this place," he said. "Two animals like those guys live here, and it's immaculate."

"Maybe Edna cleans it."

"I don't think so," Ray answered. "My read is she doesn't like them too much at this point in time."

"Wasn't real teary-eyed about Mitch," I agreed.

"Nope, not much love there."

Like in most single wides, a kitchen with a small table was right of the door. To the left, a hall led to what I figured was the bathroom and bedrooms.

Ray walked down the hall. I switched on an overhead above the couch and looked around the small room, kitchen and living room both, trying to get a feel for two men who drank and caroused all night, killed people almost automatically, and kept their home spotless.

In front of me was a heavy, wooden coffee table about four feet wide. I walked around it and sat on the couch. It was old with a green throw cover but, like everything else, looked clean. On the table was a neat stack of envelopes. I looked through it. Most were addressed to PO Box 642, Frederiksted. I went into the kitchen and opened the blinds. No bad guys outside, just a wall of green forest. I looked in the refrigerator. Just a sparse population of milk, bread, eggs, a one-pound package of bacon, an onion, and two huge mangos, probably off the tree outside. I tested the milk: still fresh. Three frozen chickens were lined up in the freezer like little soldiers next to two packs of ground beef. No hands, no feet, no heads of their enemies. I was beginning to wonder if we had the right house.

I searched through the cabinets. The small assortment of canned goods was as neat as a Marine's footlocker before inspection. I decided to find Ray. The first bedroom was empty, but he'd turned on the light. The little bathroom next to it had just an open tile shower, no tub.

I found Ray in the end room sitting on the bed. To his right was a small metal box, to his left a pile of cash. He was looking through a bunch of checks on his lap.

"You found the treasure?" I asked.

Ray looked up. "Lobster," he said.

"Lobster?"

"Charlie is making his living selling lobster."

"What do you mean?"

"These are almost all from local restaurants, and some of them say, 'lobsters.'"

"I don't see these guys selling lobster," I told him. "These are pot guys, not lobster guys."

"Mitch sold the pot. His room has about five pounds of homegrown, high-grade weed, bagged and ready to sell. But Charlie is selling lobsters, and a lot of them."

"Maybe lobster's a code word for pot?"

Ray held up a pink check, "I don't think Carambola Resort buys much pot." He picked up the checks from his lap. "Last Tuesday, the day Mitch followed you to Puerto Rico, someone delivered almost three hundred dollars worth of lobster to restaurants all over the West Side. That doesn't count this other eighty dollars in cash."

"That's a lot of lobster," I said.

Ray smiled a small smile, his white teeth just peeking out. "How'd you like to be sitting at some restaurant's back door when Charlie shows up with a bag of lobster?"

"Pretty easy take-down," I said. "But with Mitch getting killed, he might not make another delivery for six months. He might make two a week, might make ten, and maybe make zero."

"Today is Friday. It would make sense to get fresh lobster before the weekend."

I nodded, pulled the cell phone out of my pocket, and hit the speed dial for Cheri.

"Hi, hon.," she answered.

"Everything OK?" I asked.

"Yep, just fixing lunch for the troops."

"Everyone there?" I asked.

"Yep."

"Got time to do me a favor?"

"Sure," she answered.

"You know that cook out at Carambola that you helped get his green card last year?" I asked.

"Eddie Castile?"

"Yeah, Eddie. Can you give me his cell phone number," I asked.

There was only about a five-second pause, then she was back on the line. "Eddie Castile," Cheri said. "Ready?'

"Yeah," I told her as I pulled a pen and little pad out of my pocket.

"340-244-1345. That's his cell. He'll almost always answer it." Then her tone changed. "What's this about?" Cheri asked. "Eddie isn't part of this, is he?"

"No," I assured her. "I think Charlie is delivering lobster to the restaurant at Carambola, and I just need to find out what days he makes his deliveries."

"Charlie sells lobster?"

"Maybe," I said, "Ray found some checks, and they say they're for lobster."

"That's interesting," Cheri said, her voice sounding thoughtful." When I knew the brothers at Grapetree, they both hated the water."

"I guess they embraced what they feared," I told her.

"I guess so. I would have guessed they still had a

thriving pot business, but lobster I would have never thought."

"Yeah, they probably had a nice grow operation going somewhere in their back yard."

"Probably right at their house," Cheri said.

"We haven't seen any plants, but it wouldn't surprise me," I told her.

"You're at their house?" she said.

"Yep, I'm in their house," I replied, knowing how cocky I sounded.

"I leave you with Ray for three hours, and you two idiots are already breaking and entering," Cheri said, disbelief clear in her husky voice.

"Their grandma told us we could," I said, as innocent as I could sound.

"You two assholes get thrown in jail, and I may not bail you out."

I looked at Ray and told him, "Cheri says you're an asshole."

Ray just smiled.

"Get out of that house," Cheri said. "The old lady probably called the cops right after she told you that you could go in."

I thought about that. It did make a small amount of sense. I jerked my thumb toward the door in a "let's wrap this up, Ray" motion.

"Got to go, love ya," I told Cheri, then hung up.

"You in trouble again?" Ray asked.

"No, she was just kidding," I said as I shoved the phone back in my shorts.

"Time to leave anyway," Ray said as he put the checks and money back in the box. Then he slid it under the bed, stood up and smoothed out the wrinkles, and started down the hall.

As we passed the switches, Ray turned off all the lights.

"Let's call Eddie and see if there's a lobster delivery today," I said. "That would be way too easy a take-down to miss."

"Agreed," Ray said.

I dialed and heard two rings, then, "Si."

"Is this Eddie?" I asked.

"Si."

"Hi, Eddie. This is Mad Dog Cotton, Cheri's husband."

"Ah, yes." His voice turned more buoyant. "Mr. Mad Dog, how are you?"

"Good, Eddie, but I got a question."

"Si," he replied.

"Do you know Charlie Brachure?"

"Si, and heard about you and his brother. He was a *malo gringo*," Eddie said, rolling the words together.

"Does Charlie deliver lobster to you?" I asked, getting back on point.

"Si," Eddie said. "He just left."

"Just left?" I repeated.

"Si."

"Thanks, buddy. Hey, when will he be back?"

"This time Tuesday, Mr. Mad Dog," Eddie said

without hesitation. "Should I tell him you are looking for him?"

I smiled at the question. "No, Eddie. You take care."

"Good-bye, and you tell Mrs. Cheri to call. I miss her."

"I will," I said and hung up.

I looked at Ray. "Just fucking missed him." The anger and frustration were clear in my voice.

"Let's go to Frederiksted. Maybe we can catch him at another one of the restaurants, or on the road."

"He may be headed home," I said.

"That would make sense. Want to wait here?"

I thought a moment and decided against it. If the old woman told him we were at the house, or the Jeep made him suspicious when he saw it, we'd be sitting ducks on his home ground. "No. Let's close this place up and go."

Ray stepped outside and I followed. We kept our guns in our hands all the way back to the Jeep, and Ray left the big revolver at the ready until we were on the paved road again.

"All this stress makes me hungry," he said.

I looked at my watch. It was one o'clock. "Where to?" I asked.

"Coconuts," Ray said without hesitation.

CHAPTER

13

Coconuts is north of downtown Frederiksted on the west shore road. It's a little bit of Texas mixed with a perfect white Caribbean ocean view. Ray and I have both developed an addiction to its hamburgers and onion rings. It was about 1:30 when we pulled into the dirt field across the street, parking between the chunks of telephone pole scattered around to give the lot a little discipline. We ordered at the bar, then moved to one of the open-air tables to compare notes.

As we sat down, I opened my phone and called Cheri. "Hi, just checking in," I said, keeping my voice cheery in the hope she was ready to forgive me.

"You still breaking and entering?" Cheri asked.

"Naw, we saw the error of our ways."

"Doubtful," she replied.

"Honest, we're just sitting here having a burger at Coconuts and regrouping. We just missed Charlie at Carambola."

"The lobsters?"

"He delivered them just before we called."

"Look," Cheri said, her voice sounding thoughtful, "John and I checked out Chicken Charlie and the Golden Rail, where Tony might have blabbed about the coin they found. No one seemed to know anything. And the more we talked after, the more something else bothered us."

"Let's hear it," I said as the waitress delivered my diet Coke and Ray's Heineken.

"I've known the Brachure brothers a long time, and John knew them from when they were targets in one of his investigations, and we agree they can't be the brains of this deal."

"Yeah, I know that. I'm listening," I said, looking at Ray who was looking at the surf and view, seeming uninterested in anything else.

"OK. First, Mitch had to get to Puerto Rico after the airlines closed."

"Right."

"How?"

"Boat, plane," I said. "I'm still where we were at yesterday. It had to be by plane, probably private plane. And you and John are right, not something Charlie and Mitch could have pulled off themselves."

"And they'd have had even less time because Mitch

or someone had to go torture and kill Sam and Wendy first."

"Yep," I agreed, "but if some Mr. Brains was working with Mitch, he could have been getting the information while Mitch was getting to Puerto Rico. Mitch got to Jean's house about two in the morning, so he could have gotten to Puerto Rico as late as midnight. Can you rent a car in Puerto Rico at midnight?"

"Who knows? Maybe he had a friend."

"That would give him from about three in the afternoon till maybe midnight to figure out a way and get to Puerto Rico." I did the math while I talked. "That's nine hours. By a fast boat, it takes three, but the seas were rough as hell Tuesday, so I don't see a boat ride." I thought for a second and considered my logic. "Mitch had to have flown on a private plane, but how?"

"That's where John and I ended up, too. When I called a friend this morning, no commercial flights to Puerto Rico went out from the airport either," Cheri said.

I smiled to hear her, remembering all the dinners with John and Cheri over the years where the three of us had brainstormed the movements and next movements of fugitives they were hunting for the Marshals Service. They both loved the mental gymnastics, and it wouldn't have surprised me if they'd been at it all day.

"OK," I said, "we've been stuck on this plane thing, and it's a dead end. But we know the sea had to have been ten to fourteen feet going over to Puerto Rico that night, so where does that leave us?"

"Two things," Cheri said. "Either Mitch was already in Puerto Rico, or maybe St. Thomas, and it was Charlie you saw at the seaplane, or he flew by private plane from the private part of the airport without any documentation being done." She paused. "Nothing else makes sense, and I still don't see those two putting all the pieces together without help."

"Yeah, I'm with you," I agreed. "Charlie and Mitch are dumb as a box of rocks. This is out of their league."

"Not private plane material," Cheri said, "and even if Mitch was in St. Thomas or Puerto Rico already, I don't think Charlie could follow you, kill and torture Sam, and get Mitch the intel to find you in Puerto Rico without some help."

"They could have hijacked someone's private plane," I suggested, "and the authorities just haven't figured it out."

"John checked, and no such incident was reported, and again, way over the brothers' intellectual skill set."

It was clear that John and Cheri were ahead of me.

"So?" I asked.

"Our other bad guy is a pilot or owns a plane, and that's how Mitch got to you and Jean."

"So, we got a bad guy with the money and resources to arrange a plane and keep it a secret," I said, feeling an old, familiar knot in my stomach. Thugs are one thing. Rich people who are criminals scare me. "He may be very rich if Jean's theory about the pirate treasure is right."

"You got it, boss," Cheri said proudly.

"So where do we go from here?"

"John wants to know if you can go by the private part of the airfield and see if anyone knows anything."

"I think the lobster trail is cold, so that's probably our best lead right now," I said. "While we're there, we'll try to get a list of all the planes and owners – there's only a half-dozen or so -- so we can see if they know anything."

"Do you think we should check on the legitimate charter flights?" Cheri asked.

"Not now. The private plane idea makes more sense."

"Keep checking in."

"Love you, too," I said, and hung up.

Ray was still looking at the sea. "So, you and the team finally got your focus around to the rich, white bad guy," he said.

"White?" I asked.

"God, you're dumb," Ray's smile seemed to say. "Yeah, on this island, if you're rich and evil and not a public servant, you're a white guy."

I considered all the warped edges of Ray's logic and decided to play along, "So it couldn't be a rich white woman?"

Ray looked at his beer for a while. "White woman. I like that," he said.

"Or a black senator?"

"That wouldn't work," Ray said, shaking his head.

"You're fucked, Ray Man. It could be anyone. You need to give up the rich white guy thing."

"Nope," Ray said, taking a long drink.

"Nope?"

"I like the rich white guy scenario," Ray said. Then he thought for a second and added, "But I like the rich white woman, too."

"Why?" I asked, feeling the discussion tunneling into Ray's love for a good story instead of the truth.

"It's fact," he smiled

"Yeah?" I asked.

"Only way this could happen. I been waiting for you to get there," Ray said, taking my "Yeah" as agreeing with him. He drained the bottle and looked straight at me. I could see a perfect reflection of myself in his sunglasses.

"The man moving the pawns," Ray said as he stuck up a finger from his fist. "The pawns, the Brachure brothers, think they're the heavies. They don't feel the strings pulling their every move." He raised another finger. "Those boys live in a little shack and take out the man's garbage and think they're studs or something." He lifted a third finger. "They're just slaves, slaves doing the dirty work for the man." He raised his pinkie.

"If the puppet man was a black man, he'd never pull their strings without making sure they knew he was pulling. He'd have to stroke his own ego and disrespect them. And they'd never let him do that. But a white guy could manipulate the hell out of them. He'd just eat his ego and make them feel important. They'd never feel him pulling.

"This dude is a white man. Trust in your man,

Ray. He be rich -- rich white man we looking for." Ray opened out his thumb, then closed the fingers into a tight fist and smiled a triumphant smile.

I tried to see my friend's eyes through the reflection, but the glasses left me only staring back at myself. I'd never heard him talk this way before, and it made me wonder how well I really knew Ray Jones. I knew he was solid, and I also knew in my mind that the logic he was using was crap. But the pit of my stomach knew, too, that he was right.

He turned to the waves again and began talking low. "When I was young, I was a thug like the Brachure brothers. I ran with about ten other guys, and we did a lot of bad shit. Our main man was a guy about five years older than me named Brian Hamilton. He was a mean son of a bitch, and I always thought he was his own man. He wasn't much of a role model, but he was like a father to me." Ray stopped talking and sat twisting his hands back and forth on his empty beer.

I let the silence grow. I had nothing to say.

A thin smile crossed Ray's face. He was remembering. "Brian made a little money. He had a shack about like the Brachure boys, and he let us hang out there. He liked to call us his boys, and he was always good for a hot meal and cold beer. One day, we went to the little hovel and he was dead, just a pile on the floor shot about a hundred times. It took me four years to put all the pieces together, but it seems Brian got greedy, and a man in Miami ended their business. I found out my hero, Brian, was getting his marching orders from a drug dealer that moved coke through the island for years. If the Miami guy had another gang moving in or someone who just pissed him off, Brian had us take care of it."

Ray stopped talking as the waitress came over with another beer. I'd figured she'd seen him spinning the empty. She put it on the table without a word and walked away. Ray just kept looking at the sea.

He took a deep drink, then turned to face me. I saw the wrinkles, scars, two black mirrors. Was it his soul, or my own, behind them? "My mentor, my friend Brian, wouldn't say, 'That dude is stomping on the man's turf.' He knew us. He knew we didn't give a shit about the man, so he'd say, 'That scum raped so-and-so's sister' or some other shit and just get us fired up." Ray shook his head and cracked that small smile again. "We didn't think we were bad. We thought we were the good guys. God knows the cops didn't care if a young girl got raped or an old lady got robbed, so we cared. We thought we were taking care of business. We thought we were the solution."

I nodded, my voice gone, my mind reeling. I thought of the devils that chased me, and how they really chased all of us. Ray nodded back in wordless agreement: We all got devils. He knew, too.

His voice was flat when he started again. "After Brian got killed, things went nuts. My bros" -- Ray's voice began to crack, then he regained it -- "my bros couldn't handle it and started a shooting war with fantasy enemies all over the island. Most of them are dead or in prison now, all because a lousy rich guy in Miami wanted to move shitloads of coke through the island from Colombia to Miami. When he killed Brian, he turned this place into a bloodbath, but he didn't care. Every time one of my bros got shot or shot someone, they were slaves, just slaves." Ray's voice got real quiet. "Slaves knocking down the cane for the man."

Ray's face slumped. My chest felt released from a grip that wouldn't let it breathe. He turned away again, just looking back over the waves. After a while, he sipped at the beer. "You OK?" I asked him.

"Sometimes I get tired, Dog. Sometimes I just get tired."

"Tired?" I asked, not really understanding.

"Tired of being mad, tired of hating."

The burgers came, and I ate mine while Ray just looked where the far wall met the ceiling. He had another beer. I got my next Coke with rum. When the beer was done, Ray put a twenty on the table and walked back to the Jeep. His burger sat cold, forgotten and wasted. I finished my drink thinking about if I would ever be able to talk about my pain like Ray had just done. I was tired, too.

The airport is in the center of the island's South Side, so we went back east down the Melvin Evans Highway. Ray had lost interest in driving fast, sticking to a sane fifty miles per hour on St. Croix's only stretch of highway. We sat in a comfortable silence for about ten minutes. Finally, I asked, "You ever been to the private part of the airfield?"

"Yeah," Ray said. "It's not much, but there's a lot of planes that use it."

"Anything out there like a control tower or anything?"

"No, I think they use the commercial tower," Ray said, turning at a small hand-painted sign that said Private Planes. "There's just an old guy who lives there and does plane repair and pumps fuel."

Ray's description of the field was pretty accurate. There wasn't much there. The landing strip itself was paved, but the bare spots were clear as we drove across it to a single wide trailer on the far side. Hangars and planes lined both sides of the runway. I didn't see any life until Ray pulled up to the broken-down, white trailer and an old man in a grease-stained white jumpsuit stepped out. "BUDWEISER" the red ball cap on his long, gray hair proclaimed. "How can I help you guys?" the man asked as he lifted his can of Coke and walked toward the Jeep.

"Hi," Ray said. "We're trying to get some information about a plane that might have flown out of here on Tuesday."

The man eyed Ray suspiciously. "Cops?" he asked.

"Nope," I said.

He seemed to relax. "Sorry," the man said. "The goddamn feds drive me nuts. They think half my pilots are drug dealers."

"Aren't they?" Ray said with a smile.

"Maybe" the old man said, "but I don't give a shit.

I just fix the planes and give them fuel. No reason to ride my ass."

Ray pulled a wad of money out of his pants and peeled off a hundred-dollar bill. The old man looked at it. "All we want is a little information," Ray said. "We're trying to find a guy that's missing." The old man calmly took the bill from Ray's hand and inspected it, then put it in his jumpsuit pocket.

"Ask away," he said.

"You know Charlie Brachure?" I asked.

"Nope," he answered without hesitation.

"Big black man," Ray continued. "Would have been wearing dark pants and a white shirt. If you talked to him, he probably acted like an asshole."

The old man shook his head.

"Anyone leave here between four p.m. and midnight on Tuesday?" Ray asked.

The old man scratched his cheek stubble. "Wait here," he said, and walked back into the trailer.

In a couple of minutes, he was back with a leather-bound register. "This is my fuel log. The feds make me log all the fuel sales."

I nodded as he opened and studied it. "Sure, Tuesday," he said. "Jake Reid flew his single-engine to St. Thomas about four, and Leo Samuelson flew his plane, but I don't remember where. He had a passenger, but I didn't see who. He called about six and asked me to fuel him up, said he had to take a friend somewhere. I went to dinner about eight. When I got back, he was gone."

"When did he come back?" I asked.

"He was here when I got up the next morning." The old man was still staring at the log, like more information would crawl out of it.

"Can you tell us anything else about Mr. Samuelson?" Ray asked. I took out a pen and pad. Ray tried to look official without one.

"Rich asshole. Always yelling and bossy. Has one hell of a nice plane, I'll tell you that."

"Which one? I asked.

"The Pilatus PC-12 at the end." He nodded toward the runway." I don't know much about planes, but Ray must have. "Shit, a Pilatus. Nice," he said.

"Yep," the old man nodded. "Mr. Samuelson may be an asshole, but he knows his planes."

"Got an address for him?" I asked, feeling that things might be moving.

"Yeah, but you can't let him know where you got it."

"You're cool," Ray said.

The old man went into his trailer and came out a few minutes later with a page off a yellow legal pad. On it he'd written "Leo L. Samuelson," and an address in Cotton Valley, a subdivision near my marina.

As we left the airfield, Ray was quiet and distracted. When we got back on the main road, he looked at me. "You see any dive gear or lobster traps out at the Brachures?"

I thought for a second. "No," I told him.

"Can you ask someone to do some checking, see if Charlie or Mitch owns a boat?"

I thought about Ray's idea. I liked it. If there was a boat, that was a good lead on finding Charlie. He was still going out and getting lobster, so he'd have to be at his boat at some point. I hit the speed dial and called Cheri.

"Where you at?" she asked.

"Just leaving the airfield."

"Find anything out?"

"Yeah, I got a name. Can you or John run a Leo Samuelson. He lives in Cotton Valley."

I could hear Cheri talking to someone. Then she came back on. "Don't have to run him. John and I know him from HIDTA."

I was familiar with the High Intensity Drug Trafficking Areas program. When they were with the Marshals Service, both Cheri and John had been assigned to the inter-agency organization coordinating drug law enforcement.

"So, tell me about this guy," I said.

"Well, his name was always in the hat. It just never got picked. Most of the people we worked with knew the guy was dirty. We just never figured out how to get to him."

"What kind of dirty?" I asked, looking at Ray, who seemed more focused on the conversation than the road.

"Cocaine, guns, all the other happy stuff the bad guys do." Then I heard her talking to John again. "John also thinks he was tied into some money laundering," she said, "but there was never any investigation."

"Any idea about known associates?" I asked.

"No, but I'll make some calls."

"We're headed your way," I said, looking at my watch and seeing it was almost four.

"You stopping in Cotton Valley?"

"No" I said. "It's too late, and I need more information on this guy. I think it'll be a good starting point in the morning. Is John gonna be around tonight?"

There was another pause, then she said, "He'll be here till this is over, he says, and he wants to know if you're buying dinner."

I smiled. John was always game for a free meal, but it was a cheap price for what he was doing. "Tell him I'm buying, and he can pick the place," I said.

I moved the phone away and asked Ray, "Want to join us for dinner?"

He smiled back. "Got business."

"OK, looks like dinner for five," I told Cheri.

Before we hung up, I asked her to run boat registrations for the Brachures, and she said she'd also get me a Google Earth map and photo of Samuelson's home. "Thanks," I said. "Be home by five."

CHAPTER

14

As I walked down to the boat after Ray left me off, the stress of the day's hunt for Charlie Brachure finally caught up with me, and I felt completely exhausted. I climbed onto the boat, then heard voices in the salon, so I stuck my head in before I entered.

"Howdy," I said putting more energy into my voice then I felt.

"You're not looking good, Cotton," Jean said from the far side of the settee.

"Long day," I told her, then sat heavily into the white plastic lawn chair we'd moved there to make room for the bunch of us. John was on the phone sitting up on the lower helm's captain's chair and playing with the ship's wheel. He looked as beat as I felt. To my left,

Cheri and Betsy were going through some papers. They all turned to look at me.

"What?" I said

"You look like shit," Cheri said with a smile.

"You guys really know how to make a guy feel welcome," I answered as I got up and headed for a beer from the small refrigerator. "Might as well make that two," Betsy said.

"Three," John chimed in.

"Five," Jean added.

"Drunks," I said, looking back over my shoulder and eying each of them in turn. They were not a healthy-looking crowd either. I could see one reason when I looked at the second shelf, populated totally by Heinekens.

"Beer all around," I said as I set the bottles on the counter. The refrigerator under it had been keeping things far too cold lately – bad for lettuce but great for Heineken, giving all the beers a cool white frost when they hit the room's humid air. One by one, I opened them and handed them out. Then, bar tending duties complete, I sat down and looked at my motley crew.

"To life," I said, raising my beer.

"To life," they all agreed.

"We got a lot done today," Cheri said. "You want to be filled in, or you want to start?"

"You start," I said, not sure how I would describe my day.

"First," Betsy started, "I got a call from Jeff, the golf pro out at the Reef. It took him a few days to get my number from some friends who play there with me, but he said Bob's Honda was parked in the lot since Monday morning. John gave me a ride, and we went and picked it up. It's in the lot if you want to look at it."

"So, it's just been sitting there all this time?" I asked.

"Yeah," John said. "I talked to Jeff, and he saw Tony Rasser pick Bob up about eight o'clock on Monday. He said Bob threw all his dive gear into Tony's Jeep and they told him they'd be back by lunch. But they never showed." John took a frosty sip, then went on. "Got a hold of an old friend on the V.I.P.D. that investigated the wreck of Tony's Jeep. They had time to do a preliminary blood type," John said, "and none of it was Bob's."

"Anything else on the wreck?" I asked.

"A little more. Yellow paint scratched on the side of the Jeep, and they found a headlight rim in the ditch near where he went off the road that was from a Ford product. I don't expect much movement from the P.D. for a while. They had a shootout at Judith's Fancy last night, and seem to have lost focus on Tony's case already."

"Can you get me a photo of the part, and I'll e-mail it to a friend in Denver who may be able to help. If we know the year and make, it could really help us pin things down."

John nodded as Cheri took over, looking down at a legal pad full of notes. "I spent a lot of time on the phone today," she said. "Charlie has seven cars and trucks registered to him. Most of them look like old junkers that he's parting out, and none of them are yellow. Mitch had two trucks, one of them a one-ton yellow Ford."

"I told my contact at the P.D. about the yellow truck and to keep an eye out," John said, "but don't hold your breath. They couldn't even find Bob's truck, and it was in the parking lot of a golf course where two of their officers work security every night."

"Any idea when Tony's Jeep was run off the road?" I asked.

"My friend said Monday morning," John said.

"How did they know the time?" Jean asked. It was the first thing she said. She'd just been sitting thoughtful since I got there, listening knees-to-chest behind the table.

"I didn't get that information, but I got the impression they were pretty sure."

"Even if they're right, we still don't have hard evidence of someone working with Mitch," I said.

"Right," Cheri agreed, doodling absently on her pad.

Jean put her knees down and leaned forward. "I got a call from the Brendan Maza guy."

I looked at her absently, trying to remember why the name seemed familiar.

She saw my confusion. "Remember, Mr. Maza was the soldier who put the Spanish gold coin on eBay."

I nodded. "Anyway," Jean went on, "Mr. Maza talked to his sister and she had him call me. Mr. Maza had some interesting information. It seems he found the coin on the path above Isaac's Bay. He said he always wanted to come back and look for more coins but never found the time."

"So, it was on the ground, not in the water," I said.

"Buried treasure," John said. "The plot thickens."

Cheri gave him a quick look, then turned to Jean. "Did he say anything about exactly where he found the coin?"

"No. I got the impression he was keeping that little secret," she said with a smile.

Cheri looked at her notes again, then turned to me. "John and I talked to some of the guys down at DEA that knew both Mitch and Charlie, and they think like we do. The Brachure boys are just too stupid to be the brains behind this mess. But they've worked for half the bad guys on the island, so if someone is giving them marching orders, it could be anyone."

I wanted to keep my focus where the afternoon had put it. "Seems to me this Leo Samuelson is at the top of our list of people we need to talk to."

"Be careful, Mad Dog. The guy's a nut," John said.

"Thanks, but the clock is ticking, and if we're going to find Bob, we need to talk to everyone. I don't think this Samuelson guy will tell me anything, but maybe I can shake him a little and get a feel for if he's in on this."

"Have Ray shake him," John said.

"I thought you didn't like poor ol' Ray," I told him.

"You got it wrong. It's not that I don't like him. I don't trust him. But he'll be better at putting a scare into a bad guy like Samuelson than you."

"May be," I said without much enthusiasm. I knew

I'd felt wiped out when I came back to the boat, but all of a sudden, the day's impact hit me even harder. It was like a wave of exhaustion washing all over me. "Anything else important?" I asked.

"Nothing that can't wait till morning," Cheri said.

"I'm sorry guys, I'm done. I gotta get some sleep before I drop." I looked at John. "See you at two," I said, hoping I was putting up the right number of fingers.

John raised two fingers in reply. He knew when I'd be there. "Get some sleep," he said.

Cheri looked at me as I passed by heading for our stateroom. "We just ordered some pizza," she said. "I'll leave you a few slices in the fridge."

I said a weak "thanks" and waved good-bye to the crew as I dropped down the stairs to my waiting bed.

CHAPTER 15

Ray stood over me and growled like a huge bear: "Kill him!" A few feet away, Auntie Mabel sat slowly rocking in a chair twice her size. "Yes," she said in a soft, loving voice, "kill him." I looked down at my hands. They were covered in blood, and on the floor was a shapeless pile of darkness and cloth.

"Kill him," Ray roared. "Kill him!"

"Who?" I asked.

"Kill the Bastard!" Ray roared again, his eyes wide, his face contorted.

"Yes, kill him," the small voice from the chair said again. I looked toward it and saw that Cheri was now sitting with Auntie Mabel.

Suddenly I noticed I had a bat in my hand. I knew this bat. It was the Louisville Slugger my dad had brought back from a trip to Chicago. Dad had gone to a Cubs game. I listened on the radio, knowing he was there watching the Cubs beat the Dodgers 4-0. The next day, he presented me with the bat, signed by none other than my hero, Ernie Banks.

"Not with Ernie's bat!" I yelled to the room.

Then without warning, a huge black hand wheeled out of the dark mound and slammed Auntie Mable and Cheri from the chair, scattering them like cups off a table. They crashed to the floor with sickening wet thuds. Now a man rose and smiled at me. The bat in my right hand seemed small and insignificant, but when the huge shape turned on Cheri's broken body, I swung. The bat caught the beast behind the ear but had no effect.

Then the form turned toward me and charged. I swung Ernie's bat and missed. The thing hit me, and I was in the water. It choked out my air as I struggled to breathe.

My eyes jerked open. I was wide-awake, my heart racing, my bedding wrapped around me and soaked with sweat. I tried to blink the dream away, but it wouldn't die. I sucked in air again and again, and slowly my normal breathing began to come back. Through the porthole, I saw the streetlight up at the parking lot. Except for its faint glow, the stateroom was dark. The only sounds were Cheri's rhythmic breath and my still-chaotic panting. I held my hand in front of my face. It was too dark to see, but I felt no blood. "God," I thought to myself, "that was a whopper!"

The air held the scent of lemon oil and sweat as I lay there trying again to wash the dream from my mind. The Louisville Slugger -- I hadn't thought of it in years. I'd lost the bat decades ago. I reached over Cheri and picked up my cell phone. The faint light showed 1:06.

I knew it always took a combination of yoga poses and gymnastics to twist my way over Cheri out of bed from where I slept against the port wall. When I finally managed, her breathing remained deep and undisturbed. I grabbed my robe and went up into the salon. She had left my clothes on the table and a towel with my dock kit. I had to smile at her organization.

I pushed them all aside and sat down at the table, the nightmare's power still hanging on. I looked out at the marina lights and tried to relax. In my core, I felt a large, empty void, a hollowness that went down deep. Then it made me remember the pizza, and I went over and opened the refrigerator door. I was met only by blackness.

One of the wonderful things about a boat is that it gives you job security for life. You'll never run out of things that need fixing. "Damn light," I said under my breath as I reached in for the promised pizza. My fingers found a triangle of tinfoil, and I grabbed it out.

As I sat at the table and unwrapped it, I realized that the hollow feeling in my stomach wasn't fear the nightmare had brought but pure starvation. I hadn't eaten since lunch the day before. I bit into the slice with a zeal you can never quite show unless you're alone.

I grunted happily and sat back in the settee, looking emptily out the dark starboard window.

As I gazed toward the parking lot, a small light began to grow where I knew the mass of shrubs sat between the lot and my boat. I watched transfixed by the light, not knowing what it was but feeling curious, and then fascinated, by how it seemed to get bigger. Then, in a burst of thought, I knew: Fire!

The light was flames, growing quicker and quicker. And at the last millisecond, I realized they were not growing – they were speeding toward me.

I barely said "Shit!" when the light exploded against the window. The blackness outside was replaced by flame. The air was yellow, orange, throbbing with waves of heat. For a second, my mind struggled. Then I understood: firebomb.

"Cheri!" I yelled as I ran down the stairs. When I flipped on the stateroom light, she was already half out of bed and grabbing for her oversized T-shirt. Dog was bounding up the stairs with a deep growl I'd never heard before.

"Fire," I said. And then I barked, "Gun," motioning to my holstered Glock on the dresser.

Cheri pulled it off the top and tossed it to me in one smooth motion. Then she pulled the fire extinguisher off the wall and charged up the stairs, hair flying behind her.

When I burst onto the port deck after her, I could hear Dog yelping on the other side. The fire was raging there, and when I went around the back of the boat, I saw him leap to the dock. I jumped off, too, and started full-tilt toward where the light had come from. John, running over from Ed's boat, was at my side, service pistol out and ready.

"He's in the parking lot," John yelled as we rushed up the walkway toward it. A shot rang out, and we both dropped skidding to the ground. Dog kept running and barking. Then another shot, and a flash of light in front of him. Dog yelped and dodged in a clumsy leap behind the bushes.

"Fuck this," I said as my bare knee bashed against the hard cement. I scrambled back to my feet, leading with the Glock as John and I charged up the walkway. We got to the lot just in time to see a yellow one-ton truck racing out past the guard booth, too far away to be worth a shot. Dog was sitting about fifty yards away, silently watching it go.

"That was fucking Charlie," I said.

"Most likely," John agreed.

Then I wheeled and raced back to the boat. The flames were gone. Cheri was on the deck, wielding the fire extinguisher like a machine gun as she shot at flickering embers through the thick smoke. Like an idiot, I waved to her. She just shook her head and kept looking around the boat. Ed was scurrying up with an ancient red fire extinguisher almost as big as he was.

Suddenly I realized I hadn't heard any shots at the gate, but the truck had driven right by Miguel. "Shit," I said as Dog and I began running for the guard booth.

We'd gone about a hundred yards when the security

shack came into view. I couldn't see Miguel. The lights were on, but the shack was empty, and the guardrail was up. It meant he was off on his rounds somewhere. I was trying to figure where to look first when I heard the faint, familiar purr of his golf cart. Miguel emerged from the darkness a few seconds later, racing at his top speed of maybe five miles an hour.

"You OK?" I asked urgently as he pulled up.

"Si, Mr. Cotton. I was doing my rounds at the motel and I saw fire at the dock."

I jumped in next to him and squeezed Dog between my legs. "Back to my boat quick, buddy," I said. The deep relief I felt that my friend was OK seemed like one thing, but I couldn't stop thinking what Charlie Brachure would have done if Miguel had tried to stop him.

Back at the boat, a dozen or so people were gathered around Cheri, protectively touching and patting her. They all turned when I got there. "Get 'em?" Tom Conklin, a retired potato farmer, asked.

"Nope," I said, then realized I was still holding the Glock in my hand and pushed it into the pocket of my robe.

Ed smiled at me. "Doesn't look too bad," he said. "Probably clean off with a little soap and water. Cheri had it all out before I got here."

I looked over at Itchy Feet. A half-dozen flashlights were playing over the deck and cabin. I could see it was mostly paint that had burned, and I smiled back at the old man. "Could have been a lot worse," I said. Then I pulled Cheri close, wrapped my arms around her, and just held on.

Dog tried hard to make it a group hug, but Cheri kept it a twosome. Then she gave him a hard eye. "Some watchdog you are."

As I held her tight, she spoke into my chest. "Mad Dog, this asshole is beginning to piss me off."

Smelling the smoke in her hair and feeling her warmth, I could sense my own rage building. "Me too," I whispered. "Me too."

At five forty-five, I was sitting on my back deck sipping a cup of coffee and watching the sun come up. Dog was asleep under my raised legs. The way the marina faces, you can't actually see the sunrise, but that morning, I didn't care. The blends of reds and pinks and purples were dancing in the tall cumulus thousands of feet up. I just watched the colors shift from one form to another, thinking what a wonderful life I had – if I could shut my mind to the Brachures of the world.

After the fire, Cheri had made me coffee, called Charlie Brachure a few choice words, and gone to bed. The char in the air was still thick, but she declared herself too worn out to care. Sensing Cheri was still disappointed in his watchdog skills, Dog stayed up with me.

About four o'clock, after John had gone to the fly bridge to flop down on the couch and Dog had gone off to doggie dreamland, I left my post at the back of the boat and cleaned the broken glass off the starboard deck. After that, I went up to the fly bridge and got a bucket. It took the better part of an hour for me to scrub the side of the boat, but it looked pretty good now, and the work-helped calm my nerves. The fire had singed the teak around the porthole in addition to bubbling some paint, but all in all, it was nothing a little sandpaper and varnish plus a coat of paint wouldn't fix.

"You look pretty content for a guy whose boat just got firebombed," a voice behind me said.

I turned around. Ray was standing with his arms crossed and a paper bag hanging in his right hand. He was two hours earlier than I expected, but that was good.

"Them *pâtés*?" I asked.

Dog's ears went up, but he held his sleep position.

"Nope."

"Then what?"

"Danish, from the bakery."

"Got enough for everyone," John's voice came from the fly bridge.

Ray looked up at his head peeking through the stern window. "You come down big man, and I'll feed ya." Then he broke off a chunk of sugarcoated pastry and tossed it to Dog, who caught it with a lurch and laid down to pick his prize apart. The fluffy white powder coating his nose didn't seem to bother him at all.

I pointed to the thermos and a bunch of Styrofoam cups, and Ray and John poured themselves coffee and sat down. Ray sniffed. "Don't smell too bad," he said.

"Cleaned right up," I told him.

"You guys think it was Charlie?" Ray asked.

"Yeah," John answered, opening the brown bag Ray had brought.

"Don't eat them all," Ray snapped, a dark warning in his voice.

"Raspberry Danish," John said with an air of wonder as he pulled out a pastry twice the size of his hand.

"How'd you find out about the fire?" I asked Ray.

"Shirley Totan at dispatch called me. Cops show up yet?" He tossed another little piece to Dog.

"Nope," John answered between bites. A small streak of red ran across his cheek. Ray reached across and caught it with a napkin as casually as Auntie Mabel did with him the day before. John gave him a long look, then kept on eating. We all sat in silence, chewing and sipping coffee, watching the colors of the sky creep slowly into daylight.

Ray finished his Danish, carefully wiped his hands and face, and stuck his feet up on the rail. "What Charlie did last night surprises the hell out of me," he said.

"Why?" John asked between bites of his second pastry, a latticework of dough around a yellow cream filling.

Ray sipped his coffee and considered the question. "My gut just tells me it's not his style. He's an in-your-face kind of guy, and you killed his brother, Mad Dog. I think he'd want to look you in the eye before he killed you."

"Makes sense," John said.

"I'm pretty sure it was him," I told Ray. "He was

in a yellow truck, same color as the one that ran Tony Rasser off the road."

"Really?" Ray said, a sound of genuine interest in his voice.

"Mitch had a yellow, one-ton Ford, and the evidence at the accident scene looks like a yellow Ford. If you're gonna run a guy off the road, a one-ton is a good vehicle to do it with, and that's what the guy last night was driving."

"So, you think Charlie is driving Mitch's truck?" Ray said.

"Makes sense," I replied.

Ray looked up at the clouds a long while. "Makes good sense," he finally said. Then he turned back to John and told him sternly, "Leave some of those for the ladies, big man."

John raised his sugar-covered hands. "Done, thanks," he said.

"Your welcome." Ray pulled his sunglasses from his shirt pocket, put them on, and stared back at the sky. After a while, he turned to me. "I know it makes sense it was Charlie who threw that Molotov, but my gut doesn't like it. Throwing that thing was more like a warning than an attack."

I looked at the side of my boat. "Ray, if Cheri and I had both been sleeping, that could have been real bad."

Ray shook his head. "Maybe," he said, but he didn't sound convinced.

"You might have something, Ray" John said as he walked over to the edge of the boat to brush crumbs off his chest and belly. "I've read a half-dozen reports on the Brachure brothers, and they are definitely in-your-face kind of guys, and someone killing your twin brother is pretty serious stuff."

"So, who?" I asked.

"Maybe the brains," John replied.

"Leo Samuelson," Ray said, his voice going flat.

"Maybe," I said, rolling the idea around in my head but not feeling it get warmer.

"Maybe I'll be able to tell when we talk to him," Ray said.

"Cheri's got a Google Earth map and aerial photo of his house inside," I said, remembering that she'd printed it out for me yesterday along with directions to his house.

"Cool," Ray said. "I found the house and looked around last night, but I'd love to see the photo."

I wasn't surprised that Ray had been up to Samuelson's house, but I didn't like him doing something that dangerous alone. "Done," I said calmly, trying not to show my feeling as I went inside.

I grabbed the photo and a second pot of coffee I'd made and took them both outside. "I didn't realize how isolated this guy's house is," Ray said, studying the photo.

I looked over his shoulder. Ray was right. Acres of heavy bush lay between Leo Samuelson and his nearest neighbor. I didn't like what I was seeing.

"One road in and bush on all sides," I said, "with a hundred fifty feet of lawn all round the house."

Ray looked back at me, then at the map again. "If Samuelson is a real bad guy, he may not think of that as a lawn."

"What?"

The picture was clear to John. "I think what Ray is getting at is this is not just a lawn; it's a kill zone."

Ray nodded. I was just getting the point when he moved his finger along a thin line. A cyclone fence ran around the whole lawn area. Ray pointed again, and I saw two small buildings at the far end of the lawn. "What's that?" I asked.

"If I'm not mistaken, it's a kennel."

"Guard dogs," I said. "I hate guard dogs." At our feet, Dog rolled over and lifted a sugarcoated paw. "You don't count," I said, nudging him with my foot.

Ray seemed to be talking more to himself than me. "Security fence, dogs, and a nicely mowed kill zone. I don't like this."

"Kill zone," I repeated, not liking the sound of the words.

Ray moved his finger over the wide lawn. "No cover, nothing at all."

"Yeah," I said, seeing the expanse entirely from Ray's eyes now.

John reached his big hand over us and took the photo, then sat back in the chair near his coffee and studied it. With a grunt, he rolled to his left and reached into his cargo pants, coming out with a pair of beat-up reading glasses. "Getting old," he said as he put them on and began studying the photo.

"How recent is this?"

"I don't know."

"Well," he said, laying the photo on the upper part of my back deck like it was a table. "This is a pretty standard security setup. If you know where to look, it's easy to figure a lot of it out."

John pointed to what looked like the main gate. "Five'll get you ten if we drive by there, I can spot security cameras."

"They're here and here," Ray said, tapping the photo once on the far side of the road and again about thirty yards past the gate. "That's all I could see just driving by at night."

"Two security cameras," I said, not even trying to hide my concern.

"Or more," John said. "I've seen a lot of compounds like this in the states but not here." He took off his glasses and began moving them in front of his eyes. Ray took a pair of reading glasses out of his pants pocket and handed them to John. Using the two together like magnifiers, John examined the photo again. Then he tapped the corner of a small shed. "Rotating camera."

"Yep," Ray grunted.

"Fuck this, guys," I said, growing tired of the conversation, "Were going in to talk to the guy, not kill him."

"I wouldn't be worried about going in. I'd be worried about getting out," John said.

"Half the island will know we went up there," I said. "What's he gonna do?"

"Wild man," Ray said, grabbing my shoulder with a little shake. "This dude could have killed three or four people, and he might be trying to hide millions of dollars in gold. He could do anything."

"Ray is right, Mad Dog," John said, standing to his full height. "At HIDTA, we knew he was tied to coke, guns, and maybe money laundering for the Colombians. This could be not just a dangerous guy but a crazy guy."

I took a deep breath, my senses filling with the smell of my burned boat. I'm usually pretty easy-going, but I have my own crazy side, and the Molotov cocktail had bent my sense of caution. I looked at my two friends. "I talk for five minutes to this guy face-to-face," I said, "and I'll know if he's part of this. I'm gonna go to his house and talk to him."

John shook his head, a disappointed look crossing his broad features. Ray smiled and shrugged as if to say, Why not? "I'm in," he said.

"This is stupid," John said. "I'm in."

I looked at the photo and said quietly, "John, you take the girls and move them somewhere safer than the motel and the boat. If this goes to hell, they won't be safe."

He gave me a look like the kid left out of a baseball game.

"I'm trusting you with my wife and Jean and Betsy," I said, holding my hand on his elbow. "Two guys or three guys won't matter in that compound if something goes wrong, but you having my back out here means one hell of a lot."

"Gotcha," John grunted, then turned to Ray and said, "You take care of him."

Ray looked back and nodded, his black sunglasses glinting in the morning light.

"I want to get to this place early," I said. "Let's go."

It was 8:20 when Ray drove the Jeep past Leo Samuelson's house. He spoke for the first time since we'd started out: "On your right you'll see a white security camera. It's pretty obvious."

I looked right. Yep, no one was trying to hide the white camera at the end of a small clearing. I looked left and saw the gate to Samuelson's house. It was ten feet tall made of heavy steel bars. There was no attempt at beauty, just pure utility. The big red letters on the front read: "NO SOLICITORS."

"Are we solicitors?" I asked.

"No," Ray said, not taking his eyes off the road. "We're inquisitors."

He drove about another half-mile, then pulled off into some deep grass. Ray pointed to a small dirt road. "I talked to some guys last night. That's the end of Samuelson's land," he said.

"Hell of a big chunk of property."

"Man likes his privacy," Ray said as he backed out onto the road and lurched forward toward the gate again. "What now?"

"We go knock on the door," I told him.

At the turnoff to Samuelson's house, Ray went right down the twenty feet to the big black barrier that looked like the only way through the chain link fence.

He pulled the Jeep up to a small intercom and pushed the red button.

The engine's deep growl kept me from hearing what Ray was saying, but in a few seconds, the big gate swung open.

"What did you say?" I asked him.

"I said I was Ray Jones and that I was with Mad Dog Cotton, and we wanted to talk to him about the disappearance of Bob Rourk."

"And?" I asked, amazed by Ray's straightforward approach.

"He asked if you were the detective." Ray shifted gears and drove down the bushy corridor toward the house. "I said yes, and he said come on in, all nice and friendly."

I noticed the big magnum was now lying on the seat next to Ray.

"I got a plan," I said.

"I like plans," Ray replied, keeping his eyes on the road.

"You stay in the Jeep, and I'll talk to Samuelson."

"Splits us up."

"Yeah," I answered. I knew it could be bad, but it felt less risky than trying to sweet-talk information out of Samuelson with hothead Ray sitting next to me.

"Things go bad, head for the dog kennel," Ray said over the wind and engine noise.

"The dog kennel!"

"Yeah, if he has guards, they won't expect you to go toward the dogs."

"There's a reason for that," I said, thinking it was insane to move toward trained guard dogs.

"I know."

I thought about how much I hated mean dogs, and it made Ray's idea make sense in a strange way. I nodded.

We pulled out of the deep bush into a large landscaped yard surrounded by another high cyclone fence. This guy really liked his privacy. The gate was open. Driving along the crushed gravel road, I could see dramatic changes since the aerial photo Cheri had was taken. An open lawn was now dotted with palm trees and large clusters of flowering bushes. A three-foot wall ran the full length of the house about twenty feet in front of it.

The house itself was still a wandering, single-story, adobe ranch built in a classic southwestern style. A large, separate wing was on either side of an open walkway in the middle.

A black Hummer and a blue Ford pickup were parked in front of the wall. A gray-haired man in green cargo pants and a white polo shirt was sitting on the wall. Ray pulled up to him and shifted into park with the engine running. The man waved but stayed where he was.

I climbed out of the Jeep and walked over to him. The man on the wall was short, about five-six, with a slender, athletic build. "Leo Samuelson," he said, smiling and putting out his hand.

"Mad Dog Cotton," I said, shaking hands and

holding his eye contact. "This is my friend, Ray Jones." I nodded toward the Jeep.

"Yes," Samuelson said, raising an arm to Ray. Then he turned back to me. "Mr. Cotton, how can I help you?"

As a homicide cop, one of the critical skills I had to master is what my old partner, Red Blair, used to call the friendly chat. Most murderers are good liars and love to talk, gloating to themselves how much smarter they are than the cops. They think they're bulletproof, but as the years go by and you talk to about a thousand of them, you develop a bullshit meter. Maybe I wasn't the Caribbean's answer to Sherlock Holmes, but I've got one hell of a bullshit meter. To get the feel I needed for nice and friendly Leo Samuelson, I had to sit down and just talk to him.

"Do you have somewhere we can have a little chat?"

"Come to my garden," Samuelson said, waving at Ray to join us.

"You go ahead," Ray called out, his big black sunglasses covering any emotion. "I'll wait."

Samuelson smiled at Ray and led me down the walkway at the center of the house. It opened into a large garden with wings and arms of the home all around it. A small white metal table sat beside a glistening pool. Samuelson gestured toward the chair nearest the pool.

As I sat down, a large black man in white chinos and a loose Hawaiian shirt came out of the house. "Anything, Mr. Samuelson?" he asked.

"I'll have a tea, Larry. And you, Mr. Cotton?"

"Tea is fine," I told Larry. As he turned, I noticed the telltale bulge of a handgun in the small of his back.

Eager to start my interview, I leaned forward. No need for chitchat. I was ready to talk. To my surprise, Samuelson leaned forward, too. He wasn't looking worried about my questions.

"Do you know Charlie Brachure?" I asked calmly.

Samuelson's eyes brightened and moved upward as he thought about my question. "No," he said after a few seconds. "I don't think so."

Nothing about his answer kicked off my bullshit meter. Either this guy was a world-class liar or not my man.

"I'm investigating the disappearance of a man by the name of Bob Rourk. Do you know Bob?" I asked.

Again, Samuelson's eyes darted upward before he spoke. "No, I don't think so," he said. "What does he do? I've met so many people on the island it's hard for me to remember them all."

"Bob is a dive instructor," I told him.

"Nope, don't dive," Samuelson said without hesitation.

I decided to change my direction. Looking straight at Samuelson, I asked, "Where did you take your plane on Tuesday night?" His eyes immediately darted down and then to the side. Even before he spoke, my bullshit meter was ready to scream.

"I went to St. Thomas on business," he said. This was crap, and I felt I'd jumped closer to a breakthrough.

"Mr. Samuelson, you're lying to me. Why are you

lying to me?" I asked, keeping my voice level and my eyes fixed on his.

"What I was doing and where I flew on Monday is none of your fucking business," he barked back angrily. Samuelson had got pissed off fast. When you've got someone angry, experience had taught me, press the bet.

But a small nagging presence in the back of my mind started whispering, "Don't press now. Too dangerous." And if I still couldn't smell the acrid stench of my burned boat in the back of my sinuses, I might have listened to it. Like an idiot, I forged ahead and pressed. "You went to the airfield, fueled your plane, and made a night flight. Where to, Mr. Samuelson, and who was your passenger?"

His eyes jerked right and left, a clear search for a good lie. Then he stopped and let out a breath, suddenly seeming to calm down. He called out, "Larry."

Behind me, I heard a faint movement. I froze but didn't turn. I just stared into Leo Samuelson's cold dead eyes.

"Mr. Cotton," he said, "I figure you would not come up here without telling someone you were doing it. Am I correct?"

I knew this question was trouble and tried to put on my best you-don't-scare-me face. "Correct," I said.

"So, if I tell Larry to blow your fucking brains out, then have my other man kill the prick in the Jeep, I'd be wise to expect company."

A cool calm came over me that was pure combat instinct, and I looked Samuelson hard in the eye. "Real simple, Leo. You are welcome to kill us both, but it won't be cops you see next."

"A threat, Mr. Cotton?" To Leo Samuelson, it seemed, we were discussing a simple business transaction.

"A promise," I said calmly.

He considered what I said and then asked, "How much is my wife paying you, Mr. Cotton?"

I saw Larry standing about ten feet away, partly hidden by a large palm tree. It was clear he was listening, and he didn't have any tea with him. Instead, there was an old Navy Colt .45 in his right hand. Not the finest weapon on the planet but plenty effective.

I turned back to Samuelson, a little off-balance from his question, and asked, "Wife?"

"Yeah, wife. The bitch put you up to this, didn't she?" There was no hint of falsehood, only anger and raw hate in his voice.

"Who was your passenger?" I shot back, trying to gain some control of the moment.

"Debra Canton, my girlfriend, Mr. Cotton. Is that what you wanted to hear?"

His voice was flat now. I sat back and looked at Samuelson and felt like a complete jerk. It took me a second to regain my mental footing. "Where to?" I asked.

"As I'm sure you know, Debra lives in St. Martin. I flew her to St. Martin." Every sense told me that Leo Samuelson had just told me the full truth.

"Mr. Samuelson," I said, standing and extending my hand, "I apologize for the questions. It's clear you can't help me find Mr. Rourk. I don't work for your wife and didn't come to talk about Ms. Canton." I took a deep breath. I wanted him to understand that I was not in any way a threat to him.

"I got off on a bad lead that took me to you," I said. "I thought you knew something about Mr. Rourk's disappearance."

Samuelson sat back in his chair, relaxed again. Then he moved forward and put out his hand. "I apologize," he said. "My ex-wife is being a pain in the ass, and I guess I'm seeing demons everywhere."

I smiled to myself. I understood seeing demons everywhere.

Samuelson's eyes were still fixed on me. "Larry," he said. "Will you please see Mr. Cotton out. And Mr. Cotton, good luck."

"Thanks," I said and followed the hulking Larry out of the garden back to where Ray was waiting in the Jeep.

I got in, and without a word, Ray turned around and headed back down the lane to the main road.

"Nothing," I yelled over the noise of the Jeep and wind. "I'm chasing my tail."

"Not our bad guy?" Ray asked.

"Not our bad guy," I said, feeling the frustration grow.

"He is a bad guy."

"Yeah," I said, remembering Samuelson's brief burst of red-hot anger when he thought I was working for his ex-wife.

I'd gone in to face a man whose hands looked soaked

in blood. Maybe the only way I was still alive was that going in was such a mistake – a crazy, desperate mistake because I couldn't think of any other idea.

It had been five days since Bob Rourk disappeared, and the real time for finding him and giving this case a happy ending was running out.

"What now?" I asked, feeling a sense of helplessness.

"We find Charlie and shake him before we kill him," Ray said, his eyes straight ahead on the road.

"Let's just shake," I answered.

"Sure," Ray replied. But I wasn't convinced.

When we got to the marina's entrance, Ray just roared on past it. "You got ideas?" I asked as the Jeep headed toward town."

"Yeah," he said. I didn't ask what. I knew I'd know soon enough.

As we got into Christiansted, we turned right at a small outdoor Mexican restaurant and headed for the beach. It was where a lot of the fishermen land to sell their catch. Ray pulled up in front of a small boat with a sixty-something black man working on a net. We both got out, and Ray walked over and greeted him fist to fist.

"Mad Dog, meet Carlos Rubin, fisherman of the great Caribbean and sage patron of this humble beach."

I had to smile. That was vintage Ray, street hood one minute, scholar of rhetoric the next. I'd never have him all figured out. But that was OK. I could handle it.

Carlos grinned toothlessly in response and offered

his fist. I bumped it with my own, and his grin grew larger.

"So, hombre," Carlos said to Ray, "if you came to buy fish, it is gone."

"No fish, my friend," Ray said, pulling a ten-dollar bill out of his pocket. Carlos casually stuck it in his own. "Charlie Brachure," Ray said after the money had disappeared.

Carlos blinked once and then smiled in recognition.

"Where's his boat?" Ray asked.

"Boat?" the old man answered.

"He fishes for lobster, right?"

Carlos rubbed his chin and waved at a table and four chairs sitting in the sand next to his boat.

We sat down and I looked toward the surf gently lapping at the beach.

"You know Charlie?" Ray started again.

"Sure," Carlos said.

"And he's selling lobster?"

"Yes, he sells to the restaurants," Carlos answered as he pulled a Budweiser out of a battered cooler and opened it.

"So," Ray said, "where does he keep his boat?"

"I didn't know he had a boat," Carlos said.

"If he doesn't have a boat, where does he get his lobsters?"

Carlos scratched his two-day-old, gray beard. "I never thought about it, Mr. Ray," he said. "I don't know, but I have never seen him out fishing."

"I'm glad someone else knows how to bang their heads against a wall," I said.

Ray turned to me and shrugged.

"Thanks, buddy," Ray said, putting his hand on the old man's shoulder as he stood up.

"Sure," Carlos said, looking down at the stack of dominos on the table. "Want to play some bones?"

"No, not today, my friend, maybe later," Ray said, and we started back for the Jeep.

We'd gone about ten feet when Carlos called out, "You looking for Charlie?"

"Yeah," Ray said without turning back.

"He's at Piper's," Carlos said.

We stopped in our tracks, turned in unison, and looked at the old man, who had already turned his attention to the table and was absently playing dominos with himself.

"What?" Ray asked.

The old man looked up. "Charlie," he said, "Charlie is at Piper's. He got a hardon for the day bartender, that Cuban girl. He's been there every day for a week."

"You sure?" I asked.

Carlos looked hurt. "Sure, I'm sure. Charlie's been falling all over her all week." The old man pointed a bent finger at me. "You go to Piper's, and Charlie will be sitting at the bar. You listen to Carlos. I see him there every day."

"Muchas gracias," Ray said as we hurried for the Jeep.

"Por nada," the old man said, raising his hand.

"Shit, man," Ray said as we got into the Jeep. "No way we can be this lucky."

"I don't know, buddy," I said. "I think we're due."

Piper's is a little bar just on the outskirts of downtown. Ray got there in five minutes. He parked a block away, and we both looked up the street. A yellow one-ton pickup sat closer to it than we were, parked illegally on the right side of the road.

"Bingo," I said, checking my Glock for a shell in the chamber.

"In back, there's a blue door," Ray said, "the bar's back door. You need to cover it."

"I'm going in with you," I told him.

Ray Jones is my best friend, and I'd trust him with my life, but I did not trust him not to shoot Charlie Brachure as soon as he walked into the bar. He knew how bad I needed to talk to Charlie, but Ray was one man I couldn't predict. In all the years I'd known him, he was still an enigma.

I had to have Charlie alive. He was just a pawn, but there was no other link to the real bad guy. If Charlie died before he could talk, we'd never find Bob Rourk or know what was really going on.

Ray glared at me, but his resolve softened. "OK," he said. "We go in fast. It's a small place. We can be on him before he even knows we're there if we're lucky."

"Agreed," I said. "He gonna look like Mitch?"

"Yeah, beefier, meaner, same dumb face."

I slipped my Glock back behind my back, and Ray did the same with his revolver. We pulled our shirts down over the guns as we climbed down from the Jeep and walked toward Piper's bar and Charlie Brachure.

I looked up and down the street. "No cars," I said. "Maybe we're lucky."

"Yeah, Charlie don't want to be here when there's competition for that girl."

At the small blue door in front, Ray stopped and closed his eyes. It dawned on me he was adjusting them to the dark he expected inside. After a moment, he held up his right hand, one finger showing. Then, two fingers. Then three as he jerked open the door and disappeared into the darkness. I entered quickly behind him. The light was dim, like Ray figured, as I squinted into the shadows. I waited at the door while Ray moved the twenty feet to the back of the room. The woman behind the bar was tall and slim, with long black hair, dark flickering eyes, and a large pouting mouth. She had on cutoff Levi's and a tight Corona T-shirt. I could understand why Charlie was coming to Piper's.

As my eyes adjusted, I realized she, Ray, and I were the only ones there. At the far corner of the bar was a half-drunk Corona. The woman looked at Ray, then at me, and smiled, asking silently what we'd like. Ray put his finger to his lips and pointed at the chair in front of the beer. The woman's eyes grew as Ray pulled out his huge revolver. She gestured toward the men's room just as we heard the toilet. Charlie must not have been into washing his hands because as soon as it flushed, he stepped out.

I was only five feet in front of him. Ray was ten feet

behind him. "You," Charlie exclaimed, automatically moving one-step back. He froze for just a heartbeat, and then surged forward with his hands reaching out. But his charge was clumsy, off-balance. At ten in the morning, Charlie was drunk already.

As he got to me, his right fist came around in an arc, but I ducked to the side and got away. The swing took him past me, and I smashed a hard left cross to the back of his ear. Charlie stumbled forward into the table and two chairs next to Piper's front door.

Before I could move again, Ray was next to me, and as Charlie lay bent over the table with his back to us, Ray kicked him squarely between the legs.

The bartender squealed, and I heard the back door slam the wall as she jerked it open. I looked up just in time to see her disappear at a full run.

When I turned back to Charlie, he was lying in a fetal position rocking back and forth between the two overturned chairs. Ray had the big revolver in his right hand and was expertly moving his left over Charlie's body, looking for weapons. He pulled a small revolver from Charlie's back and slid it across the wooden floor. A white pearl-handled switchblade came out of a sock and slid after it, stopping a few inches from my right foot.

I looked at the back door, and Ray nodded. "Yeah, I know," he said. "Hard to know who she's gonna call, the cops or half of downtown to back up Charlie."

He stood up and went to the back door, then dropped the two-by-four next to it in the steel slots that keep it shut. "I don't think Charlie's got a lot of friends," Ray said, "but just in case."

On the floor, Charlie was moaning. "OK, time to talk," Ray said as he hoisted the big man into a chair.

Still doubled over, Charlie looked up at him. "Fuck you," he said in a choked grunt that sent a stream of vomit out onto the floor inches from my feet. Ray moved gracefully to the right.

"Shit," Charlie said, choking again. "I can't breathe."

Ray grabbed him by the neck, leaned down, and whispered in his ear. Charlie's eyes grew huge, and his lips drew back in a grimace. "Bad, you fucking asshole!" he screamed and rose into Ray, pushing him back toward the front door. But Ray just stepped aside like a matador dissing a bull, and Charlie stumbled awkwardly toward me, hands reaching out, rage and hate etched across his face. He took two steps, then the third landed square in his puddle of puke. In an instant, the foot flew forward and the rest of him flipped back.

For a long second, Charlie wheeled his arms trying to catch his balance, and then wind milled himself into a wooden barstool next to me. His head met its back with a dull thud, and Charlie slid limply to the ground.

"Yuck," I said, wondering if the rancid liquid all around his head was deep enough to drown in.

Ray was beside me now, his big gun back under his shirt. "Check his pulse," he said, looking at Charlie's motionless body.

I couldn't see any part of Charlie that would have a pulse that I wanted to touch. For a second, I felt sorry for poor old Charlie, lying in his own puke on that raw wood floor in the dirty windows' dim light. Then I brightened up. I was almost sure he was alive, and with Ray standing only a few feet away, that was a small miracle.

"Nope," I said, knowing that what I was looking at – and its stench – had me a split second from losing my own breakfast all over Charlie's back.

"What a mess" Ray said as we heard the police sirens. He turned to me and smiled. "Never thought I'd be happy to hear that," he said. I just smiled back at him as the tires screeched to a stop outside.

The sexy young barmaid never did come back, so Ray and I were forced to get our own beers out of the cooler. But as he pointed out, it saved us the tip.

When the cops finally got to the bar, their guns were drawn and their attitudes agitated. First, they demanded we get on our knees and put our hands above our heads. They seemed surprised by Ray's request to finish his beer, Officer Michaels pointed his gun and told him to "freeze," as he lifted the ice cold Bud to his mouth.

Ray and I both agreed later that it was overkill, even though a bloody Charlie had come to and was expressing that we were guilty of a multitude of crimes.

Against my advice, Ray found it necessary to comment on one of the officer's parentage, something I'm sure was a paramount factor in his need to handcuff both of us. It took till two in the afternoon to get cleared by the police.

Initially, they were more enamored with the thought of Ray and I going to jail than Charlie, but when the deputy chief showed up, calmer heads prevailed, and the cuffs came off Ray and me. Even the deputy chief was reluctant to arrest Charlie on his bond violation, but after Cheri made a call to the U.S. attorney and told him about this guy out on bond carrying a .38 special that could be a murder weapon, the police interest in Charlie increased dramatically.

The last Ray and I saw of Charlie, two uniformed officers were leading him out of the bar, half carrying him and doing their best not to touch him. Poor old Charlie had a bandage the EMTs had put around his head and what they said was a mild concussion. Both they and the officers all thought the injury to Charlie's manhood would recover as well. Watching his slow, stooped walk, I had my doubts.

"You tagged him," I said to Ray as the three of them passed by.

"I feel bad," he said with a small smile. I raised my hand, and Ray gave me a high five. We hadn't had any chance to get answers from Charlie, but as days go, this had been a good one.

"Hey, what did you say to him anyway at the bar when you had him down?" I asked as we walked to the Jeep.

"I just told him to get ready to meet Mitch," Ray said casually, "that Mitch was a *maricón* and so was he." I don't know a lot of Spanish, just enough to get me killed at a bar. But I stopped and laughed in the street at that one.

When we left the hospital, the first stop was back at Piper's to check over the yellow pickup outside. Still no ticket on it, but there was no missing the white paint scratched along the left side, or the deep hole where a headlight used to be. Then I saw the gas can lying in the bed. "Enough," I said. "Let's get out of here."

As Ray drove, I kept seeing the boulder on the scrub brush hillside where Tony Rasser's truck had met the Caribbean sky on its way to the black rocks below. At a Cost-U-Less, Ray came out with a case of Bud that he took over to the boat beach and presented to Carlos. The old fisherman was a happy host, as an impromptu party got under way.

Pulling east out of Christiansted, I speed-dialed Cheri. Ray and I each had a beer at our side, and a three-pound fillet of mahi from one of the fishermen lay in the back of the Jeep wrapped in a plastic bag of ice.

"Hi," I said, then filled her in a little. "We couldn't get a statement but may have a chance later."

"Figures. Nothing before the cops showed?" she asked.

"Nope."

"Where are you?"

"I'll be home in fifteen minutes," I said. "I'll tell you all about it. And can you start the grill? I'm bringing home dinner." I hung up and took a sip of the cool beer. I felt better than I had in months.

Ray was thinking as we drove by the grade school

and the Pickled Greek's. "The real bad guy is still out there," he said.

"I know, but we're moving forward, and it feels good."

"It does" Ray said and lifted his beer in a silent toast.

I clinked my can with his. "Wonder if they got the puke off Charlie yet."

Ray laughed out loud. "Did you see those two prima donnas leading him out of the hospital? You'd think they never saw puke before."

We both laughed, and then Ray got serious. "Mad Dog, Charlie won't talk to us or anyone else."

"The U.S. attorney has him by the balls. He'll talk," I said.

"How long you have been on this rock?"

I thought for a second. "Seven years"

"And you haven't learned a thing. Guys like Charlie don't talk. They're not like your hoods in Denver. Charlie won't say a word. It's the way he is. It's the way they all are."

I thought about what Ray was saying. He was right. Cruzen men like Charlie were their own strange blend of stubbornness, honor, and hate. The reality was that I didn't have to worry about Charlie anymore, but we were no closer to finding Bob Rourk.

"What now?" I asked.

"Dinner," was all Ray said as he took a long draw from his beer and powered the Jeep toward the marina.

CHAPTER

16

The next day, Cheri and I went down to the seaplane port and saw Jean off to Puerto Rico. Betsy went home, too, knowing, I think, that she had lost Bob but keeping a brave face. Ray said he needed to finish some boat work at the marina, and the search for Bob Rourk sadly ground to a halt.

On Tuesday, they had the funeral for Sam and Ann. I was amazed how many people showed up. Cheri cried all day, and it wasn't much easier for me, knowing how much of the fault was mine.

With Charlie in jail, I worked on the boat, spent time with Cheri, played with Dog, and kept glaring at the pieces of the case going round and round in my head. In my gut, I knew I didn't have enough of them to put the puzzle together. Cheri complained about how far away I was, and I knew how much it hurt her that I was only half there. Usually, I'm not prone to depression, but even though Charlie was off the streets, the funeral and the knowledge that I had failed Bob Rourk kept me shrouded by a black cloud.

Ray and I talked. Though we knew the Brachure brothers were just pawns and the real bad guy was still out there, neither of us had any idea what the next move should be. We moped and sulked as it all went stale.

Then, with day after day after day of this just building and driving me crazy, we got a break.

I was sanding the rails of Itchy Feet, getting ready to put a third coat of varnish on them, when John came walking down the dock holding a manila envelope.

"Got a second?" he asked.

"Sure," I said, dusting off and reaching over to shake hands.

"You need to read something," John said, handing me the envelope.

"Come on board," I said, and we walked to the back of the boat where I had a small cooler sitting in the shade.

"Sit," I said, pointing to a folding chair. John plopped down his big body, folded his hands, and just looked at me. I set the envelope down, opened the cooler, and pulled out two diet pops.

We opened them, and I took a long sip, eying John the whole time.

"Read it, Mad Dog," he said, his voice flat and emotionless.

I opened the envelope. There were four sheets of paper inside, the last with a newspaper article clipped to it.

I took them out and started reading. The first paper was a fingerprint report.

"Where…?" I began to ask.

John raised his bear-like paw to stop my question. "Read," he said again.

It was a standard fingerprint report, detailing what was found on the yellow pickup. The police had taken it in an abundance of caution after they took in Charlie, and then got a warrant to check for prints because of the damage on it. There were no surprises. "OK," I said. "Charlie's prints are all over the truck. So what?"

"Last paragraph," John said.

I read it again and realized what it was saying about a second set of prints in the truck and on the gas can in back.

My heart rate picked up, and I turned to another sheet. It was an FBI report, just one short paragraph identifying the second set of prints in the truck as belonging to "Clark Jamison." It was no one I knew, a name I'd never seen before. I looked at John.

He just nodded and took another drink of pop.

The third page was a report from the Atlanta Police Department dated December 8, 1985. It identified the fingerprints of one Clark Jamison as being found on several walls and a laundry list of objects, including a chain saw and various hand tools.

The final page was a one-paragraph missing person

report for a fifteen-year-old boy named Clark Jamison. Paper-clipped to it was a newspaper article from the Atlanta Journal. The article described a brutal crime scene where a local district attorney, Paul Jamison, and his family had been found murdered in their suburban home. The dismembered bodies of Jamison, his wife, and four children, ages seven to thirteen, were scattered through the house. A fifth Jamison child, Clark, was missing.

I read the article again, and a shiver ran down my back.

Finally, John broke the silence. "I tracked down the lead detective," he said. "He's retired and lives in Arkansas now. He remembered the case and told me that he and the other detectives were sure the kid, Clark, did the killings. But he was never found.

"The guy kept a copy of the case file and said he'd try to send it to me sometime this week, said he had to drive to his son's in Atlanta to get it out of an old file. And this isn't all. The kid's prints were found at four murder scenes in Atlanta the year after, and then he just disappeared. Two of the murders were drug-related."

"Cocaine?" I asked, the skin on my back beginning to goose bump.

"I didn't ask," John said.

"Description?" I asked.

"He was a kid. Who knows what he looks like now? Green eyes, brown hair, fair complexion. The guy I talked to said his parents were short, so I guess this Jamison's probably not real tall. No scars, et cetera."

"We need a set of prints from Mr. Samuelson, I'm thinking."

"I thought you said the guy was OK after you talked to him," John replied.

My mind shot back to Denver and a conversation like the one I'd had with Leo Samuelson. For the first time in years, the scar that ran across the base of my ribs itched, and a small ache began deep in my gut. "I've been fooled before," I said, "and the guy you're describing is clearly a sociopath. No one can lie and hide better than a real sociopath."

"Never ran into one, I don't think," John said, looking down at the papers in my hands. "If this is the guy, seems to me you and Ray coming away from Samuelson's compound alive was a stroke of luck."

When John said that, a fragile part of my mind seemed to break. I was back in time. Back in another place. I saw a dozen women. Beautiful women, and the lawyer who in a ten-minute interview had gone off my list of suspects. I thought of that lawyer, not knowing my mind had cleared him, slipping a gun into my side in the elevator of the Denver district courthouse and pulling the trigger. In a sickening flash, I was sitting on that elevator floor again staring up at Harvey Lance. A cruel smile formed across his face as he snarled, "Stupid fuck, see you in hell!"

"You OK?" John said, touching my shoulder. I realized I'd sat down, and felt the cold sweat running off my forehead.

"I don't know," I said, trying to shake off the

feeling of faintness that had come over me. As a cop, I had blundered and walked intentionally into plenty of dangerous situations but sitting down with Leo Samuelson may have been a meeting with true evil.

"Just sit there, I'll get some water," John said, touching my shoulder again and starting around the boat to the galley.

"No," I said, still feeling off balance but recovering. "I'm OK. I was just thinking how bad that trip to see Samuelson could have gone."

"Yeah," John said. "If this Leo Samuelson guy is really Clark Jamison, God only knows how many people he's killed over the years, and you and Ray were up there pulling on his strings like a couple of kids pulling on a pit bull's ears."

"Yeah," I answered, breathing deeply.

"Think we should go to the feds with what we've got?" he said. I could hear the doubt in his voice, and I felt it, too.

"We don't have shit, John."

"Yeah," he agreed.

"This would be a nicely wrapped up little package if we had Samuelson's prints," I said, my mind beginning to spin on how we could get them.

"We can't give the feds enough for a judge to sign a warrant," John answered. "All we really have is a guy flying a plane to God knows where on an evening when Mitch somehow got to Puerto Rico."

I thought about what John said. Our evidence against Leo Samuelson was almost nonexistent. It was a trail of breadcrumbs based on half-baked leads – maybe nothing more than coincidence. I stuck out a finger to start ticking off what we had – or didn't. "Samuelson leaves St. Croix in his plane about the same time Mitch could have left for Puerto Rico, and we can find no other plane flying out of St. Croix without a flight plan that night."

"That's something."

"He has green eyes." Another finger up.

"Same as maybe twenty percent of the population."

"Brown hair." I put a finger up, and then took it back down, smiling at John and shaking my head.

"Lives in a fortress." I put the third finger back up.

"OK, that's a little off," John, said, warming to the idea.

"Bodyguard," I said, but I didn't bother with a finger.

"Not much there," John answered, "but based on what I learned from HIDTA, he's a probable for being mixed up with using the island as a conduit to smuggle drugs. And two of the Atlanta murders were drug-related."

I raised another finger and looked at my hand. "My gut says he's our guy."

"Gut can't be on a search warrant and won't be evidence at a trial."

I nodded. John was right. "My gut also tells me the coin is a key part of this, or why did Mitch go to Puerto Rico in the first place?"

"If Samuelson is involved in the gold, his buddies

in the drug trade are perfect partners to get rid of it," John said.

"Have either of you two Sherlocks asked why they were chasing the coin in the first place."

John and I turned to the voice behind us. Cheri was standing at the rail of the boat in cutoff jeans and her black T-shirt declaring, "THE LIVER IS EVIL AND MUST BE PUNISHED." Her hair was pulled back in a ponytail, and she was holding a quart-size red coffee mug.

"I thought you were sleeping," I said.

"I was," she said, pointing at the companionway to our stateroom. "Until two master sleuths decided to brainstorm right over my head."

"Sorry," I said.

"Yeah," John agreed, raising his hands in surrender.

Cheri made a shooting motion at each of us in turn. "Bang. Bang." John grabbed his heart and sank slightly. I just smiled. She'd shot me with the red cup before.

"Now, you two. It's bad enough I have to listen to you, but now I have to straighten you out, too. Do not fixate on Leo Samuelson. It would be a serious mistake to build evidence to prove his guilt when, we don't have a shred of valid evidence that he's the guy."

John picked up the papers he'd come with and held them toward her. "I think these will prove Samuelson is our guy, but we need his prints."

Cheri sat down and skimmed the four sheets. Then she looked at both of us. "OK, from what I see here, this Clark character is a nut ball that's lived long enough to get his fingerprints in the Brachure brothers' truck and on the can that may have held the gas that was used to catch my boat on fire."

"Right," John answered.

"Kills like a sociopath, has green eyes, brown hair, into drugs maybe, and might be short."

Then she handed the papers back to John. "You two couldn't get a warrant from Judge Roy Bean with that garbage," she smiled.

"No, but it's a start," I told her.

"Agreed," Cheri said. Then she turned to John. "So, let's think about what more we need to get the feds involved and maybe a judge to sign a warrant."

"Prints would be huge."

"You're right," Cheri said. She was about to go on, but then her looked turned more thoughtful. "I hate to change the subject here," she said, "but how's that help Bob Rourk if he's still alive?" She turned to me. "That's the job you were hired for, remember?"

"Maybe in the search we find him," I said.

"Maybe you get Leo Samuelson fired up and he kills him, or one of his minions puts him in the ocean."

"So?" John said.

"Samuelson is a recluse. To get his prints, you'd probably have to break into his home or plane," Cheri said, then took a sip of her coffee.

"OK," I said.

"It may make you feel warm and fuzzy to know Samuelson is Clark what's-his-name."

"Jamison," John said.

Cheri rolled her eyes. "But that evidence you want is just going to get you two in trouble, and even though neither of you are cops so you're not violating Samuelson's rights, his lawyers will have a field day with how you got the prints."

I am a veteran of dozens if not hundreds of shady searches, and I knew Cheri was right. Samuelson had plenty of money to fight in court, and if we messed up, his lawyers would have the tools they needed to raise havoc.

"So, we just sit on our hands," I said, beginning to feel hopeless again.

"No," Cheri said, "you go back to your original instincts."

"OK, that was a while ago. What were my original instincts?"

"Where was Bob Rourk going the morning he disappeared?"

"One of the East End bays, probably Jack's or Isaac's," I said.

"Where did the soldier find his coin?"

"Isaac's Bay," I repeated

"Why would someone kill Tony and maybe Bob?" Cheri's questions continued.

"So, they didn't tell anyone about the coins," John said, a hint of understanding coming to his voice.

"There have to be more coins or clues up at East End that the bad guys want to keep secret," I said.

"Bingo!" Cheri said as a confident smile crossed her face, "and we know that the bad guys are keeping an eye on the bays because they must have seen Bob and Tony Rasser the first day they found a coin."

"If I'm Samuelson…" John said.

"Or the bad guy," I corrected, wanting to keep the field open.

"If I'm the bad guy" John went on, "I've had a week and a half for things to calm down, and it's time to go back to the East End bays now and do whatever it is that I do."

"Can you still get access to those night vision glasses?" I asked John.

"Yup," he answered, a broad smile coming to his square face.

"It's the cleanest way to do it," I said. "Back to doing it the hard way, good old legal police work."

Cheri nodded and looked at me. "If you spot someone at the bay and you follow them, they could take you straight to Bob, or at the very least give you more evidence to take to the feds. Also, you don't stir up a hornet's nest, and if you two are careful, the risk is minimum."

"We sit up on the hill and watch the bays for a couple of nights and see what happens," I said.

John winced. "My ass is already getting sore."

"Take a blowup mattress" Cheri said, smiling at her old partner.

"Thanks."

"OK, what's the game plan?" I asked.

John got up and shifted toward the dock. "I'll go

round up some equipment," he said. "Meet you here about three."

As we watched him go, Cheri asked, "Where's Ray?"

"He's off on one of his wanders, but I'll give him a call. I think his tired old bones would probably love to go play watch the bay."

Ray answered on the second ring. "You, why you bothering me, Dog?"

"Going out to the East End to do some surveillance tonight. You in?"

"What time?" came his reply.

"Meet at the boat at three."

"See you at three."

I snapped my phone closed. "Ray's in," I told Cheri.

She sipped her coffee, and then looked up. "Good, let's go fool around. Looks like we've got the boat to ourselves till three."

At noon, I woke from a dreamless sleep. The stateroom was dark, and I could hear Cheri's gentle breathing. I lay still and savored the warmth and love in our tight little hideaway. Cheri and I had been together for seven years now, and I was still awed by the deep peace she could fill me with. Gently, I reached across and put my hand on her shoulder. She stirred and rolled over to face me.

Softly, she murmured, "Go get ready, Cotton. I love you."

I got out of bed, slipped on my shorts and shirt, and climbed up the companionway. When I opened the door, a beam of light shone down on Cheri, looking up and watching me. With a small wave, she rolled over and went back to sleep.

I went up into the salon and grabbed a diet Coke out of the fridge, then went to the forward compartment where I had all my gear packed.

In the small confines of the forward berth, I packed my black backpack, double-checked my Glock, and slipped it into my belly pack. When I was finished, I went back into the salon. Cheri was sitting on the settee brushing her hair.

"Let's go to lunch," she said as she snapped a rubber band around her ponytail. "I'm starved."

On the drive over to Cheeseburgers and through most of lunch, Cheri was full of small talk. But when we sat back afterward, she began to get serious. "If we're right and the bad guys are doing something out at the East End," she began, "they have to be doing whatever their doing at night."

"And they may keep a lookout," I said.

"Right."

"I think our best bet is to get into the area around five and settle into a high spot where we have cover and can see the whole bay area, but I'm going to concentrate on Jack's and Isaac's. It might take a few nights."

"They may be using boats," Cheri said.

"That makes the most sense, but for now, we just need to figure out what's going on."

"And if you figure out they're using boats?"

"Then we'll have to figure out a way to follow them."

"If you guys get spotted, it could get ugly."

"They won't. We'll be careful, and they want to be ugly, I'll just sic Ray Man on them."

Cheri smiled but then gave me a serious look. "I think you should take the shotgun," she said.

When Cheri had retired, she used her law enforcement contacts to buy a short-barrel, twelve-gauge riot gun for protection on the boat. "Too heavy," I said, but, I hated the shotgun and had never taken the time to become proficient with it. I felt more comfortable with my Glock.

"It would be the best weapon in the bush," she argued.

"No, but thanks," I said closing the discussion.

The waitress, a slim, black woman with a teasing sense of humor, brought over our bill.

"Mad Dog," she said with a big smile. "When you gonna get rid of this woman and start running with me?"

Cheri smiled back at her. "Don't ask for what you don't want, Judy."

They both laughed. When I got finished paying, I turned to Cheri. She was sucking on a straw and looking at me.

"What?" I asked.

"Love ya," she said with a faraway look in her eyes.

"You OK?"

"You know, I miss you," Cheri answered, her hand touching my arm.

"I'm right here," I said, looking into her deep brown eyes.

"No, you're not. You're already up on that hill."

I began to protest but stopped. This was our time, and she was right. I'd been lousy company during the meal -- planning, plotting, and worrying over the coming night. "I'm sorry," I said. "I can't help running everything over in my mind."

"It's OK," Cheri said. "I love you just the way you are, even if you are a space cadet."

I smiled at the term. "Space cadet" was what we used to call some of Cheri's co-workers when they were off in another reality, and now she was calling me a space cadet.

"I miss you sometimes," she said, tightening her grip on my hand. A softness came into her eyes.

"I'll be OK," I said.

"Sure."

"When this is over, we'll run away and take the boat to Virgin Gorda for a month or so. Sound good?"

"Yeah," Cheri said. "Maybe just you and me for a month would be good."

Suddenly, I wanted to walk away from this case as fast as I could. I wanted to get in my truck, drive back to the marina, climb onto Itchy Feet with Cheri, and just motor out to sea. Suddenly, all I could feel was the exhaustion of the last ten days pulling on me. I dropped my head and had to take a couple of deep breaths. I'm sure that when I raised my head, my eyes were moist, but I didn't care. "I've gotta finish this," I said.

"I know," Cheri answered, squeezing my hand hard. "I just need you to know I want you back when you're done."

"A hundred percent," I said.

"I'd take fifty percent if I could really get it."

She stood up and started toward the door. "Let's go. John and Ray will be at the boat at three."

When Cheri and I got back to Itchy Feet, John's ratty old red truck was parked at the head of the walkway to the dock. In the back was a large black backpack. Sitting up on the front seat was a short-barrel, black assault rifle. Cheri tapped the truck's window as we walked by. "See, someone is organized," she said.

"I'm not taking a damn shotgun," I told her, a little too strongly.

Cheri ignored my testy tone and waved to John and Ray, who were perched in our folding chairs on the bow. John had his big, black combat boots propped up on the rail. His bald head was covered with a black cap, and he wore a black T-shirt and black cotton pants. He was clearly in stealth mode. Ray was in his usual garb: black tennis shoes, black pants, and a black T-shirt topped off with his black sunglasses.

"Get those hooves off my rail," Cheri told John as she stepped onto the boat, giving him her stern but playful smile. John smiled back and casually raised his hand. He didn't move his feet, but then, we both knew he wouldn't.

"Look comfy," I said to John.

"Am," he replied.

Ray just smiled.

"I need about ten minutes," I told them as I went down the port companionway.

Inside, Cheri was pulling a plastic bag out of the fridge. "Put this in your backpack. It's water and a few diet Cokes. I'll make you some ham sandwiches while you get ready. I'll make enough for all of you."

"Thanks," I said.

"I'd feel better if you'd take the shotgun," Cheri told me again.

"No," I answered. "I'm fine." I pulled my Glock out of my belly pack and held it up. "Man's best friend."

"What happened to dogs and wives?"

I held up the gun again and corrected myself. "Man's second-best friend."

"Who's first?" Cheri asked, trying to corner my nimble mind.

"I don't want to get into this in front of Dog."

Hearing his name, the blue heeler rolled over and stuck a leg in the air to remind me, "I'm number one."

"Mutt," Cheri grumbled.

Dog rolled back and resumed his imitation of a sleeping dog.

I left the two of them in the salon to iron out their differences, got my backpack, and took it into the master stateroom to get ready. The bottom dresser drawer there was crammed with all my old work clothes. I took a worn pair of black combat boots out of a storage chest and set them next to the bunk, then laid out a black T-shirt, black cargo pants, and a black baseball cap. I pulled out my old flak jacket and looked it over. Modern flak jackets have gotten a lot more protective and lighter as time's gone by. I bought mine twenty years ago, and it must weigh a good thirty pounds. I didn't think long before I stuck it back in the drawer. Then I took out a small black-sheathed knife and a .22-caliber pistol in a nylon holster and set them on the bed next to my clothes and pack.

As I pulled my T-shirt off, my right shoulder gave a sharp complaint, reminding me that I was a chubby, old ex-cop and not the man I used to be. I rubbed the muscle between my arm and neck, and it thanked me by letting the pain subside. I could feel my heart thumping in my chest, and in the half-dark of the closed stateroom, I could sense the anticipation -- and the fear -- growing. This, I knew, could be a long night of pure boredom ahead. But it could also be the end of the hunt.

I had known all along in the back of my mind that at some point, I might have to do a night watch at the East End bays, but I had not looked forward to the discomfort or the danger. Now that the time was upon me, I felt the mixture of hope, anticipation, and worry.

I took off my boat shoes and sat for a second considering the night ahead. I had decided to do a long march into the bays from the ruins at Grapetree Resort so no one would be likely to see us set up our surveillance position on the hill. We would have to pick our way through the desert-like thorn bushes that cover the hills of the island's Far East side. I thought about whether a machete would help but vetoed the idea. The three of us would look weird enough with our black outfits and black backpacks without me carrying a machete, too.

"Better hurry," Cheri called from up above, "or it'll be dark before you get settled in there."

I reached for my cargo pants, pulled them on, then realized I was out of socks.

"Can I borrow a pair of your socks?" I yelled at the closed stateroom door.

"Sure. Get a move on."

I had to smile. She was either pushing or pulling all the time. She just couldn't help it. Sometimes I wanted to say, "Back off. I'm a big boy," but why deny a lady the right to be what she was? I knew I wouldn't have it any other way. We were a team, and if she had to be in charge, that was fine.

I lifted my pants leg and strapped the knife to my right calf, then the pistol to my left. I had carried the two small hidden weapons for most of my career. Once they'd even saved my life and putting them on gave me a feeling of familiar comfort. I could feel the blood flowing to my hands and chest, the old sense of the hunt coming over me. The strong leather smell of the combat boots brought back my hundreds of nights working the dark streets of Denver. A small adrenaline rush quickened my heart. I reached back, grabbed my black T-shirt, and pulled it on. The old cotton still had the faint smell of gunpowder and resin.

When I opened Cheri's dresser drawer, the socks and bright-colored panties were clear in the dull light. As I rifled through the pile till I found a pair of black cotton socks, a faint scent of lavender mixed with the smell of my clothes. Together they were erotic and sensual. For a moment, I considered luring Cheri into the stateroom, but then I remembered Ray and John lounging on the front deck, and her urging that I hurry. I shook my head, not quite believing what I was thinking at that moment. "Mad Dog, what are you doing down there?" Cheri called out.

"Thinking about sex and going through your underwear," was my silent answer. "Be right up" was the one she heard.

Sitting on the bed lacing up my boots felt strange. For seven years on the island, I've lived in shorts, T-shirts, and boat shoes every day and most nights. I imagined how badly the old boots would probably blister my feet trudging the two miles to our hiding spot above the bays.

I hefted the backpack, feeling how light it was, and looked inside. The water, and ammo seemed lonely, and the sandwiches probably wouldn't help much. "What the heck," I said to myself and stuffed in the flak jacket from the bottom drawer. Then I went up on deck.

Cheri and Dog were still sitting across from each other. "You took long enough," she said.

"Got hung up in your dainty drawer looking for those socks," I told her.

"Take them off."

"The socks?" I asked, confused.

"No, the panties," Cheri said with a stern look on her face.

The Gold of St. Croix

"Honest," I said, setting down the heavy pack and raising my hands, "no panties. I left them unmolested."

"You're slipping," she teased.

"Just old age," I answered.

"That fucking John's pacing is going to wear through the deck. Would you please get going before I brain both of them?"

"I'm out of here," I said, moving across the room and kissing her. As I pulled away, Cheri didn't, holding and kissing me longer. Dog grumbled a light half-growl. "Hush," she said as she released me and looked down at him.

"We should be back by eight in the morning," I told her.

"OK," Cheri said. Then her tone changed. "Oh, shit. I about forgot. Take this," she said as she pulled an orange device about the size of a cigarette pack off the galley counter. "It's got new batteries in it."

I looked at what she handed me, but it took a few seconds to identify. "That's the thing you got me for Christmas, right?"

"Yeah," Cheri said. "It's called a Spot locator." She clipped the orange box to the side of my belt. A small light on it was blinking about every five seconds. "OK," I asked her. "What's it doing?"

"I read about it when I bought it for you, and it's cool as hell."

"How so?" I asked.

Cheri turned the laptop on the table so I could see the screen. On it was a satellite photo of the marina.

"Google Earth," I said.

"Yep," she said and pointed at a circle on the marina where the boat sat. "I just set this up after I made the sandwiches. I marked that spot with the Spot locator I just hooked to your pants and it not only identified the location but put it on this map."

I thought about the device on my hip. "GPS tracking," I said with a little wonder in my voice.

"Yep."

"Cool."

"Yep." A proud little smile snuck across her face.

"What do I have to do?" I asked, looking at the blinking device.

"Keep it where the satellite can see it and push one of the buttons, and that's it," Cheri said.

"And?" I asked.

"Whenever you want me to know you're OK, you push this button, and it will send me an e-mail you're OK and show me where you are."

I pulled the little box off my hip and looked at it. "I just push OK. And it tells you where I am and that I'm OK?"

"Yeah. And this is the help button," she said, pointing to one in the lower left corner. "You push that if you want me to help with something, and I'll know you've got a problem, and I'll come find you." The only button left was marked 911. I could make a good guess what that one would do. "That's nine-one-one," Cheri said. "It contacts a nine-eleven operator in the states, and they send the cavalry. And I'm notified, too."

"Let's go already," a voice boomed from the port companionway. There was a hard scowl on John's big face leaning in toward us.

"Want to see something cool?" I asked like a kid with a new toy.

"No, damn it. I want to go. I'm not dancing through the bush at night.

"OK," I said. I kissed Cheri, waved at Dog, and hefted the pack onto my back.

When I got outside, Ray was still sitting feet up on the back deck as John hurried off the boat. "Big Guy is in a hurry," he said as I walked past him.

"Yep," I answered, tapping him on the shoulder to get him moving.

"He needs to chill, could blow a gasket."

"You'll think blow a gasket, Ray Man, if I have to haul my fat ass into the East End in the dark," John said from the dock.

"Be cool, be cool, Big Man," Ray answered as he gracefully vaulted over the rail to land just in front of John. "This'll all work out. No reason to work up a sweat."

John smiled at Ray and then looked expectantly at me. "Well," he said. I looked back at the two guys who were supposed to be my backup. "I'm not jumping over the rail," I told them.

"Good thing," Ray said as he started toward the parking lot. "You try that, and we'd be going to the hospital instead of the East End."

John and Ray set a fast, silent pace to the truck.

John swung in behind the wheel as I put my pack in the bed. "Gonna be a long night," he said.

The low sun was shining bright as John drove out of the marina to the main road heading east. "You want to take the north or south trail?" he asked.

I'd made my decision earlier: the south way from the old Grapetree Bay Resort. But now I wasn't so sure. It was less treacherous but also longer. The north trail is steep and rocky all the way as it winds to a hill overlooking Isaac's, drops to the bay's white sands, and then climbs again to Jack's Bay on the island's southern corner. But it would only take us about half an hour.

I checked my watch and saw that we had less than an hour of daylight left. "Go to the trail by Point Udall," I said, thinking the shorter route would let us set up our little camp before the sun went down. The day was moving to its end much faster than I'd realized.

CHAPTER

17

The three of us drove in silence up the road to Point Udall, each lost in his own thoughts.

Going up the steep incline to the East End of St. Croix, the road deteriorated from blacktop with potholes to potholes with blacktop to miles and miles of dirt. Covering the hilly terrain was the kind of foliage that usually dominates a desert. We passed huge clumps of gnarled cactus and thick fortresses of thorn brush. At the narrow pullover where the trail to the East End bays begins, John stopped and parked.

We climbed out and got the gear from the bed of the truck. As I swung the heavy backpack over my shoulders and buckled the waist belt, I could feel the little knife chafing my calf already. It took only a moment's thought about the walk ahead before I unstrapped it and put it in a pocket.

John fumbled through his pack until he found a small, crinkled, and shapeless short-brimmed canvas hat with a shoelace chinstrap. He put it on and smiled at Ray and me. I fought back the urge to tell the big man how stupid the gray cap looked on his bright red head. To my surprise, Ray had nothing to say either. He just shook his head and started down the hill. When John, in a final insult to any semblance of style, tightened the lace around his neck, I couldn't restrain myself. "Disneyland?" I asked as I walked on after Ray.

John just gave me a wordless, "What?"

I stopped and pointed to the rag-like blob. "Get that at Disneyland?"

"Bush cap," he answered with a smile.

I looked again at its perch atop his big bald head. "One size fits all, I take it."

"Yep," John said, signaling an end to the conversation by hefting his pack onto his back and starting down the steep, rocky trail. I followed, watching out for the loose rocks littering the long hill to the beach. The bright ball of the sun dipped over the western hills. "Better hurry," I said.

John only grunted. Ray seemed not to hear. We picked our way down carefully to the bottom where East End Beach stretches south for two hundred yards. As we walked out on the deep sand, I checked for footprints. There were only our own. The beach was deserted, and no one had been there since the last high tide. The only sign of life was the trail of a small sea turtle dragging itself down to the crystal water. The Atlantic waves rolled noisily toward us. We walked in silence through the deep sand toward the rocky trail at the far end of the beach. Ray led and John and I followed, each of us sunken into our own thoughts.

Midway down the beach, John stopped to wipe the sweat off his face with the canvas hat. Holding it, he looked at the western sky. "Timed this perfect," he said.

"Yeah," I agreed. "I just want to get to the top of the hill and settled in before it gets too dark."

John replaced the hat, tightened the cute little string, and began trudging again after Ray. I shook my head and decided it was a victim of John's clothes-washing skills.

The next time John stopped, Ray was waiting. Above us, the trail rose quickly for two hundred feet, all loose stone, steep black rock, and sharp, broken ledges. "This could be a bitch at night," John mused, imagining the need to hurry down it in the darkness. I realized that the soldier in him was already forming an exit plan from our little surveillance post.

"Yeah," Ray said, "but bad for everyone, the ones running and the ones chasing them."

"We have flashlights," I said reassuringly. "We should be OK."

Both men turned to me and smiled. "Use lights a lot when people with guns are after you?" Ray asked.

"I see your point," I said. I realized that going up the rocky trail to where we could have a full view of Isaac's

287

Bay also was putting ourselves in a position where retreat would be difficult if not downright dangerous. What worried me was that Ray and John had sensed this problem almost instinctively, and I hadn't seen it till they pointed it out.

"We got no choice," John said as he started up the hill.

I gave the rocky trail a long look, and then followed him, hoping I wouldn't have to come down it until daylight.

We moved single file, mostly walking but at two of the larger rocks, hand-over-hand was the only way. At the top, John was standing on a flat, bare patch of ground gazing down at Isaac's Bay. Ray was sitting on a big rock overlooking the beach. To the east and north, huge white puffs rose thousands of feet. The rolling water below was beautiful in the late light of day, shimmering as small waves created a multi-faceted latticework of blue, green, and white. Around the bay, the surf looked like lace breaking over the shallow reef, and behind it, the sea stretched forever. "Damn, I love this place," John whispered.

A lone frigate bird soared toward land and swooped a hundred feet over our heads. It brought my thoughts back to the hilltop, and why we were there. "Let's get set up," I said. "I think we'll watch Isaac's tonight since Bob was heading here, and if we don't see anything, we can move and set up between Isaac's and Jack's tomorrow night."

I looked up the hill to the east of the path separating

the two bays. From a grassy area about twenty yards off the trail, all but the most northern part of Isaac's Bay would be in sight. "There," I said, "under that small grape tree."

Ray glanced at the tree, and then stared into the growing darkness on both sides of it. "You two stay there," he said. "I'm gonna take a tour of the bush behind us. At least one of us should be somewhere else. All together ain't the safe way to go."

"Mad Dog and I'll set up under the grape tree," John said, "and you've got our back. We can switch off during the night, so we all get watch and some sleep."

Then Ray was gone, silently disappearing into the bush. The spot John and I set up at was ideal. We could see anyone who came up the hill, and they wouldn't notice us in the dark. The grassy area was above the steep rock trails on both the East End Bay and the Isaac's Bay side, so we'd hear anyone struggling up the rocky trail long before they reached our lookout. And with Ray in the bush behind us, I couldn't see any way someone could ambush us.

"Looks good," I said to John.

"Good cover, and that little bit of grass'll be a lot softer than the rock."

John dropped his pack on the deep green patch that would be our home for the night, and then covered it with a large canvas tarp he took off the pack and unrolled.

I set down my own pack and looked over the position. The bay was fifty feet below. We could see anyone coming to it by foot or boat. "This is perfect," I said. I took out my flak jacket and put it close to the south side of the tarp to use it as a pillow while I watched the bay.

I laid my Glock between the folds of the jacket, and strapped the knife back on my calf. John watched me work. He looked at the flak jacket. "You carried that all the way up here?"

"Last-minute decision," I said, as if that explained it, then I pushed the heavy jacket with my foot.

"You're nuts."

Another affectionate kick.

John plopped down on the tarp and sat Indian-style looking out over the unobstructed view. "This tree'll give us good cover, too," he said. The big-leafed tree between the bay and us stood only about six feet high but was probably twenty feet wide. We could easily see between the leaves but there were enough of them to cover our position.

I nodded in agreement and began emptying my pack. I put the four clips of spare ammo in the stretch pockets of my jacket and laid out the plastic bag with sandwiches and pop on the tarp between us.

"These might come in handy," John said, taking out a pair of night-vision goggles. "Got them from a friend at DEA."

"Cool," I told him as I pulled out a pair of binoculars and a spotting scope I kept on the boat. I set the scope on its short tripod in front of the flak jacket, and John leaned against the jacket and looked through it. "Nice," he said as he adjusted its focus.

Behind us, Ray appeared out of the bush. "You two getting cozy?" he asked as he set his small pack next to ours.

"Night vision, nice," Ray noted, running a finger over the metal casing.

"You want it up in the bush?" John asked.

"Nah, Big Man. Plenty of moon tonight. I'll be fine."

After playing with my scope a while, John grunted and went back to pulling things out of his pack, most of them food or soft drinks. Finally, he took out the short-barrel black assault rifle and laid it against a fork in the tree. It was something John had bought just before he retired. I remembered when he and Cheri had shown up at the boat beaming at their new purchases. Cheri had gotten the short-barrel riot gun, and John had his ugly little Bushmaster M17. They'd unwrapped their prizes like kids at Christmas, and then talked guns all through a night of beer and pizza. Me, I'm not a big gun guy. The only ones I owned I had with me. John, and Cheri, had a love for the fancy tools.

He took out four clips and laid them next to the rifle. "Nice," Ray said with admiration.

"Enough ammo?" I asked, trying to imagine what kind of raging battle would take that much.

"Boy Scout at heart," John said, pulling a foot-long survival knife out of his pack.

"You'd be better off with Band-Aids," I told him, eying the wicked-looking knife.

"Yep," John agreed, and then pulled out a six-inch-square first aid kit.

"Want a quick lesson on the Bushmaster?" John asked Ray and me.

"Nope," I said, knowing I'd never use it as long as a handgun was available.

"Pretty simple," he said.

"Nope."

Ray put out his hands and took the gun from John. In a matter of seconds, he had it apart and was examining the inner workings. Just as quick, he reassembled it and returned it to John. "Good," he said. "Cleaned, oiled, and ready to kill. I like a man that takes care of his shit."

"Thanks," John said, continuing to pull food out of his pack. "We're only here for the night," I told him as the potato chips and candy bars piled up on the canvas.

Then, over John's shoulder, I saw movement on the far side of the bay. I touched him on the shoulder. "Look," I said as I lay down in front of the spotting scope.

The light was fading, but the scope gave a clear view of the figure climbing out of the surf and moving quickly up the beach away from us. Even without it, though, I could tell the figure was PADI. My nimble little friend had a net catch bag in one hand and a spear with a large fish in the other. With the grace and agility of a cat, he moved across the Isaac's Bay beach and up the steep rock trail on the far side that led to Jack's Bay.

"Headed for his cave," I said, watching him top the hill and disappear.

"Or his penthouse," John said. "That guy is full of secrets."

"I wish he'd have come this way," Ray said. "That looked like a big enough fish for us and him."

"Yeah, I could use a little fresh fish, and maybe a nice roasted lobster," John said with something close to lust in his voice.

I smiled to myself. Some people only think about sex or money. John's every thought was centered on food.

"Yep, a little grilled snapper would have been good," I agreed.

"Oh, well, got Cheetos," John said as he pulled a large orange bag out of his pack.

"Cool," Ray said, pulling a silver flask out of his own small backpack. "Brandy, keeps you warm." He took a small sip and handed it to John, who took a quick sip and pointed the flask at me, but I raised my hand and shook my head.

Ray and John grinned. "Cool, more for us," Ray said.

I pulled out the plastic bag of ham sandwiches Cheri had made for what she called our little camping trip. The food reminded me of her, and that reminded me of the Spot locator. I pulled the orange box off my belt and pushed the on/off button. A small, blinking red light appeared. I pushed the OK button, and two lights began to blink. I put the device on the tarp and let it blink away. When I turned back around, I noticed that John had quit digging in his pack. He and Ray were both staring at the locator. I picked it up and offered it to them.

"Just don't punch any buttons," I warned, not sure what would happen. John took out a small set of reading glasses and examined the little box in the dim light. He turned it upside down, like that would reveal some unseen mystery. Then he lifted it to the light, and even took off his glasses and held them to the back of the device. "Can I take it apart?" he asked with child-like innocence.

"No!" I said, knowing from experience that he probably couldn't put it back together.

"What's it doing?" Ray asked, reaching over and taking it from John.

"Right now," I said, "it's telling Cheri where we are and that we're OK."

"Why not just call?" John asked.

"No go here," I told him. "We're nowhere as far as Verizon is concerned. We're on our own."

Ray didn't seem to mind that. "I like your toy, man," he said. "How's it work? What happens if you push help?"

"Cheri knows something has happened and we need help."

"And if you push nine-one-one?"

"The cavalry comes."

"Cool."

I checked the time. It was seven forty-five. "I'm gonna send an OK message to Cheri every hour or so.

At quarter to nine, I'll send another. Mind doing the same on your watch?"

"Sure," John said like a kid allowed to play with a new toy.

"Fucking high tech, man," Ray said. "I thought my little GPS locator was cool, but that thing I gotta own," Ray said.

Then he got up and grabbed his pack. "I just came down to let you guy know I'll be up in the bush," he said, pointing to a spot about fifty feet up the trail. "Found a nice little hidey hole, and I got your back." Then he headed off into the thickets.

The gulls shrieked flying inland for the evening as John and I arranged our gear and settled in. The last hint of light was gone when John whispered, "If they come, they have to come by boat."

"Yeah," I said, remembering that Cheri and I had thought about that, too. "These trails are way too dangerous to come in and out at night, and even if they do come by land, between Ray's position and ours, we'll know it."

"You know that fucker is not what he seems," John said.

"What fucker?"

"Ray," John answered, lying down on the tarp and looking toward the beach. "He's serious ex-military, Cotton. He moves like a fucking ghost out here in this thick bush, and the fucking Bushmaster is my gun and I can't field strip it half that fast."

"We all have our secrets, buddy," I said, knowing

that one of the foundations of my friendship with Ray was not asking too many questions.

I settled down on my belly, looking at the long, white line of foam where the Atlantic swells crashed into the shallow reef "I'll take first watch," I told John, "and I'll wake you about midnight, OK?"

In reply, he put his hands behind his head and stretched his full frame across the tarp, then shifted side to side like a cat settling into a pillow and pulled his ugly little hat over his face. Through the canvas, he said, "If our Mr. Samuelson really is Clark Jamison, he is one seriously dangerous man."

I looked out over the bush and thought about what John had said. The darkness made all the undergrowth and the bays below just a mass of black. In my mind, I saw a fifteen-year-old boy so deranged he could kill and mutilate his entire family. In that moment, there was no doubt that if Clark Jamison and I came face to face here, one of us would die. The thought made my stomach tighten, and the quiet darkness seem ominous as a chill ran through me.

"I know, buddy," I said, "Get some sleep. Ray and I got your back." John turned away and curled into a semi-fetal position. I wondered if he would sleep. I knew that no matter how tired I might be, sleep wouldn't find me that night.

I watched the sea rise and fall in the moonlight. John's slumber sounded deep and complete. Ray had been right. The moon was nearly full, and the long, white beach and shimmering ocean were clear. At midnight, I didn't wake John. I knew I wouldn't sleep and just kept my silent vigil. I wondered what Ray was doing. I didn't think he was sleeping either. My back felt covered.

I suspect that everyone has some pet paranoia. That night when my mind should have been fixed on bad guys and serial killers, I was spending most of my waking thoughts on millipedes. Lying there on the open ground in the dark surrounded by the bush, my skin quivered with the unreasonable fear that any second, one of the multi-legged stinging insects would appear and attack me. Grown men should be past such fears, and I knew there were more dangerous beasts around, but that night sitting listening to the silence and looking out into the darkness, my heart and soul were centered on millipedes.

At twelve forty-five, I turned on the Spot locator again and hit the OK button. The red lights seemed reassuring, making me feel closer to Cheri. I shut it to keep saving the battery and rolled over on my back. The clouds had cleared, and the stars were bright and perfect. I realized suddenly that though I'd felt wide-awake not long ago, now my eyes were heavy. I gave John a little nudge. He groaned a deep growl. I nudged harder, and he woke with a start.

"What!"

"You're up to bat, big guy." I took off the Spot locator and handed it to him. He took it groggily and moved to my place on the flak jacket.

"Heard from Ray?" he asked.

297

"Nope."

"I need to push this at one forty-five?"

"Yep." And then, to my surprise, I fell into a deep sleep.

Mad Dog," John said, "rise and shine. If we're gonna get going at sunrise, we need to start packing." I was deep in a sweat-soaked sleep when I felt him nudge me. I lifted my head groggily and looked around. A tiny glow was edging the eastern horizon.

"Man, I passed out," I said, sitting up and trying to clear my head.

John was sitting cross-legged facing the coming light. Empty candy bar wrappers and potato chip bags surrounded him.

"Leave any for me?" I asked.

Without comment, he tossed over a bag of potato chips.

"What time is it?"

John looked at this watch. "Five twenty. It should be bright enough to hike out in about ten minutes."

"Hear from Ray?" I asked.

"Not a peep."

I looked at the sky. Since I'd gone to sleep, a full moon had risen, sparkling over the still-black Atlantic. The sea birds were beginning to move, and the air was full of their calls as they grouped together for the flight out to sea. The morning was fresh, and the view from our little hideout felt alive as the sun inched into the new day.

I thought about telling John I wanted to wait to see

the sunrise, but I knew he was ready to go. It would be just as spectacular, I figured, if we saw it from the beach below.

John was hurriedly packing the wealth of empty wrappers and other garbage in his pack when I heard a rustle of bushes below me. I looked up, expecting Ray. The lone figure twenty feet away was just silhouette, but even in the dim light, I knew who it was -- it wasn't Ray.

PADI stood stark still, his waist-length hair and beard bulking out his slender body. Even in the dead light of the morning, his eyes, smile, and light swim trunks were clear in the shadows.

Before I could move or speak, PADI's right hand lifted, and I saw a brief flicker of light. In the split second it took to know what I was seeing; my world went crazy. My mind barked "Gun!" as I dove to the left, away from PADI and toward John, who was kneeling on the tarp happily filling his backpack.

As my body hit him, a loud explosion erupted from where PADI had been standing, and the roar of a Magnum came from the hill where Ray was.

There was no mistaking the thud as a bullet hit just below me. John screamed in pain. Before I could get off him, I heard a second shot from PADI's direction, and the grape tree limb just over my head burst in a shower of bark and fragments.

In the half-light of dawn, I looked toward PADI and saw what Ray's gun had done. His left arm hung loose, and the hand was leaking blood as he ran toward John and me. In his other hand, he held a black pistol, but he was shooting up the hill, not at us, firing two quick shot at where Ray was hidden.

To my amazement, PADI leaped gracefully to the right, seeking cover from Ray's higher position just as another round from the Magnum tore into the bush where he'd been. Then, moving back left, PADI lowered has gun and fired twice more toward John and me.

I pushed off John toward my gear on the other side of him, landing on the flak jacket. I could hear PADI crashing through the bush the last twenty feet toward us. Helpless, I whipped up the jacket in front of us as a shield against what I knew was coming. Another shot burst out, and a dull thud told me John was hit again. I could feel the impact as the slug pounding home while I tried to block the next shot with the flak jacket. The Glock fell out of its folds, but I couldn't get to it. I couldn't even look. I just knew I had to keep the jacket between PADI and us, though I couldn't even see where he was. John's body was moving, though, trying in powerful crablike motions to get to the tree where the Bushman was leaning.

Another shot came from close in front and to the left, tearing the vest from my hands as it hit. Somewhere, PADI was struggling through the virgin bush. It was both friend and enemy, keeping him from getting closer but hiding him from Ray's sights.

In a surge of adrenalin, I pushed away from John and dove for the Glock. As I hit the ground behind his scrambling mass, I looked up and saw PADI, his face clear in the growing light. There was no madness, no hatred, just a calm smile. The blood still dripped from his arm. He was standing at the edge of the tarp.

With a satisfied look on his face, he carefully aimed his black pistol at my head. I tried to duck behind the vest while I fumbled to get control of my gun, knowing I was dead.

Then Ray's big gun roared a third time from the hill above us. Instead of a shot from PADI, I heard the thud of its round hit the tree next to him. PADI's head jerked toward Ray. As it did, John rolled toward him, and just as PADI turned back to face us, John's huge black combat boot shot out in a vicious kick slamming into his gut.

PADI flew back, bent in half with shock and amazement. Another tree splintered as Ray's gun roared again. I knew in that moment that if not for John's kick; the splinters would be PADI's flesh and bone.

As John kept crawling to his rifle, my hands found the Glock. I stumbled to my feet, holding it in both hands, and fired at the little man ten feet away. To my amazement, he tucked and rolled instantly, and the shot ripped a path through the brush inches to his right.

Never leaving his crouch, PADI lurched toward the path and crashed into the heavy brush. Before I could aim and shoot again, he was swallowed from sight. John was firing now from his knees, unleashing a semi-automatic torrent into the green wall. My target was the sounds of a body racing through the thick cover as I fired my Glock again and again.

From somewhere in the brush, I heard a loud

"Fuck," then silence. John was bent in half, holding his calf with his right hand and leaning on the Bushmaster.

"Where else are you hit?" I asked, unable to see his wounds in the shadow his body cast.

"Little fucker shot me." John spit out the words through gritted teeth as he straightened to his knees and fired again into the bush where PADI had disappeared. I put my hand on the barrel of his gun. "John, stop. He's gone."

"Fuck, I know. Just had to see if I could get lucky." He sank down against the grape tree.

"John," I said, grabbing his shoulder and asking again. "Where are you hit?" My mind was whirling. I was sure he was hit at least twice.

"Calf," he said, barely above a whisper. His bloody left hand pointed to the wound. In the dull dawn light, all I could see was a dark stain, but I knew it was blood.

I heard a gun roar again from where Ray was holding his position on the high ground. I looked up and saw PADI, who I knew now was Clark Jamison, weaving among patches of cover and running for the path to Isaac's Bay about a hundred yards down the hill. Ray fired again. His gun had to be out now. Then I heard the sharp pops of his Glock, but I knew his target was beyond its range.

I pulled the knife from my right calf and gently slit John's pants up the leg to above the knee, then cut around it to get his lower leg clear. "Where else are you hit?" I asked.

John looked up in confusion, and then realized what

I meant. A faint smile crossed his eyes as he pushed his backpack to where I could see it. A neat hole was almost dead center in the black fabric. Around the hole, the pack was wet. I hesitantly touched it with my finger and smelled it. Nothing. I tasted it and knew immediately. "Lemonade," I said flatly.

John's pain turned to anger. "He shot my thermos!"

I almost laughed out loud, but a crash of brush stopped me as Ray emerged with a gun in each hand.

Far away, we heard a loud voice. "Cotton, you fucker. Cheri's dead. You hear me, you fucker, dead." I looked down to Isaac's Beach at least two hundred yards away. PADI was standing in full view, facing up toward us. But it wasn't PADI. There is no PADI, my mind insisted. I watched Clark Jamison turn and run toward the path to Jack's Beach.

"Seriously fucking crazy," John murmured as he held his hand over his calf.

Ray nodded. "A first-class sociopath."

I turned back to John and took out my mag light. The three of us gazed at the wound in the meat of his right calf. I wrapped the pants leg I'd cut off around it, then a couple of strips of duct tape I got from John's pack. Somewhere, I remembered, he had a first aid kit in there, too, but nothing looked like I needed it.

"Bummer," he said.

"No bone," I told him. Then I remembered the exchange of shots between Ray and …who was that madman? He wasn't the PADI I'd known so many years, yet that was the only way I could think of him.

"You OK, Ray?" I asked.

"Yeah, just pissed. Give me that fucking rifle and a clip. Time to end this."

"Yeah," John said, pulling his leg away from me, picking up the Bushmaster, and twisting so he could see the little figure, now three hundred yards down the beach and still running. "But you're not ending this, Ray Man. I am."

John winced in pain as he tried to pivot around into a prone shooting position.

"No," Ray said, stopping John's tortured movement. "He's mine," and he gently lifted the rifle from John's hands.

Ray took the Bushmaster and walked to the edge of the hill, standing erect as he aimed. Before he could fire, we watched in astonishment as PADI turned and shot twice in our direction. Instinctively, John and I ducked at the sound, but Ray stood unmoving, the rifle still trained on the beach.

"Too far, you crazy fuck," I said as the little hermit started running down the beach again.

"Yeah," Ray muttered, "that pea shooter can't hit shit, but this can." Three quick shots jumped from his gun.

The sand in front of PADI exploded in a rain of sand. He stopped and turned, looking toward the rocky outcropping Ray was shooting from.

The full red sun was over the horizon now. I reached for my pack and pulled out the binoculars. Ray fired three shots again. Even that far away, I could see clear as the sand to PADI's left leaped up. The little killer seemed unconcerned. He just stood there instead of running again, looked at the spot in the sand where the bullets had hit, then reached down as if he were brushing sand off his leg.

"Slow and easy, soldier. Slow and easy," John said in a low voice behind me.

In a swirl of his graying brown hair, PADI stood erect and shoved his bleeding left fist to the sky. I didn't have to see it to know a middle finger was shoved higher. Ray fired a third three-shot volley.

From the beach three hundred fifty yards away came what seemed like a faint yelp of pain. PADI spun to his right. The bloody hand grabbed his ear. The sun was on him now. The blood was unmistakable as it coursed down the left side of his beard.

"Yes!" I yelled.

"Now finish it," John said, his voice flat. "Slow and easy, Ray Man."

The assault rifle barked three quick shots again. One hit the sand in front of PADI, but the others staggered him back. He stood unmoving, left hand still clutching his ear. I knew he was hit dead center and waited for him to drop. Instead, his right hand raised the pistol and fired quick, not stopping until it was empty.

Ray just watched. PADI looked down at the gun like it was a bad child, then shook it violently and threw it angrily toward the sea.

"Fuck this," Ray said and fired another series of three fast rounds. PADI turned and began running in a zigzag down the beach, his mat of hair waving with every quick turn.

Again, Ray sent a volley at his target. PADI pitched forward and fell, then lay motionless.

Ray pulled the rifle from his shoulder and stared at the still form. I lowered the glasses from my face and turned toward him. Suddenly, he growled, "No! Fuck you."

I looked back down the beach as the body rose and first staggered, then hobbled, moving farther away with surprising speed.

Ray lifted the rifle and fired again, not stopping till the Bushmaster was dry.

"Wow," I said as the little figure made it to the end of the beach and started up the long hill to Jack's Bay.

"Tough little guy," John said, admiration in his voice.

"Way tough," Ray said. "Crazy tough."

"No brain, no pain," I agreed.

Ray lowered the rifle again and just looked at the hill where PADI had disappeared. "I guess I'm out of practice," he said.

John shrugged and pulled his cell phone out of his cargo pants. He opened it and punched buttons. Then he stared at it blankly and turned to me. "Fucking Verizon."

"Big surprise," I said.

Ray still stood at the edge of the hill. "You OK?" I called out to him.

"Except for my pride."

"He ain't going far," John said. "A man doesn't take a solid hit like that and go far."

I pulled the Spot locator off my belt and pushed the on/off button. The light blinked red. I pushed the nine-one-one button, and two lights blinked.

John looked from the lights up into my eyes. "You're not carrying me home, are you?" He knew the cavalry was on its way. Help would be here. They'd get us out and finish the job.

I didn't answer. I could only think of what PADI had said about Cheri. Retreating, regrouping, reinforcements – it might be John's way, but it wasn't going to be mine.

"Ray'll take care of you," I told him. "He'll take you up the trail. I'm not finished."

I looked at Ray, and he nodded. He'd left the edge of the hill and was just staring at the bare patch of ground where we'd spent the night. "How did that fuck get by us?" he asked, shaking his head.

"He just knows this bush." I bent down and checked the makeshift bandage on John's leg. The bleeding had slowed. "Only one of us can go," I said as I straightened up.

"That's crap," John said. "None of us should go. Let the police get him."

To my total astonishment, Ray walked over to John, leaned over to take hold of his arm, and helped him to his feet. Then he effortlessly hefted the big man up over his shoulder in a perfect fireman's carry.

"I'll get him home," Ray said. "You go kill the little fucker."

I hooked the Spot locator to Ray's belt. "Thanks" was all I could think to say.

"You leaving all this stuff here?" John asked, looking around the camp.

"I'm carrying you," Ray answered. "That's enough."

John just shook his upside down head as Ray turned and started walking.

For a second, I stood and looked south toward Jack's Bay. I pushed the catch, and the partial clip fell from my Glock to the sand. I pulled a fresh clip out of my pants and slapped it into the pistol with a loud click.

Then I walked over to the flak jacket and slowly put it on. I fastened each of the four Velcro straps and, without looking back, started down the rocky trail. As I walked, I could hear Ray moving steadily the other way.

I'd only gone fifty paces or so when I saw a bright red drop of blood. "Yes!" I thought, knowing there'd be more and more. The Glock felt light and warm in my hand. "Should have never threatened Cheri, you little fucker," I said. I knew my prey couldn't hear me, but he'd know I was coming after him.

I walked steadily across the beach PADI had run across only minutes before. My eyes stayed fixed on the sand, on the small bare footprints, on the blood.

At the base of the hill at the south end of Isaac's Beach, I could feel the sweat running down my back. The sun was climbing now, and the flak jacket squeezed and baked me. The view to the east was blinding. As

I started up the steep trail on the hill to Jack's Bay, I wondered if the murderer was waiting at the top. In a way, I hoped so. I was tired. I wanted this over. I wanted to put PADI away, put Clark Jamison away, and go home to Cheri.

A long time ago, I realized I was a bad man. A long time ago, I realized I could kill and not care. If the man I killed needed killing, he wasn't a man, just an object. I watched other officers get angry or go into depression after shooting someone. I didn't feel anything. I guess we all have black holes in us. Cheri and John always wondered why Ray and I were friends, but as I slowly walked up that hill, I knew. Ray could hate at a level they couldn't comprehend. But I could understand it. I knew what it was to care nothing about a life. All Clark Jamison meant to me was a thing I had to hunt down and kill before I could go home. My little friend, the crazy hermit PADI, was gone, as though all the days we shared never existed. I knew Clark Jamison could stand up from behind a bush and kill me at any second and drown every person who loved or cared about me in a flood of grief. I didn't care. Today, one of us would die, but there was no emotion in the retching hole I felt inside. I didn't care.

At the top of the hill overlooking Jack's Bay, there was no gunshot, no attack. I surveyed the landscape for movement or some other sign of my prey. There still was nothing but footprints and the occasional drops of blood. In the distance, I heard sirens. "Good," I thought.

But I didn't look back. I lowered my head and started down the bush-covered trail to Jack's Bay.

To get to the beach, you follow the trail through a deep cut in the native rock. At the top, I had to put the Glock in my pants and use both hands to go farther. I turned my back to the beach and began slowly climbing down. At a deep drop-off, my handhold was a pool of wet gore. I didn't need to smell the copper or even see the red to know. My prey was bleeding badly. He must have stopped here to rest. I wiped my hand on a clump of grass and continued climbing down.

To my surprise, the small tracks crossed the full distance of Jack's Beach and went up a long steep trail to the top of the next hill. Halfway up, I had to stop. My shirt was soaked. The sun roasting me in my flak jacket was almost more than I could stand. I sat a long time on a chair-like rock formation. I sat long after my breathing had calmed, and the ocean breeze had cooled my body. Again, I heard sirens in the distance. "No," my mind yelled to the sirens. "He's mine." I stood and trudged forward.

At the top of the hill, a line of boulders and a black wrought iron fence blocked the path. A huge pink house loomed above me. I knew this place. It was the north entrance to the Bays. PADI had led me to the outskirts of a residential area. I hurried my steps, praying no joggers or early morning hikers would stray into the madman's path.

I went around the fence and was on a paved road. The light was just beginning to bathe the western side of the hills. Dogs in yards and houses joined in a cacophony, maybe at me, maybe PADI, maybe just the sun. I passed a thick, wet smear on the pavement. PADI was down this road, and I didn't care where it took me.

The first time I felt the rage, I was nine. A sixth grader named Salvatore Rico had beat up my little sister. Sal was big and mean, one of those sad kids that only understood violence and hate. Cheri would have felt sorry for him. As I had walked down our neighborhood streets looking for him, all I felt was the rage. It took me four long hours to find him outside a Stop and Shop at the corner of Poplar and CY Streets. He was sitting on his bike like a little king talking to a couple of buddies, older kids I knew from school. I remember the three of them looking up and sneering as I walked toward them. I didn't change my pace. I zeroed in on Sal Rico. He said something but I don't know what. In a single motion, I kicked out the flat of my foot and smashed it against his knee. I kicked again and again as it stayed trapped against the bike. I remember the sound of snapping before Sal fell to the ground. I grabbed his long, black, greasy hair and began pounding his head on the cement.

I remember being held by Sal's two buddies and the store manager while the police and ambulance came. My father got me, and we had a long talk. He and my mother were not happy. I went to a ranch owned by a friend of my dad's to spend the summer working. That summer, Lee Coffman, the owner of the ranch, dubbed me Mad Dog, and the name stuck. I never let it go. I became Mad Dog.

The trail of dark stains continued past million-dollar homes and tall fences. After about a half-mile, I knew where we were going, and I quit looking for blood.

In 1989, the Grapetree Resort was a multimillion-dollar miracle, a monument to the tourist Mecca it foresaw for the new St. Croix. The high-end bungalows and exclusive resort existed only to pamper their guests. That all changed on September 17, when a Hurricane called Hugo spun over the island with sustained winds of two hundred miles an hour. Two days later, St. Croix was a broken remnant and the Grapetree Resort a hollow shell.

For twenty years, the gutted cement ruin was only a mecca to looters and salvagers. As I walked across the rubble-strewn cement to what was once the entrance to a grand resort, I saw a single drop of bright red blood.

Stepping over the fallen beams and twisted metal, I thought back those twenty years. Cheri and PADI had worked here together. I wondered how close she had come to being one of his victims. I wondered if Sue Horn – Cheri's friend, PADI's lover – had vanished not in a hurricane but as a result of a psychopath's madness. How many people had fallen prey to him in the twenty years since then? My stomach turned, and I had to stop for a second.

In the middle of the parking lot, I came to a big, broken piece of concrete. I stepped over it and sat down, staring at the two stories of dark caverns in front of me. Somewhere in there, my hunt would end.

I could almost hear the lives that once moved and breathed in the old building. Huge cement pots sat on each side of the gaping entrance. Wild thorn weeds overran them and most of the building's walls. A white plastic shopping bag blew lazily into the entrance. It winked and fluttered in the shadows like a ghost ready for the carnage, ready for me to enter. Then a current blew it high and it was gone.

No bird called. The surf was silent. Only the sun seemed alive as its heat pressed in and I cringed from the glare. The rest of the world had stopped. I could feel the ruin sucking its energy into the dank, dead, evil shadows.

Every ounce of common sense told me to wait for backup. But a deeper voice said, "Go." I was calm, empty. I rose and walked toward the entrance, my right arm hanging loose, the Glock a part of it, my mind focused only on my prey.

The entrance was a concrete arch twelve feet high. I walked through it slowly and deliberately into the dark building. My head was down, my eyes scanning the broken half-light of the old reception area.

On the dust-covered floor, a story emerged. Small bare feet moving in a crab-like gait, the right one clear and distinct, the left dragging and leaving a thin, dark trail. I didn't hesitate. I followed it up the stairs. I could envision the man ahead of me hopping, one step at a time, clutching the broken metal rail.

He was a wounded animal, as dangerous as a man could get. My mind was locked on him. My heart was cold. I felt nothing else.

Halfway up the long, wide staircase, a smear of dust and blood told me he had sat. The gore was wet and fresh. I turned and looked out the entrance. I saw the broken concrete I'd rested on in the parking lot. He had sat there, on that step in the shadows, and watched me outside. He knew I was coming. I walked slowly, purposely, up the stairs and sensed that the time had come.

From the top of the stairs, the tracks in the heavy dust went down a long cement balcony. The black rusted rail was twisted, and in some places, it was gone. A hundred feet away, the balcony itself had collapsed.

Between the end of the cement and where I stood were four room doors. He was in one of those rooms, and today one or both of us would die there. I tightened the flak jacket and wiped my sweaty hands on my pants. In a crouch I moved forward.

The trail of footprints passed the first room. All the doors had been removed and salvaged or stolen years ago. Inside, the room was light and dark, black and gray, pattern less and crazy, like PADI.

I looked past the next naked jamb. Once, the room was opulent. Light came in thirty feet away through a gaping hole where the front windows had been. Through it, I could see waves crashing against a bulkhead. A pelican sat undisturbed on its cement.

These had been apartments, I knew bedrooms,

baths, kitchen, living area. Looters had ravaged the sheetrock, torn out appliances, ripped ragged holes to get the plumbing and wire. Streaks of light shone through the walls now, and broken fragments of blue and white tile littered the floor. There were a hundred places my wounded prey could hide. I followed his trail down the balcony.

At the third room I stopped. PADI was in there. His trail ended at the inky darkness. I looked up above it. The numbers were gone but still were clear in the unpainted cement.

It was time. I raised the Glock, crouched low, and moved into Room 2004 of the Grapetree Resort. There was no light. Someone had covered the large windows that once brought in sun and sea. I peered into the black room. In another space beyond it, a single ray pierced the dusty air from a hole the bone pickers had ripped in the roof. The room's savaged skeleton was a patchwork of light and shadow.

I froze and listened, straining to pull as much of the room as I could into my eyes. Doves cooed somewhere toward the sea. Rot and decay filled the space -- and something else: the faint smell of coppery blood and sweat. He was here.

Crouching low, I crabbed into the room. By the light from the inside balcony, I could make out another room to the right, a bedroom. I bent low looking for the trail of dust on the broken floor. My prey had gone past that door. There were only the tracks of a rat in its own little Sahara.

I looked into the deep shadows of the other rooms. A hallway was in front of me, about eight feet long. Then a half wall that I figured was once a kitchen counter. Its frame had been ripped and torn by the scavengers and salvagers. I squatted for a moment at the end of the hall, and then crabbed in front of the ravaged counter. Its whole front had been busted out, and the tile and sheetrock sledge-hammered into rubble. As I peeked through the torn gap, I realized I could see the shadows of the kitchen behind it.

I sniffed the air, listened, and then moved in front of the torn gap under the countertop. I heard a rattling exhale of breath close beside me. In that split second, I knew my mistake. The dim light from the open door left me a perfect silhouette for someone crouched in the recesses of the kitchen. I spun around, the Glock coming up to aim into the dark void. A strange twang came from the blackness only five or six feet in front of me. The Glock fired blindly, as a ripping impact slammed against my right shoulder, just beyond the shield of my vest.

The Glock dropped in a clatter. For a long agonizing moment, all I felt was the searing pain. I tried to move, to reach down for my fallen gun, but something held me back. I twisted from my crouch, and the pain in my shoulder ripped more. Nearly fainting, I crumbled to a sitting position, sliding to the grit-covered floor. I could hear my flesh tear as claws of pain stabbed into it. I closed my eyes and tried to breathe deep again and again.

When I opened them, I was sitting on the floor in the dark, my right arm pinned to the wall, raised in a grotesque wave. My hand flapped over my head on a broken puppet's arm. Gazing through the torn wall of the kitchen counter, I saw two cloudy green eyes staring back. The eyes blinked. I waited as my own began to adjust. A white slash of teeth appeared, and then the clump of gray-brown hair matting PADI's chest began to take shape. He was sitting with his legs extended, leaning back in a recess that once held a stove. Beyond the blink and the smile, he didn't move.

I looked to my right, and my forehead brushed against a metal object. The pain in my shoulder flashed as my head touched it. I looked up. A half-inch diameter shaft of steel was rammed into my shoulder, pinning my arm at its inhuman angle. "Spear gun," my mind said absently.

A thin voice in the gutted kitchen said, "Sorry."

Somehow, I didn't believe it. I looked at the ghost-like apparition, realizing what had done this to me.

I pulled forward; the steel rod didn't move. Only the pain moved – higher! I was pinned like a bug to the wall. "Shit," I muttered.

PADI moved his head. I saw a moist mass of hair.

"Hit you in the head," I said.

"Ear gone," the voice answered weakly.

"Leg."

"Butt."

"Ouch," I said

The figure's arms began to move, and reflexively I

tried to duck, but the spear held me in place. I winced in pain. The dark arms disappeared under the mass of PADI's hair. When he raised the huge mass of his beard and dreadlocks, the hair that showed was wet with black shiny blood.

In the dimness, I could make out a hole in his chest. Each time he breathed, the light caught the shimmer of foamy bubbles. Maybe a second hole was oozing even more just below his right-side ribs. His chest was breathing slow, labored.

"You killed me," he rasped.

"Good," I said, remembering the wild shots I'd fired into the bush, wondering if I had hit him, too, in addition to Ray.

"You're like me," he whispered.

"How's that, Clark?"

His smile disappeared. Did he know he was Clark? How long since he'd been Clark in his own maddened mind?

"Clark," he said flatly. He gave a long unblinking stare.

"Clark Jamison."

"We're both hunters, predators," he said, seeming to ignore my use of his name.

"I'm not like you."

"I knew you were a predator the first day Cheri brought you to me."

I was tired of listening to the evil little fuck, and I twisted into the pain to try to reach my lost Glock, but the spear held me in place.

"That's gotta hurt," he said. I gasped in pain and sank farther.

As he smiled at my pain, I reached down my left leg. Could he see me? Did he know what I was doing? My hand crept along the leg, pulling even more on the spear, the pain ripping past my shoulder, across my chest, deep into my gut. But I kept reaching.

I pulled up the cuff of my pants and slipped the little .22 out of its nylon holster. I had no breath left. In a surge of pain, I leaned back against the wall and closed my eyes.

When I opened them, I could see the blur of PADI and the bright metal outline of a spear gun pointed straight at me. As I stared down the barrel, I could see the rubber band lying loosely at its front. A spear was in PADI's right hand.

"Want to give a guy a hand?" he said.

"Nope," I answered, raising the little pistol and pointing it carefully an inch above his eyes.

"Why?" I asked. Could he see what I was doing? Or was it too dark? Was he too lost in his own pain?

"Why?" he repeated, confusion in his voice.

"Why kill all those people?"

"They wanted to stop me, stop my dreams," he said.

"So, you just killed them?" I asked, feeling the invisible plague of his evil crawling across the small space between us.

"I am free," he said as if that explained something.

"Free?" I asked.

PADI started to cough. Each time he retched, his

body convulsed. When it stopped, he dropped his head until it rested on the mat of beard and dreadlocks. Finally, he lifted it.

"I am free, and they were sheep. Sheep are born to die, and when they take from a hunter, they seal their fate." It made no sense, but I knew that to PADI, it was all the sense he needed.

"Am I a sheep?" I asked, realizing he was more than a madman. He was pure evil.

"No," he said. And he smiled. "You're a hunter, and I have killed you."

My .22 still was aimed at his head, but he showed no fear. He only smiled.

"I'm not like you," I said, and lowered the pistol to my lap. I closed my eyes, and the world went black.

CHAPTER

18

I remember Cheri standing over me. I remember opening my eyes and seeing her face. She had slapped me on the right cheek. "Cotton, goddamn it. Wake up."

When my eyes opened, all I saw was her face. I could smell her soap and feel the sting of the slap. I raised my free hand, leaving the pistol in my lap.

"Why?" was all I could say. I couldn't understand: Why she would slap me?

"Damn it, look at me," Cheri said.

"I'm OK," I said. I was still in the dark recess. I motioned through the hole in the cabinet toward the other body.

She hadn't seen the form opposite me. When I gestured to the man in the shadows, she rose and went toward him. I couldn't see much. I saw her tan pants go around the counter into the kitchen. I saw her stoop and push her hand through the mat of hair.

"PADI!"

"Clark Jamison," I said.

He opened his eyes and smiled at Cheri. "Hi lady," he said, like she had just walked up on the beach.

"Fuck you, PADI!" Cheri said. I heard the metallic click of handcuffs and the sound of the spear gun and spear being thrown across the room. When she stood and moved away, I could see she had cuffed his left wrist to a bare steel pipe. He didn't seem to notice.

Cheri came around the corner of the kitchen counter, knelt next to me, and put a piece of cloth gently around the shank of metal and the wound in my shoulder. Then she looked down at the pistol in my lap and back up at my face. "You couldn't kill him?" she asked, softness in her voice.

I knew that wasn't right. I could kill him. No problem. Then I realized: The need had left me. At some point, the black, unyielding desire to kill the trash in front of me had fled. "I could kill him," I said, looking through the torn hole in the sheetrock at the two green eyes. "I could kill him, but I decided not to, because I'm not like him." The eyes blinked and closed.

Cheri leaned closer and ran her hand through my hair, then kissed my lips gently. "I'll be back," she said, and stood and walked out of Room 2004. Again, the blackness closed in.

CHAPTER

19

The beep kept annoying me till I woke. "Get the alarm," I rasped. A hand touched mine, and I opened my eyes. Cheri was sitting there. She had on a blue flowered shirt and was wearing her reading glasses. She took the glasses off and looked at me. "You're back," she said.

"What's that damn beeping?

Cheri smiled. "Monitor," she said, pointing at the flashing machine next to my bed.

"Means I'm alive," I told her.

"Yep."

"John?" I asked

"Down the hall still trying to learn to eat hospital food."

"PADI?"

"Dead when I got back after I called the police."

"Did you get me here? How'd you find me?"

"The Spot locator. I ran into Ray hauling John out, and he said you went the other way. I just followed your trail."

"Oh," I said. Things in my head kept moving. "I feel loopy," I told her.

"Pain meds."

"I think I like them."

Cheri patted my hand, and I closed my eyes and fell asleep again.

It was my third day in the hospital when Dr. Orcot finally said I could see the gang. The first day, he cut the end of the spear out of my shoulder. The second, I spent in the post-surgery clouds. The day after that, he proclaimed his work a success and said I'd be a free man "soon." That wasn't soon enough, so Cheri decided we should all get together there in my room and not waits who-knows-how-much-longer.

It was ten in the morning. Betsy showed up first, still wearing her cast and sling. She was gaunt, and her eyes seemed red, but she had a big kiss for a bright smile and me. We talked for a while, and I told her how sorry I was about Bob. Cheri had told me the night before that an FBI team found his body in a shallow grave on the hill above Jack's Bay.

"You did everything you could," she said gently, running her hand across the stubble that was starting to grow on my cheek.

I was just saying my thanks when Cheri and Jean walked into the room. Cheri was wearing a bright blue sundress I'd bought for her birthday, and Jean had on long blue jeans and a white shirt. They both gave Betsy a hug, and then they all sat down around me.

It was more attention from three lovely ladies than any man had a right to. As Ray said when he walked in a minute later, "You don't deserve this much love, man."

I offered my friend my left hand, and he took it in both of his. "Next time you wait for the Ray Man when you go hunting, understand?"

I smiled and looked at Cheri. "No next time, man," I said.

"I'm cool with that," he answered and offered me his fist. I pressed the one I could move against it.

Still, a player was missing. We joked around for about five minutes, then John hobbled in. "You finally finished sleeping?" he said. "Every time I come in, you're just snoring away."

When I saw that big form again and heard that big voice, my throat tightened up. I couldn't really speak, so I just held up my left fist. John bumped his own against it. "Love ya, man," he said, and then took my fist in both hands. When he let go, I wiped my eyes and looked at all my friends sitting around me.

I still didn't understand what had happened the last couple of weeks. "Does it all make sense?" I asked. "Does anyone know yet what the story really was?"

Jean took a deep breath. "We spent all last night trying to drink all your rum, and I think we have most of it pieced together."

"Most of it," Cheri echoed, "but not all yet."

"PADI was Clark Jamison," John began. "The coroner made a positive ID from the prints. When he went down, it cleared ten murder files just in Georgia. And a tourist murdered in San Juan in 1988."

"San Juan?" I said.

"Yeah, a guy by the name of Steve Lord. It was his dive instructor card and identity that Jamison was using when he got the job at Grapetree back in '88."

"Killed him."

"Knifed him in downtown San Juan and hid the body," John said.

"It gets worse," Cheri added.

"After our little shootout," John went on, "the V.I.P.D. went into the hills and found Jamison's cave. Between my contacts and Ray's, we've got a pretty good picture of what was going on, but the governor's office has a tight chokehold on the media, so hardly any of it is public knowledge."

"And …" I said.

"Brother, they're finding bodies all over that hill," Ray said, shifting his chair in closer. "A girlfriend of mine in the coroner's office told me the FBI has sent over a full forensic team that's taken over a whole wing in the basement of the hospital."

They were all eager to share a piece of the tale. "The FBI has been scouring the hills by Isaac's for two days," Cheri said, "and if Ray is right, they have fifteen possible homicides."

I felt the blood run out of my face. "Fifteen," I said.

"It may just be starting, Mad Dog," John said.

"Yesterday, they found a tunnel system under the old resort. Probably, that's why he was going there."

Betsy knew about this, too. "A friend of mine is a V.I. cop, and he says there are tunnels all through the underside of the resort. That little bastard had been tunneling for years."

"I just found something out this morning," Jean said. "Last week, a colleague of mine called and told me he'd been hired by the FBI to do an appraisal on some coins in St. Croix. He wanted to know what it was about. I told him I didn't know anything but I wanted to hear what it was about after he got here. We met for breakfast this morning, and he said he's valuing a hoard of gold coins that he described as a king's ransom. He said it might be the largest cache of uncirculated Spanish coins ever found in the Caribbean. Jamison was piling up what he found for years, protecting the treasure in his own crazy mind."

"Probably how he was paying Mitch and Charlie," John said.

"I don't think so," I told him. "I think I have a piece of the puzzle. Ray, you remember when we went to the brothers' house in the forest?"

"Sure."

"It's always bothered me that those guys were making a living selling lobster and none of their clothes or shoes are anything like a fisherman's, and they didn't have any of the tools of the trade. No traps, no boat, no dive gear, nothing. Someone had to be supplying them with lobster."

"Jamison," Ray said, snapping his fingers.

"They brought him supplies and he gave them lobster, and maybe fish to sell that he was catching."

"Yeah," John said, "that must be what those pre-paid cell phones were for that they found in the cave. That was how he and the Brachures kept in touch."

"My contact at the P.D. said they found over four thousand dollars in three glass jars in his cave, along with a hoard of jewelry from people he killed," Ray said.

"And Steve Lord's ID," John added.

"So he could pay the Brachure brothers cash if he had to," I said.

"And get Charlie to loan him his truck when he firebombed our boat," Cheri said, her voice rising in anger.

"When we just missed Charlie at Carambola," Ray explained, "he was with Jamison. Jamison rode to town with him and then took the truck for a couple of days. That's when he bombed your boat."

"Actually," John said, "my source at the P.D. told me when Charlie found out about all the bodies on the hill, he cracked like an egg so he wouldn't be accused of killing them, and has been spilling his guts for two days to anyone who'll listen. Seems it was Charlie that ran Tony off the road."

"But how did Mitch get to Puerto Rico?" Jean asked.

"Easy," Ray said, slapping me on the forehead gently. "He caught the late flight to St. Thomas and the nine o'clock flight from there to San Juan."

"No private plane?" I said.

"Nope."

"And Sam and Wendy?" Cheri asked softly.

"Mitch went back to their shop. Charlie may have been in on it and just covering up, but I'm betting it was all Mitch."

"So, my friend," John said, looking around the room, "we just stopped one of the worst serial killers in history."

Cheri turned to me. "Like John said earlier, it seems like the governor and FBI have put a huge lid on all this. They're scared it would make the tourist trade even shakier than it is. So don't expect to be on Larry King Live."

"Fine with me," I told her.

"It may get a little bit of press," Betsy said softly.

We all looked at her, sitting quietly at the foot of the bed.

"I found a lawyer in Florida," she said, "that says that he thinks Bob and Tony could get salvage rights for finding the treasure. I gave him all your names as my partners. He'll be calling you sometime this week."

We all stared at the little redhead.

"Pirate treasure," Ray whispered. "Goody!"

The End

Check out our website for more information of
The Gold of St. Croix at: www.tomsedar.com

Also watch for Tom's next book The Snow of St. Croix
scheduled for publication in the Spring of 2021.